"The scar will never heal, will it?"

Sabrina didn't answer Ramsey, and her silence was like a kick in his chest. It hurt to know she hadn't expected him to understand her suffering.

"It isn't that painful anymore," she said slowly. "Not like it was. I lost Tess's childhood, but if I'd kept her, she might not have had one. I've seen it happen—children having to grow up too fast because their parents are children themselves. I'm so glad she had you."

Before he could say anything, his pager beeped insistently. The night was definitely over. Smiling diabolically, he disconnected the machine and lobbed it into the waste can across the room. Starting today, things were going to change. Tess needed more than a token father. He needed more than a token life.

They both needed Sabrina.

ABOUT THE AUTHOR

Connie Rinehold decided to pursue a writing career after years of working in retail sales and management, and relegating a natural aptitude for writing to the status of "hobby." Connie, who makes her home in Colorado, reports that she has the full support of her husband, who typed the final draft of her Superromance, and her three children, who bought her a computer for Mother's Day!

Silken Threads

CONNIE RINEHOLD

Harlequin Books

TORONTO • NEW YORK • LONDON
AMSTERDAM • PARIS • SYDNEY • HAMBURG
STOCKHOLM • ATHENS • TOKYO • MILAN

Published October 1989

First printing August 1989

ISBN 0-373-70374-0

PROLOGUE

SABRINA FELT as if she'd misplaced a few years, become lost along the way and suddenly emerged in a world somehow different, out of sync. Logically she knew better. Only the seasons changed with such predictable regularity. Crumpling the empty plastic bag, she scattered the last of the crumbs and nuts on the ground. Even the behavior of the squirrels was predictable. She'd lived here so long that she actually found them on her porch every morning, expecting their breakfast to be served, while she waited for the teakettle to whistle.

Raising her head, she studied the landscape, wondering why she suddenly felt an urgent need to fight life's currents instead of going with the flow. Winter's promise whispered to her senses in the fresh strawberry scent of imminent snowfall, the crisp chill nipping at her flesh through her quilted robe, and in the clouds that swathed the peaks of the Teton Mountains like fluffy gray hair. Tomorrow the trees would no longer blaze with autumn fire. Tomorrow her world would pale to the colors of a dying year.

Change.

Sabrina had always enjoyed the transition from one season to the next, especially here in the part of Wyoming known as Jackson Hole, where the seasons asserted themselves in breathtaking splendor. Until now her appreciation of nature's cycles had always been detached, objective, as if they had no relationship to her own existence. But this morning she was taking it personally, feeling the changes rather than merely watching them....

Shivering, Sabrina mounted the steps leading to her enclosed back porch. Her large cedar home offered warmth, security, luxury. The many trees growing on her land shielded the house from the road, providing privacy and an added measure of peace. Why couldn't she absorb it, savor it and be content? She had everything she wanted. Almost.

When she had come here it had been enough. Then she'd needed peace, time to heal. The teakettle whistled as she entered the kitchen, and as she brewed her tea, she thought of the last sixteen years. They'd been good years. She had healed more than she'd thought possible, accomplished more than she'd expected. And she'd come a long way, but not far enough to leave her ghosts behind.

An aroma of mint drifted upward from her mug. She would drink her tea, make breakfast, then follow a long-established schedule. Her days were made up of such rituals—to be performed in a life that had itself become a ritual, well-ordered and disciplined....

As incomplete as a half-furnished room.

The ringing of the doorbell broke the silence. Sabrina frowned, automatically tightening the belt of her robe as she left the kitchen to answer its summons. Who could it be at this hour?

She looked through the peephole before releasing the dead bolt. A fleeting glimpse of blue-gray eyes under winged brows sent a sense of déjà vu rippling over her, as if the past that had dogged her footsteps for half her life had suddenly emerged from the shadows to lay a hand on her shoulder. A young woman's tall figure and tousled black hair reinforced the feeling. She closed her eyes and shook her head. It was a trick of the light . . . a trick of the mind.

Opening the door, she looked more closely at her visitor. Shock paralyzed Sabrina. Her heart seemed to stop beating. The world temporarily ceased to exist as she confronted the source of so many haunted memories.

Her visitor's eyes widened, first with curiosity, then with recognition and finally apprehension. Once, Sabrina had fallen in love with eyes like these, eyes that shimmered with a touch of silver and darkened to smoky gray with turbulent emotion.

"You're Sabrina Haddon?"

Like her own, the voice was husky. Unable to speak, Sabrina nodded.

"I'm . . . my name is Treasure . . . Tess Jordan." The girl continued to stare at Sabrina.

Treasure indeed. Wealth beyond price had been given by Sabrina to two nameless, faceless people for nothing more than payment of a hospital bill and a promise to love her daughter unconditionally. Even as she tried to reject the truth, she knew this was the name she'd wondered about until she'd thought she'd go mad.

A curious mixture of girl and woman looked out at her from a face reflecting too much desperation for her years. It was a familiar face, with dimples that winked when she spoke, a wide mouth that tilted up at the corners, a nose that was a little too short. . . . How many times had she seen that same face in the mirror? Except for the eyes—a legacy from Johnny—the features were her own.

Johnny. So handsome, so exciting, so beguiling, looking at her with admiration and desire, beckoning to a young girl free for the summer from the strictures of her elderly parents. Sabrina had mistaken his attentions for love. He had mistaken her intelligence and outgoing personality for sophistication. Then he'd left her—to face alone the results of his deceit and her own gullibility. How long had it been? Seventeen years?

A thousand dreams ago.

The moment stretched between them, strained by uncertainty. What should she say? What could she say? How did one cope with something like this? The pragmatism and common sense it had taken Sabrina thirty-two years to acquire deserted her. She was self-conscious in a way she'd never been before. Years of dreaming about a moment like this had not prepared her for its reality.

Seeing the girl's shiver, Sabrina focused on the light jacket Tess was wearing over a cotton shirt and jeans. Winter came early to northwestern Wyoming. "You must be freezing," she said with a catch in her voice. "Come in."

"You know who I am." Tess's statement betrayed no surprise.

"Yes." Sabrina's throat ached. Her heart constricted, trying to close around the emptiness left by the past—an emptiness she hadn't been able to fill with her fantasies of watching her child grow and sharing in that growth. That emptiness could never be filled by anyone but the girl standing in her foyer.

Tess drew her brows together in a frown as she looked down at her feet. "I didn't think. I should have called or something."

Emotion ripped through Sabrina, leaving her breathless. She had felt it before, whenever she'd allowed herself to imagine, to wonder, to wish. Unconsciously she raised her hand to touch and comfort the teenager, recalling that when she was no older than Tess, she had reached out to smooth the head of the crying infant she'd held so briefly—the only time she'd seen her child—until now.

Tess raised her head at Sabrina's movement and backed up a step. "I didn't mean to intrude," she said firmly, defiantly.

Sabrina lowered her hand. No, this was not her child. This girl-woman who looked at her with a blend of wariness and stubborn independence belonged to a family named Jordan.

Releasing a breath, Sabrina concentrated on the present. Needing to reassure Tess as well as herself, she forced a smile to her lips. "You're not intruding. I was just about to make breakfast. Are you hungry?"

"Mmm." The girl's eyes searched as much of the house as was visible from the entry.

Sabrina answered the unspoken question. "I live alone."

"I'm starved. I drove straight through."

Grinning in spite of herself at the reply, Sabrina stood aside. "Then come in, before we freeze to death and food is no longer an issue."

She settled her guest at the kitchen table and poured her a cup of tea. Sabrina was surprised to find that her own tea was still warm. It had only been a few minutes since she'd answered the door. A few minutes and one instant of recognition were all it had taken to change her life—and those of how many others?—irrevocably.

"I guess I'd better let Daddy know I'm okay. He's probably calling everyone in Cheyenne looking for me by now."

Nearly dropping her mug, Sabrina stared at Treasure in horror. "Cheyenne? You drove over four hundred miles to Jackson? Alone? At night?"

"I'm a good driver," the girl mumbled as she stared down at the tablecloth, her finger tracing random patterns over the linen.

"But all the way from...?" Dozens of questions adding to her confusion, Sabrina's voice trailed off. Where should she begin? With Daddy? From Tess's words, it sounded as though he was her only parent.

Tess wrapped her hands around her mug. "I've been on my own a lot since Mom died. Daddy has to travel in his business."

Sabrina struggled to keep her outrage from overflowing into her voice. How much was "a lot"? She hadn't given up her baby so that she could be left to her own devices at such a vulnerable age. What business could be more important than a daughter? Through gritted teeth, Sabrina asked, "How long has it been?"

"Almost two years." Her guest's indifferent shrug contrasted with the emotion that Sabrina saw shimmering in her eyes.

What kind of man was he...this...this Daddy? Cautioning herself not to jump to conclusions, Sabrina turned away. Surely there was more than the sketchy picture Treasure had drawn. She hoped there was.

Squeezing her eyes shut, she asked herself the same question that had plagued her for sixteen years. *Oh God, what if I've entrusted my child to people who don't care for her?*

CHAPTER ONE

OH, GOD, she's sixteen, a baby. Please keep her safe.
Ramsey Jordan raked his fingers through his hair and
glared at the address book lying open on the desk.
Choking back a knot of fear, he repeated the only hope
he had. *She hasn't gone far. I'll find her.* If he held onto
that thought instead of other, more frightening possibilities, he might make it through the next few minutes. Ramsey closed his eyes in anguish. *Tess, where are
you?*

Reaching the *Z*'s without finding any names he might
have missed the first dozen times, he slammed the book
shut. He'd called everyone they knew, hoping that Tess
had gone visiting and he'd simply forgotten her plans.
Knowing it was a plausible assumption made him sick
to his stomach. Between expanding his business in
Denver, arranging for his father-in-law's funeral here in
Cheyenne and sorting through the papers it had taken
Bill all his adult life to accumulate, his mind was satu-
rated with enough details to keep him busy for a year.
Too busy to pay attention to Tess.

Ramsey rejected the idea. Sure, he'd been preoccupied, but not to the extent of forgetting his daughter.
He'd always made a point of knowing exactly where she
was and what she was doing....

Sure, Jordan. So where is she now?

Staring at nothing, Ramsey wished his father-in-law were still alive. His would have been a logical mind in a frantic, gut-twisting situation. But Bill was gone; he'd left Tess and himself with no one but each other.

Tess had loved her grandfather to distraction, and Bill's sudden death had devastated her. But she had seemed to be handling it. That should have been his first clue. No one handled death that well. His lip curled in self-disgust. Why hadn't he seen that she was keeping her grief inside, where it could hammer away at her without disturbing anyone but herself? It had been the same when Claire had died. Tess hadn't shed a tear, though she and her mother had been close. At least, he hadn't seen any tears.

But then, Tess had certainly had a bad example to follow—namely himself. The only things he'd let himself see in the last few years were contracts and financial statements. He and Tess should have held each other, shared their sorrows and their strengths, grown closer. Instead, he'd pursued his work as if it were all he had to live for. And last night he'd told Tess that he couldn't take the time for a vacation. She'd just stood there looking resigned then had left the room without a word.

That was the last time he had seen her.

He should have explained how sensitive his negotiations to expand Ram Air Couriers were. After years of building his capital, slowly increasing his fleet of airplanes, assembling the best team of employees he could find and searching for prime airport facilities, he was within a thought's breadth of realizing his dream. Surely Tess would understand.

Yeah, Jordan. She'll understand that hangars and airplanes are more important than she is. What reason had he given her lately to believe otherwise? And for what? Money? He already had more than he could spend in a lifetime. The truth made him wince. It wasn't about money, but safety. All his business required from him was a commitment of time, brainpower and energy. He could keep his heart to himself. Great. After two years of emotional blindness, he was suddenly blessed with twenty-twenty hindsight. And that, he thought derisively, might buy the hole in a doughnut.

Sitting back in Bill's executive chair, Ramsey forced himself to calm down, think rationally, search his memory for clues.

He and Tess had spent yesterday cleaning out Bill's study. She had been sorting through the papers in the desk. She'd grown quiet, thoughtful....

Ramsey's brow furrowed. Now that he thought about it, she had acted as if she wanted to say something, but had apparently changed her mind. Feeling hassled by the growing mound of details needing his attention, he'd barely noticed. Later that afternoon, he'd found Tess sitting on the floor in front of the bookcase, leafing through the telephone books Bill had for every community in the state. He'd remarked on how bored she must be....

Following that train of thought, Ramsey's gaze fell to the shelves in question and fastened on two wads of paper, half-hidden under the bottom shelf. In his desperation, even they looked sinister. Bending over, he picked them up and smoothed them out on the desk, willing them to reveal Tess's whereabouts.

Suddenly he felt as if an army was walking on his grave with hobnailed boots. Numbers blurred, then came into sharp focus. Suspicion became an itch he didn't want to scratch. The name he'd never heard leaped out at him and filled him with inexplicable dread. And the dates on the papers . . . He was reaching—he hoped. It was crazy, just a coincidence, impossible.

It scared him to death.

He read the figures again, missing not so much as a comma or decimal point. He'd never forgotten that date, or the particular dollar amount that the second paper showed. Sixteen years ago, he had gladly, jubilantly written a check for that sum. Claire hadn't been able to carry a baby to term. After her fourth miscarriage and the resulting radical surgery, adoption had been the only way left for them to have a child. They would have willingly, without regret, given everything they owned for the treasure they had received in return.

Treasure. Tess. His daughter in everything but blood.

With hands that hadn't stopped shaking since he'd discovered Tess missing, Ramsey grabbed the telephone and punched in the number of Chester Simmons, his friend since childhood. He had also been Bill's law partner for the last eight years.

A metallic, recorded voice with a western drawl answered on the second ring. Damn. He hated talking to a machine. "Chet, this is Ram. Call me as—"

A click and a live voice cut in. "Do you know what time it is, Ram? Ten o'clock. Saturday morning. I have one hell of a headache, and my teeth feel like they're wearing sweaters. This had better be good. . . ."

"Chet, Tess is missing."

"What?" The fuzziness in Chet's voice cleared instantly. "Tess? When?"

"Last night, this morning. I don't know. She went to bed at ten, and I fell asleep in the study around midnight. When I woke up this morning, she was gone. So is the Blazer." Tremors shook him as he thought of what could happen in twelve hours. Tess could be alone, in need of help, reaching out in the dark and finding nightmares. Or nightmares might be finding her. . . .

"What about her friends here? Did you call them? Maybe she went home to Denver."

Propping his elbows on the desk, Ramsey rubbed his forehead. "I checked with everyone." He swallowed. "The hospitals and police, too. Nothing."

"Since she obviously took the car, it's unlikely she's been kidnapped." Ramsey heard Chet take a deep breath, plainly hesitating. "You haven't received any ransom demands, have you?"

Ramsey could almost hear the circuits engaging in Chet's brain and he found a small comfort in that. His own mind was on overload, incapable of any thoughts but those colored by fear, panic and grim imagining. "No. Nothing, except—" Two pieces of paper, yellowed by age, crackled under Ramsey's hand, reminding him of what he dreaded asking. "Chet, does the firm have a client named Sabrina Haddon?"

Chet's silence lasted a little too long for Ramsey's peace of mind. "Not for years. Why?"

Ramsey's heart turned to lead and sank to his feet at the brevity of Chet's reply. His old friend was a detail man, who never took the shortest route from question to answer if he had enough information to take him around a bush or two. Something told Ramsey that he had plenty of information. "Who is she, Chet?"

"A former client, Ram. Privileged information."

"Cut the crap, Chet. You can take privileged information and shove it in your . . . trash can. We're talking about Tess—my daughter, your godchild."

"All right. Why do you want to know? What does this have to do with my godchild?"

"You tell me!" Ramsey roared, then forced himself to relax, letting calm wrap itself around him like a strait jacket. He'd rave like a lunatic later. "Tess was cleaning out Bill's desk. I found some papers. I'm afraid Tess found them first. The dates and—"

"Slow down, Ram. I gather Sabrina Haddon's name was on these papers. What were they?"

Hearing a click, Ramsey knew Chet was lighting one of his favorite cheroots, a sure sign that he was going into his legal eagle mode. "One is a personal memo, reminding Bill to 'Get a medical history from Sabrina for Ram and Claire.' The other is a hospital bill for Sabrina Haddon—a cesarean section on the day Tess was born." His voice came out thick and hoarse. "Chet, tell me this is a twisted joke. Tell me I'm getting punchy and seeing something that isn't there."

"I can't, Ram." Chet's quiet answer held a note of apology.

Suspicion turned to a hard lump of certainty in Ramsey's chest. His tension level increased as he steeled himself for what he knew would follow. "Then tell me what you can."

"Okay, Ram. Bill left some documents with me. He wanted the information available for Tess, when or if she ever wanted to know about her birth mother. But only after she turned eighteen. Sabrina agreed to this, with the stipulation that you should have full knowledge of and support for Tess's decision. In keeping with the agreement, I couldn't give you or Tess the information until she was of age." Chet sighed. "I guess it doesn't matter now. Hold on while I get the file out of my safe."

Waiting for his friend to return to the phone, Ramsey wondered how Chet could think so quickly and talk so slowly.

One minute stretched into two, then five. Ramsey's nerves stretched with them until he thought they would snap. As surely as he knew that he'd driven her to it, he knew Tess had run to Sabrina Haddon. But he didn't know whether to be relieved or give in to fear of a different kind.

"Ram? Are you ready?"

No! his mind screamed as Ramsey pulled a pen out of his shirt pocket. "I'm ready. Shoot." A shiver rippled over him at his own choice of words. He felt like a sitting duck as Chet began firing information at him.

"Sabrina Renée Haddon, a change of life baby, born in a small town forty miles north of Cheyenne. Age: thirty-one. She's single...black hair...blue eyes...five foot nine...." A wolf whistle came over the line. "There's a picture here."

"Forget the measurements, Chet. I want to know about her."

"You don't know what you're missing." Chet coughed and mumbled something about his cheroots. "Sorry. I'll stick to facts."

"Today, Chet."

"Uh-huh. Let's see. Her mother died when she was fifteen. Her father was confined to a wheelchair. She quit school to nurse him and have the baby. He died three years later. Bill handled the estate, which consisted of the old homestead and not much else. She went to Denver, worked her way through high school and the Art Institute by waiting tables. She studied fashion and commercial art and was subsequently hired to design and make clothes for a small boutique."

"And?" Ramsey prompted when all he heard was the rustle of paper.

"Bill gathered quite a collection of newspaper and magazine articles on her. She made it big, Ram . . . has a high six-figure income. Her boss at the boutique made her a full partner, and they set up a classy operation in Denver."

"She lives in Denver?"

"No. She owns a custom-built house on a prime lot outside of Jackson, Wyoming. Her partner runs the manufacturing plant—Sabrina handles the creative end of it and commutes several times a year. That's about it, other than the usual trivia."

Ramsey shook his head in disbelief. "You sure, Chet? What about the brand of perfume she wears or the name of her great-grandmother's pet chicken?" he asked peevishly. Listening to the bits and pieces of the woman's life, he'd felt a grudging admiration for what she'd accomplished. Sabrina Haddon sounded like a respectable woman with a lot of guts. She'd come a long way. On the one hand it eased his worry. On the other, it irritated the hell out of him to think she might be getting somewhere with Tess.

"Can't help you there, Ram. Bill did compile a medical history on the last three generations of her family, though. These private adoptions can leave a lot of loose ends to trip over."

"Why in bloody hell didn't he sever his connection with the Haddon family after the adoption?"

Chet's sigh was as eloquent as a shrug. "Bill and Sabrina's father were old army buddies. My guess is that Bill felt responsible for her, since she refused remuneration other than medical expenses for having Tess." Chet's lighter clicked again. "For what it's worth, Bill did turn her over to another law firm, once he knew her future was secure."

"Okay. I get the picture." Closing his eyes, Ramsey stared at other pictures of times long past: of Claire and himself viewing Tess through the nursery window; of the two of them taking their baby home and fumbling with the logistics of diapers and formula and the snaps on baby sleepers. A smile tugged at his mouth as he thought of Tess's first tooth, her first words and all the other firsts. They hadn't always been estranged.

The smile faded, and pain took its place as he thought of the unhappiness that had taken the pleasure out of family life. It had happened so gradually that he hadn't realized it until it was too late. But by then he'd lost his sense of belonging, and hadn't known how to get it back. Was the danger of losing Tess the price for his blindness, his stupidity?

Ramsey couldn't accept that. "Dammit. Tess is *my* daughter." He blinked, realizing he'd spoken aloud, and struggled to keep his anguish from slipping through the cracks in his control.

"Ram?" Chet's voice was rich with friendship and compassion. "I'm going to give you the address and phone number in Jackson."

Ramsey scribbled the information on the desk blotter. His daughter had driven over four hundred miles out of misery and desperation—because of him. After hanging up the receiver, Ramsey pressed his palms against his eyes, and his shoulders heaved with a grief he could no longer contain.

SABRINA'S PHONE RANG just as Tess was finishing her tea and could no longer put off calling her father. Frustrated by the interruption, Sabrina crossed the room to pick up the phone on the breakfast bar. "Hello."

"Sabrina Haddon?" The voice was deep, its tone impatient, antagonistic. It was a voice she had never heard, yet she recognized it with the same sense of déjà vu she'd experienced earlier.

"Yes."

"Ramsey Jordan. Is my daughter there?"

"Yes, Mr. Jordan, she's here." Out of the corner of her eye, Sabrina saw Tess slump back in her chair. "I'll call her for you." She wanted to ask how he'd known her whereabouts, but thought better of it. He didn't sound in the mood for explanations.

"Not yet, Miss Haddon. How is she?"

"Tired, hungry and upset."

"Well, she can join the club."

"Yes." Sabrina motioned for Tess to go into the bedroom, where she could use the extension in privacy. "I can imagine how difficult this is for you, Mr. Jordan. Hopefully we'll all have calmed down by the time you arrive to pick Tess up."

Ramsey glared at the telephone. That all-inclusive "we" made him feel as if she'd just patted him on the head. The last thing he needed was gratuitous comfort. And he had a sneaking suspicion that her calm, husky voice had carried a subtle reprimand. He resented her apparent control, when he was hanging onto the edge of rationality by his fingernails. "Calm and runaway daughters don't go together, Miss Haddon."

Sabrina sighed, understanding his anger even as she rebelled against it. If she were in his shoes, she'd be walking on the outskirts of reason, too. "Mr. Jordan, I—"

Ramsey's sigh echoed hers. "Will you put Tess on the next plane to Cheyenne? I'll reimburse you and make arrangements for her car."

"No."

"No? What do you mean, *no*?"

"I told you, Mr. Jordan, she is exhausted—emotionally and physically. If I put her on a plane, she won't be alone." Startled by her own vehemence, Sabrina leaned against the bar. Her response had been automatic, natural, as if she had a right to see to Treasure's welfare. But she didn't ... she didn't.

"Isn't it a little late for maternal concern?" Ramsey inquired dryly. He heard her sharp intake of breath and the suffering it conveyed, but firmly told himself to ignore it.

Crimson rage warred with long-endured pain. Late? It had been too late sixteen years ago. When would it stop hurting?

"I'm sorry, Miss Haddon, that was uncalled-for."

"Yes, it was," she agreed crisply, unwilling to pursue the topic.

Ramsey interpreted the message correctly and changed the subject. "Has Tess told you how she found out about you?"

"No. I gather the same way you have."

"Bill Jarvis."

"But he's the attorney who handled the adoption."

"He was also my father-in-law. He died last week, and Tess found some papers in his desk," he explained with weary fatalism.

"I'm sorry to hear that." Groping for the bar stool behind her, Sabrina clenched her fingers around its back and sat down heavily. Bill Jarvis dead? Ramsey Jordan's father-in-law? She remembered their conversations and how, each time, she had stopped herself from asking if he knew anything about her child until she'd been shaking from the effort. Sensing this, Bill had suggested a complete elimination of contact. "I don't understand. Bill wouldn't have been so careless."

"No, he wouldn't. It was just a freak thing. The point is, Tess has found you, and I wish to God she hadn't."

"At least she's safe, Mr. Jordan."

"Is she? Can you guarantee that, Miss Haddon?"

With a jolt, Sabrina realized that he considered her a threat. Her thoughts hadn't gone that far beyond the chaos Tess's appearance had created. It was hard to accept. She'd never thought of herself as a danger to anyone. "I won't hurt her," she promised quietly.

For some reason Ramsey wanted to believe her, but until he knew more, doing so would be a mistake. And he'd made too many of those already. "I hope not, Miss Haddon."

Sabrina gripped the receiver and reminded herself that Ramsey Jordan was recovering from what had probably been the worst scare of his life. "Shall I expect you to come for Tess today?"

"Yes. I'll leave here as soon as I can have my plane serviced," he said wearily. "And, Miss Haddon? I'd appreciate it if you didn't ask Tess for information you shouldn't have."

Before she could reply, Sabrina heard Tess pick up the extension. Without waiting to hear more, she hung up and slammed a cast-iron skillet onto the stove. His request grated after all the years, all the effort, she'd spent not asking for information. And it angered her that information about her seemed to be up for grabs to anyone who wanted it, while Ramsey and Treasure Jordan were protected.

Sensing she wasn't alone, Sabrina looked up. Tess stood in the doorway, tears running down her face. "Tess—?"

"He said he loves me," she sobbed.

"Did you doubt it so much, Tess?" Alarmed by the building storm of crying, Sabrina allowed instinct to take over and pulled the girl into her arms. It felt strange to be holding her like that, rocking her as if she were a small child with a hurt to be soothed.

You can miss what you've never had. In that brief moment of sharing, Sabrina felt the hole in her life filling—and wished it didn't have to empty again.

As if she just couldn't hold it in anymore, Tess poured out her fears and unhappiness. "After Mom died, he stopped...being Daddy. I keep thinking—what if he didn't want me? And now that Mom is gone, he doesn't have to pretend anymore. We used to have so much fun. Is something wrong with me? You gave me away. Mom and Grandpa died, and Daddy..." She shuddered, then stopped, as if she suddenly realized how much she was revealing.

Grasping her shoulders, Sabrina stepped back to look at her. "I didn't give you away. I gave you up. There is a difference. You give away things you don't want or need. You give up because you recognize that you've done the best you can, and there's no other choice." Sabrina knew she was oversimplifying, but her feelings ran too deep to be easily put into words. "And if your father doesn't love you, he gave an award-winning performance to the contrary on the phone."

Tess stared at Sabrina. "He did?"

"Yes." Sabrina breathed deeply as sudden weakness overcame her. It had all been too much. They were all functioning on pure emotion. Especially Ramsey Jordan. She couldn't doubt his love for his daughter. It had underlined every word he'd said to her, and had been emphasized by guilt and raw pain.

Smiling gently, Sabrina dared to smooth Tess's hair. "I didn't mean to lecture you. Would you like to take a shower while I make breakfast?"

The girl nodded, then stepped back, apparently realizing that she'd just confided in a virtual stranger, and that stranger had held and comforted her as if she really cared. "I'll get my duffel out of the car."

Tess's departure from the kitchen plunged Sabrina into deep, disturbing thought. Soon the teenager would be asking painful questions, searching Sabrina's past for answers to her own insecurities. She'd have to be scrupulously honest. The idea of reaching back sixteen years to feel the pain and disillusionment all over again made Sabrina cringe inside. Having to put the memories into words and then to say goodbye again only made the prospect worse.

Cracking eggs into a bowl, Sabrina heard once more a deep, angry voice, so clearly that she nervously glanced over her shoulder to make sure he wasn't standing behind her. She was never nervous or self-conscious or uncertain. She never lost her temper, either, yet she had come dangerously close to doing so today.

For years she'd had the reputation of being calm, always in control. For years she'd concealed her negative emotions by speaking quietly, precisely, articulately— exactly the opposite of the reaction people expected. For years she'd been in complete control of herself and

her life. The whisk bounced as she tossed it into the sink
a little too forcefully.

To her way of thinking—reasonable or not—Ramsey Jordan had a lot to answer for.

CHAPTER TWO

"SOMETHING sure smells good."

Startled, Sabrina looked down at the food on the table with no recollection of having prepared the meal. "Oh... yes. It's ready. I hope you like ham and eggs, Treasure."

"Tess. Only my mother called me Treasure."

Sabrina fell still; she felt as if the slightest movement would shatter her into countless fragments of brittle glass.

"I mean..."

"Don't worry about it, Tess." With a joyless smile, Sabrina sat down and invited Tess to do the same. The silence grew awkward as they ate. An obstacle course of unspoken thoughts and unvoiced anxieties stood between them. They were strangers with nothing in common but a mutual curiosity about each other. The importance of what was happening, what could happen, what might begin between them overwhelmed her. Swallowing a bite of food that seemed to have grown in her mouth, Sabrina forcibly reminded herself that today was the only beginning they would ever have.

"Why did you give me up?" Tess asked, still staring down at her plate as if she were afraid to hear the answer.

Apprehension rushed at Sabrina. She knew how crucial her answers would be to both of them. Would Tess understand? Tearing her toast into small, uniform pieces, she tried to read Tess's expression. Could she accept the truth? It seemed so weak now and she wished with all her heart that things had been different and she had chosen another course so long ago.

A thousand regrets ago.

Hardly feeling courageous, Sabrina began to speak in a monotone. "I was fifteen. My folks were elderly, poor and in bad health. My mother died when I was six months pregnant. The income from her sewing business was gone. I buried her and my illusions on the same day. I couldn't work, go to school, take care of my father and raise a child. I was still growing up myself."

"Why didn't you have an abortion?"

"I couldn't do that. I wanted you too much." Sabrina's voice faded to a whisper. It had never stopped being true.

"Then why?"

"Tess, the world isn't like a black and white photograph on glossy paper. I intended to keep you—I wanted it to be you and me against the world. The statistics were against me, but I believed I'd be the exception to the rule. When you kicked for the first time . . ." Sabrina's composure frayed as she recalled the wonder of experiencing a separate life moving within her, depending upon her. "You were a human being, not something to play house with and dress up like a doll. My responsibilities toward you went beyond giving birth and trying to prove a point."

"You were scared," Tess stated flatly, accusingly.

"I was scared," Sabrina agreed. "I had a responsibility to myself, too. If I'd kept you, chances are we both would have suffered. I couldn't take the risk."

The chair screeched across the floor as Tess stood to carry the plates to the sink. "What can I call you?"

Of all the responses Sabrina had expected, this wasn't one of them. Was this Tess's way of putting off judgment until she knew more? Sabrina prayed for it to be so, even as she wished for an immediate reaction. "Sabrina is fine," she said, relieved and frustrated all at once.

"I'm glad I came, Sabrina."

Did that mean Tess was glad because she had her answers, or did it mean that she accepted her? Sabrina knew she wanted too much, too soon. "How did you find me, Tess?"

Plunging her hands into the soapy water, Tess related the events leading up to her arrival in Jackson.

Appalled at the simplicity of it, Sabrina wanted to laugh hysterically. All the precautions, all the care Bill Jarvis had taken to keep everyone anonymous had been made futile by two old scraps of paper, lost and forgotten behind a drawer. "You came here with no more to go on than memos your grandfather had written to himself?" she asked incredulously.

"Why else would Mom and Daddy need someone else's medical records? Why would they pay your hospital bills? It made sense to me." Rinsing the dishes, Tess stacked them in the drainer.

Sabrina leaned against the counter next to her. "Tess, you took a gamble coming here. What if I'd thrown you out?"

"You didn't," Tess pointed out defensively.

"No, but I could have. Not all women in my position are pleased to have this happen. They can be hurt by it as much as or more than the children involved. The laws are designed to protect all parties concerned, not just the adopted child.''

Tess stared out of the window. "When you answered the door and I saw the look on your face...I knew I shouldn't have just popped up like that. Are you mad at me?''

"No. I'm not angry." Noting her too-pale skin and the charcoal smudges of fatigue underlining Tess's eyes, Sabrina smiled gently. "I am worried about you. You're worn out. I think you should take a nap before we do any more talking.''

"I don't..."

Daring to reach over to lay her hand on Tess's, Sabrina spoke softly, raggedly. "Tess, I'd appreciate some time alone. I'm feeling pretty threadbare right now.''

RAMSEY INDULGED in a spate of creative cussing that would have put a seasoned stevedore to shame. All he wanted was an airworthy plane. It wasn't much to ask, since he owned a whole fleet of them—unless his Cheyenne-based planes were either coming or going and Hap, his chief mechanic, had put his Piper Cherokee onto the sick list. His hand tightening around the receiver, Ramsey listened to Hap tell him all the reasons why he couldn't have the plane ready within the half hour.

"I didn't like the way she was sounding, Boss. The magneto is shot.''

"Then put in a bloody new one!" Ramsey roared.

"Ain't got one. Had to send to Denver. The boy is flying it in on his way to L.A." The "boy" was Seth Jamison, Hap's nephew and Ramsey's general manager.

"Los Angeles is in the other direction, Hap.''

"Yup. Told him that. Said he'd make a detour."

Ramsey shifted impatiently on his feet. "Look, Hap, see if you can rent me a plane. As it is, I'll be lucky to miss the cold front moving in by a squeak and a prayer."

"Bad idea, Boss. You're asking for somebody else's problems. The way I see it, you got enough of your own."

"Aargh!"

"What's that ya say? Couldn't make it out."

"Never mind. Just find me some wings with an engine attached."

"Sure, Boss. Have the Cherokee ready for ya by one."

Ramsey gave in with a muffled curse. By the time he rounded up another aircraft, Hap would probably have his own repaired.

He tried to kill time by sorting through the last of Bill's papers. Throwing down a folder in disgust, Ramsey stood and rotated his shoulders to work out the kinks. He kept remembering a husky voice suggesting that he calm down. Privately he'd called Sabrina Haddon a bitch; he knew he'd been unfair.

But knowing he'd been unfair didn't make a helluva lot of difference. Sabrina Haddon wasn't a helpless teenager now and, from what Chet had told him, she had the kind of star quality that would attract a young girl like Tess. She presented a very real threat to him. He couldn't blame her for Tess's running away. He *could* blame her if she took advantage of the situation. Damn. Why hadn't she married? With a different name, she wouldn't have been so easy for Tess to find.

Feeling twice his thirty-nine years, Ramsey left the study to wander aimlessly through the house, stopping in the doorway of a frilly red and white bedroom.

Tess. She was turning into a spoiled brat. No. That wasn't fair, either. Wise beyond her years in some ways, stubborn, impulsive, responsible—Tess was all these things, but not spoiled and not a brat. She missed her mother. He missed Claire, too—what they'd once had, what he'd hoped to reclaim—until she'd died and all second chances had been canceled. The only difference was that while Tess had been reaching out, he had been pulling himself in, tucking away any stray emotions, so they couldn't be stepped on. His lip curled in self-disgust. He'd stopped listening to his daughter.

Walking across the room that Bill had let Tess decorate herself, he stopped at the old-fashioned vanity. Fingering the pots and tubes of cosmetics, he wondered when she'd traded baby powder and finger paints for perfume and lipstick. Next to the lamp, a book lay face up, a man and woman in a torrid embrace on the cover. He looked at it from a different angle. When had she given up Dr. Seuss in favor of romances? Tess was growing up, and he'd almost missed it.

Well, no, not quite, he amended. He hadn't missed the way Tess watched his general manager with her heart in her eyes. He'd just let the knowledge fly past, convincing himself that Tess would outgrow her crush on Seth, that this was just a phase, that the high school fullback she'd been seeing lately would divert her attention. Was that part of the reason she'd become so desperate? First love was bad enough, but Tess had been hit by the big three afflictions of growing up all at once—first love, love for an older man, and unrequited love.

Why hadn't he talked to her about it, let her know that he was available and not so old that he couldn't remember what it was like? Ramsey turned away from his reflection in the mirror. He knew why. He'd felt awkward, inadequate to deal with the problems of a young girl. But girl or boy, what difference did it really make? Both were human beings with human feelings and the same capacity to be hurt. It didn't take a woman to understand that. All it took was someone who cared.

It was about time he let his daughter know just how much he did care and how much he was capable of understanding. *About time,* he repeated mentally, refusing to believe it might be too late.

The pager hooked to his belt went off. Ramsey ignored it, fighting the urge to chuck it across the room. He'd called his office to tell them he wouldn't be available until Tuesday, and he'd meant it. Damn it to bloody hell. He was the boss. His employees were supposed to listen to him. But then, how many times had he taken time off, only to show up anyway? Claire had been so efficient when it came to handling home and hearth that he'd wondered if she needed him at all.

Shaking his head at the futility of such thoughts, Ramsey glanced at his watch and left Tess's bedroom. He could do something about her, share with her, help her over the rough spots....

And maybe his daughter would help him a little, too. He could use a little help, he reflected.

He checked his watch again, this time paying attention to the position of the hands. If the plane wasn't ready, he'd bloody well fix it himself.

The Cherokee was ready just before two. Grateful that the airport was small and didn't have outgoing aircraft stacked up on the runway, Ramsey took off with a minimum of hassle and Hap's weather prediction echoing in the cockpit.

He couldn't care less about the weather. It was the memory of the warmth and brightness in his daughter's voice that was tearing him up. *She's nice, Daddy. We look alike.* Wasn't that just dandy—physical evidence of Sabrina Haddon's connection to Tess. Maybe after spending some time with her, Tess wouldn't like the woman....

Scanning the horizon, Ramsey radioed for a weather update. As he checked the instrument panel, he frowned. He was losing oil pressure. Seeing a light mist form on the windshield, he cursed under his breath and read his charts. He had to land, preferably on a runway. Fortunately, the storm moving down from Canada was still a safe distance away and Casper wasn't socked in. As he approached the Casper airport, Ramsey muttered that he could have made the trip faster on roller skates.

A mechanic waited in the open doorway of the Ram Air Couriers hangar to guide him into the building. Grinning at the plump, fiftyish woman dressed in grease-stained coveralls, he jumped to the ground. Next to Hap, Lenore Harris was the best aircraft mechanic in the business.

"Hey, Lenny, am I glad to see you!"

"You're always glad to see me when you have problems. What is it this time?"

"Oil cooler, I think."

"Okay, I'll get on it." Lenny began to unscrew the engine cowlings. "There's coffee and sandwiches in the office."

Ramsey nodded. "I could use them. Thanks, Lenny. I'll be right out to give you a hand."

The top of Lenny's head barely reached Ramsey's shoulder. She squinted up at him, planting her hands on her hips. "The hell you will. Go put up your feet and eat some of my sandwiches. I'll take care of this."

Before he knew what had hit him, Ramsey found himself in the office, staring down at enough food to feed his entire ground crew. He smiled, listening to Lenny talk to herself while she worked on the Cherokee. She'd fix it all right—if she didn't cuss it to death first.

As he reclined on the old cracked leather sofa, his third sandwich fell from his hand, and his arm slipped over the edge of the cushions. He awoke to find slanting sunbeams shining in his eyes and Lenny's small, callused hand shaking his shoulder.

"Come on, Ram. She's ready. I knew you'd want to check the innards before I put the covers back on."

He shook off the effects of sleep and followed her into the hangar. "It's looking good. You're one hell of a mechanic."

"Unless you can tell me I'm skinny, gorgeous and look twenty-five, I don't want to hear any flattery."

Laughing, Ramsey gave her a big, smacking kiss before climbing into the cockpit. "Lenny, when are you going to make some man happy?"

She stuck her head in after him. "When I find one as big and handsome as you, only younger," she retorted. "Oh, I threw a case of oil into the back, and here's a thermos of coffee. You've got some heavy weather ahead."

If she only knew. Grimacing, Ramsey signaled acknowledgment and continued his preflight check. He radioed for clearance and waved as he taxied to the designated runway. He felt better for the nap, even though he wished Lenny hadn't let him sleep so long. His mouth quirked into a smile. Coffee for him and oil for the Cherokee. She was always mothering him, just as she did his airplanes.

Urgency coursed through his veins as he left Casper far below. It was late and the sky had an ominous cast. He had to get to Jackson and separate Tess from Sabrina Haddon. *Jordan,* he told himself, *you're acting as if she were Caligula in drag.* The truth was simpler than that. He'd blown it with Tess, and he was afraid that Sabrina might offer her everything he'd withheld.

The closer he came to Jackson, the more his mind turned to Sabrina Haddon. She'd been so calm on the phone. Her voice made every word sound like a secret shared in the dark. His spine tingled as if long, slender fingers were brushing up and down his back. It was the same sensation he'd had while talking to her. If she were any other woman, he'd swear it was . . . awareness. The very idea lit a fuse to his temper. Never mind that she'd seemed concerned about Tess and sympathetic to him. She was probably as hard as marble and just as cold. He was in no mood to like that lady. She didn't belong in Tess's world, and he'd make damn sure she knew it.

With tribal instincts overruling reason and a strong sense of unease clutching his heart, Ramsey approached his destination.

SABRINA STOOD at the window in her workroom, breathing deeply, absorbing the silence into her troubled mind. The land appeared to be waiting, gathering strength for the storm to come. Golden-crowned and ermine-barked aspen trees swayed gracefully, their medallionlike leaves shimmering with each movement of air, appearing to wave a final goodbye before being stripped by bitter winds. She couldn't help but selfishly hope that the weather might further delay Ramsey Jordan's arrival, giving her more time with Tess.

He'd called from Casper to tell her he'd had mechanical difficulties and would be late. It was a reprieve—and a reminder that she only had Tess on loan for a few more hours.

The sound of his voice touched her memory as night touched the land; his words had been dark with hidden meanings and forbidding expressions. His frustration over the delay, his anxiety for Tess and his insecurity about the future of his relationship with his daughter had all been in evidence. . . .

"Oh, awesome!" Tess entered and walked around the room, running her hands over the equipment.

Turning from the window, Sabrina smiled and nodded toward the machine Tess was investigating. "That's a serger."

"I know. And that one is a blind hemmer, and the other one is just like mine."

"You sew?"

"Yeah. When you're built like me, it's hard to find what you want in the stores. Either the buttons gape on the blouses, or the skirts are too short. You know what I mean." Tess paused when she saw the drawings on the walls. "What exactly do you do?"

Amused, Sabrina looked at the denim skirt and shaker sweater Tess was wearing. "I design those, among other things."

"Cachet Fashions by. . . You're that Sabrina? I've been wearing your stuff since I grew bumps. They're the only nice clothes I can find that fit right."

Sabrina glanced down at her own tall, voluptuous figure. "That's why I'm in this business."

"Who makes them all?"

"My partner and I own a manufacturing plant. I design and make the patterns and samples—Marty runs the plant. We sell to retailers all over the West and just issued our first catalog."

Tess flopped into a chair at Sabrina's drafting table. "Is he gorgeous?"

"Who...Marty? Yes, she is." Sabrina thought of Martine Jensen, one of the world's truly good people, beautiful to her soul.

"Oh. Is there a he?"

"Not really. I seem to have more of a talent for making friends of men than—"

"Lovers? What a bummer."

"Men make wonderful friends, Tess."

"And lovers."

Sabrina's muscles tensed. Sickness washed over her. Tess was so young. Too young. "I hope you're just guessing."

Clutching her chest dramatically, Tess sprawled back in the chair. "Of course. I'm saving myself for the man I love."

The breath she'd been unconsciously holding escaped Sabrina's lungs. "I hope he doesn't come along until you're much older."

Tess's eyes took on a faraway expression as she spoke almost to herself. "Mmm. Much older...I wish I was."

Sabrina had the feeling that the source of Tess's wish was both masculine and older than was acceptable for a girl of sixteen. A teacher? Family friend? She wanted to ask, but Tess had already confided more to her than she'd expected.

"I hate to say it, but I'm hungry."

Sabrina grinned. Evidently Tess had inherited her own healthy appetite. "I have a beef stew simmering. All we have to do is toss the salad and make the dumplings."

"I'll do the salad. Daddy says my dumplings are like rocks."

In spite of Tess's appetite, she ate little. Sabrina didn't do much better. She couldn't. No matter what happened, she knew their unguarded moments wouldn't be repeated. Right now they were both tired and emotional; the barriers were down. Once Tess had time to think about it, and Sabrina actually accepted the transient nature of their relationship, they would be more restrained, less at the mercy of their emotions. Sabrina was all too conscious that this would likely be the first and last time she would enjoy girl talk with her daughter.

After cleaning up the kitchen, Sabrina lighted a fire in the living room, while Tess selected a tape to play on the stereo and advised her on the merits of compact discs. The room glowed intimately with candle- and firelight as Tess sat on the floor with a cup of hot cocoa. Sipping a glass of wine, Sabrina felt a creeping chill as the clock ticked off minute after minute.

"Do you think Daddy's all right? It's snowing pretty hard."

"I'm sure he is. When he called from Casper, he said it might take a while to complete repairs."

"I'll bet he's turning the air in his flight path blue." Tess sorted through a stack of old record albums. "He hates being hung up like that."

Sabrina had guessed that much about Ramsey Jordan. She wanted to know more. Again she couldn't ask. Her position at best was precarious; if she asked one question, she was afraid of asking others, whose answers she had no right to know. *Sometimes,* she thought wryly, *doing the right thing is a real bitch*.

The stereo clicked off, but Tess didn't seem to notice. She sat with her back to the fire, cocking her head in a way that made Sabrina feel as if she were seeing herself from a long time away.

"How did you feel when your father died?" Tess asked in a hushed, troubled voice.

With a trembling sigh, Sabrina relived the days following her father's death—days full of grief, loneliness, regret. "Lost . . . guilty . . . relieved."

"Me, too. Mom wasn't sick very long, but at the end she looked awful. It took two weeks, and she faded away an inch at a time. I hated watching her suffer, but I still begged her not to leave me." A single tear fell onto the back of Tess's hand. "Afterward . . . I was glad it was over, and resented her for giving up. Daddy wouldn't talk about it. I guess I resent him for leaving me, too."

"Maybe he couldn't talk about it, Tess. He and your . . . mother—" Sabrina stumbled over the word, hating it, feeling cheated by it. "She was his mate. It must be incredibly painful to lose a part of yourself like that." Sabrina sipped her wine. "Tess, you felt abandoned. So did he. Can you imagine how he feels now?"

"You mean now that I've run away?"

Sabrina nodded. "What you did has to be a father's nightmare. If you wanted to see me, you should have asked him first."

"I was afraid," Tess said bleakly, haltingly. "If he hadn't listened, or acted like he didn't care . . . All I wanted was to talk to someone. I wanted to know the truth about you...me...instead of always wondering."

Wanting to shake Ramsey Jordan until his teeth rattled, Sabrina counted to ten. She had no doubt that he cared about Tess. His ability to show it on a daily basis was something else again. The situation shouldn't have had to reach crisis point before he could show his daughter he loved her. If things continued as they were, Tess would spend the next few years of her life in a constant state of desperation until, one day, it would turn to an anger she would never outgrow.

"He passed your test. You shook him up good, Tess. But did you ever stop to think what you would have done if he'd failed?"

"He's really mad at me."

"I should hope so. What did you expect? Groveling? Did you think he'd thank you for risking your safety, your life, just to get his attention? Or were you hoping he'd feel guilty?"

"I didn't mean to hurt anybody," Tess mumbled.

"I'm sure you didn't, but it happened, just the same."

"Did I hurt you, too?"

Ask me that after I disappear from your life like the latest fad. Sabrina didn't dare anticipate any other outcome. It had been sheer despondency that had driven Tess to seek her out and open up to her. She'd needed desperately to talk to someone, and had reached out to the only other person she felt linked with besides her father—a father who had been emotionally absent from her life for two years. For Tess's sake, Sabrina hoped that would change.

But she couldn't think about that. Not when now was all she had. "Tess, I wouldn't trade today for all the hunks in Hollywood."

Tess's smile brightened the room. "I think you're crazy, but . . . thanks, Sabrina."

Knowing reality would intrude soon enough, Sabrina turned the conversation to subjects near and dear to a young girl's heart: fashion, music and Hollywood hunks.

"Soon enough" came with the increasing frequency of Tess's yawns. Despite the early hour and her own reluctance to end the evening, Sabrina suggested that Tess go to bed. "Your father might not make it tonight. The storm looks more like a blizzard."

Tess nodded in agreement. "Daddy's impatient, but he's also careful." She stopped halfway across the room. "Do you think we could see each other again? I'd really like to. . . ." As if she'd realized that Sabrina couldn't answer that particular question, Tess lowered her head and walked away.

"So would I, Tess," Sabrina whispered, staring into her glass until Tess disappeared down the hall. Leaning her head on the back of the sofa, Sabrina thought that if Ramsey Jordan had heard his daughter's request, he'd grind his teeth to nubs. Though he hadn't said it in so many words, his meaning was clear. She had no rights where Tess was concerned. She was to stay away.

And his rights were guaranteed by Sabrina's signature on a legal document that had been followed by sixteen years of his loving and nurturing Tess. She was his daughter in all the ways that mattered. Sabrina's common sense and moral code wouldn't allow her to think in any other terms. It was too late to reclaim what she had willingly relinquished, too late to expect more than a walk-on part in Tess's life.

As she listened to the rhythmic whisper of snow brushing against the house, Sabrina closed her eyes and allowed the tears to run freely down her cheeks....

CHAPTER THREE

AN IMPATIENT POUNDING on her door jerked Sabrina from her uneasy slumber. A glance at the hand-painted clock on the wall showed that an hour had passed since she'd fallen asleep. She heard agitated cursing, muffled by solid wood. Her stomach lurched with sudden apprehension. Ramsey Jordan had made it through the storm. But then she really hadn't expected otherwise.

"Just a minute." Dropping back to the sofa until circulation returned to her protesting limbs, she used the seconds to smooth her indigo sweater and matching wool trousers. Then forcing herself to move, she rushed to the door before he pounded it off the hinges.

A raised fist met her in the doorway, as he prepared to knock again. She backed up. He checked the forward motion of his arm and stared at her with an expression she couldn't decipher. Her gaze traveled upward to see dark, arched brows above eyes the color of fine brandy.

First impressions of Sabrina Haddon hit Ramsey fast and hard, like multiple blows to his solar plexus. Impressions of black hair, deep blue eyes, fair skin and a body that matched her voice—provocative and designed for intimate expression.

No wonder Chet had whistled when he'd seen her picture.

Ramsey had expected a slim fashion plate, with a full complement of cosmetics and not a hair out of place. The woman before him wore no makeup that he could see, and her hair was loose and natural around her face. Her clothes were elegant and feminine rather than severe or flamboyant.

Aside from her striking features and dramatic coloring, he had an immediate impression of the kind of class that no amount of training or cultivation could simulate. She stood straight and tall, radiating confidence and success. Her expression was calm and controlled. Then he noticed that her hands were pressed flat against the wall behind her, as if she needed something solid to hold on to. The edge of his antagonism dulled considerably.

Ramsey's jaw firmed. He shouldn't be noticing these things. And he definitely shouldn't be drawing such positive conclusions about her with no more than twenty seconds of up-and-down inspection. Damn. She'd upset his balance from the start. Extending a hand, he stepped forward. "Miss Haddon? I'm Ramsey Jordan."

Sabrina looked at his hand as though she wasn't quite sure what to do with it. She did know, but was reluctant to follow through, afraid of... what? Her fingers wrapped themselves around an impossibly big hand. Heat moved up her arm and sizzled through her body.

"Yes, Mr. Jordan. Please come in," she whispered. He didn't look like a father, husband or any domestic breed of man she'd ever seen. He made her think of a sinfully rich dessert, guaranteed to satisfy any woman's fancy.

He nodded. "Thank you." Removing his hat with his free hand, Ramsey felt a quickening in the pit of his stomach. Disgusted at his reaction to her touch, he broke contact and with both fists clenched at his sides, walked into the house as if he were storming the gates of hell. "Where's Tess?"

While his baritone voice was pleasing, the demanding tone of his question was not. "She's asleep," Sabrina answered stiffly.

A lock of wavy, coffee-brown hair fell over his forehead, compelling her to study him more closely. Coffee and brandy—warmth and intoxication. Evidence of frequent laughter radiated like sunbeams from the outer corners of his eyes. Long, curved dimples never quite disappeared from his lean cheeks and bracketed a perfectly shaped mouth that seemed more accustomed to smiles than his present scowl.

Only now did Sabrina realize that she was looking up at him, something that was a luxury for a woman of her stature. He appeared to be at ease with his size, which, Sabrina knew, many tall men weren't. The gentle firmness of his handshake proved to her that he had learned to control the strength of his well-muscled body.

Ramsey unfastened the buttons of his shearling coat and placed his hands on slim, jean-clad hips as he scanned the room.

Smiling was as difficult for Sabrina as forcing her gaze away from him. She had to remind herself of who he was, why he was here. "May I take your coat?" she asked. Thank heaven for formality; it filled the void where rationality and quick-wittedness should be.

"No. Tess and I aren't staying." Ramsey swallowed, feeling victimized by her . . . presence. In every way, Sabrina Haddon was more than he'd bargained for.

"Wouldn't it be wise to let her sleep through the night and take her home in the morning?" Sabrina marveled at how normal she sounded when she felt so unstrung.

"Wise? It isn't wise for her to be here at all, Miss Haddon."

Sabrina sighed in exasperation, threw up her hands and walked to the fireplace. At least his attitude gave her an excuse to turn her back on him and put some distance between them.

"For heaven's sake," she said, "I'm not the Wicked Witch of the North."

"West," he corrected her absently, watching her jab at the burning wood with the poker.

"What? Oh...whatever. Anyway, Tess has been around me all day. If there was damage to be done, I've had twelve hours to do it." Sparks flew as she poked the largest log.

"Watch it." Ramsey rushed to her side, snatching the poker out of her hand as he stomped on a hot cinder. "Did you do any damage?" he asked, lifting his gaze from the smudge on her cream-colored carpet.

Straightening, Sabrina looked at him. "To my carpet or to your daughter?"

"Dammit. I'm talking about Tess and you know it." Clamping his mouth shut, Ramsey wondered if he really was the guy acting like a first-class jerk, and stifled anything else he might have felt like saying.

Indignation encroached on the calm that Sabrina had vowed to preserve throughout their meeting, and her next words emerged through clenched teeth. "Mr. Jordan, kindly remember you are in my home. If you want to talk, take off your coat, sit down and stop acting like a..."

"Jackass?" he supplied helpfully.

Sabrina's eyes widened. This man was full of surprises, not all of them unpleasant. For the life of her, she couldn't decide whether to agree with him or not. "I wouldn't go that far," she said graciously.

Ramsey rocked on his heels, studying her through narrowed eyes. No one had spoken to him in years as she just had. He wasn't prepared to like her, yet every dark thought he'd had about her brightened as he stood there, receiving the most open, forthright stare he'd ever experienced. This was no shady lady of questionable character, he finally conceded. She was simply a lady.

And he was supposedly a gentleman. At least, his mother had tried her best to raise him as one.

To Sabrina's amazement, Ramsey placed his hat on one of the sconces that bracketed the mantel. After draping his coat over her desk chair, he sat down in one of the cream-, blue- and rose-striped chairs in front of the fireplace, and looked at her with self-mockery in his eyes.

"Would you consider offering this jackass a cup of coffee?"

Sabrina opened her mouth, found nothing to say and shut it again. Why did she see an engaging little boy requesting a treat, instead of a big man who had entered her home in an extreme state of agitation?

"Please? It's been one hell of a day, Miss Haddon." He smiled wearily. "I'll try to behave."

Sabrina turned on her heel without a word and headed for the kitchen. *What a disturbing man,* she mused. Just when she'd built up a full head of steam, he had put on the brakes. She sighed and measured coffee into her old-fashioned blue enamel pot.

Warning lights flashed in her head. She'd best not allow him to lure her into a false sense of security. He was fighting for his young, and, as with all animals, that made him dangerous. Never mind that she had no intention of going against his wishes concerning Tess. He didn't know that yet.

Placing mugs on a tray along with cream, sugar and a thermal carafe, Sabrina frowned. It went against the grain for her to be so suspicious. Always expecting the best from people had exposed her to hurt more than once, yet she preferred that to cynicism. But was she being cynical now—or understandably careful?

Careful, she decided. It was the only sane way to be around a man as unsettling as Ramsey Jordan. After pouring hot coffee into the carafe, she picked up the tray and returned to the living room.

Setting the tray upon the table between the chairs, she glanced at him. "Here's your..." The words trailed off as she saw his closed eyes and heard his slow, deep breathing. He was asleep, long legs stretched toward the fire with ankles crossed. She knew she was gaping, but couldn't help herself.

For some odd reason, she'd pictured Ramsey as an older man with a thickening waist, maybe even a paunch. Her gaze traveled to his flat, trim middle and lingered on the callused hands clasped loosely on top of his belt. They didn't look like the hands of an office executive, yet Tess had given her the impression that he held a white collar position.

A demanding growl came from his stomach. Sabrina smiled. That very human sound of hunger made him seem less threatening, more approachable....

His eyes opened to stare directly into hers. He'd probably been watching her watch him the whole time. Flustered at having been caught, Sabrina turned away to pour coffee.

"What did you tell Tess?" He didn't move a muscle except to take the mug she handed him.

"The truth. She wanted to know why I gave her up."

"And?"

His solemn tone made Sabrina uneasy. She had trouble thinking straight with those brooding, intense eyes fixed on her. She answered crisply. "Mr. Jordan, Bill Jarvis told me that he had informed you and your wife of all the facts surrounding Tess's birth, including how I felt about it. Nothing has changed."

"How did she react?" A curtain dropped over his expressive features, a curtain that didn't quite conceal his emotions. He'd known all along how badly she'd wanted to keep her child. The knowledge couldn't help but alienate him further.

Holding her mug with both hands, Sabrina sat down in the chair facing him. "With acceptance, I think. In some ways Tess is a very mature young woman—"

"How nice for you. What's next? A bid for visitation rights?"

"Aren't you being a bit dramatic about all this?"

Sliding upright in his chair, Ramsey leaned forward, draining his mug before thunking it back onto the tray. "It's a dramatic situation, isn't it? Misunderstood adopted daughter travels across the state to escape fiendish father." He looked down at his hands, which were hanging loosely between his outspread knees. "Arriving at her destination, she runs straight into the sympathetic arms of the woman who gave birth to her." He raised his gaze to Sabrina. "I feel like I've wandered onto the set of a soap opera, only someone forgot to give me a script."

Although he was trying to hide it, Sabrina detected his hurt and confusion from the look in his eyes, the break in his voice. This man needed reassurance every bit as much as Tess did. Sabrina wanted to give it to him, yet she couldn't forget Tess's unhappiness. "Don't cast me as the heavy, Mr. Jordan. Tess came here for answers...." She broke off, not knowing what to say, not knowing what exactly he wanted to hear. No one had offered her a script, either.

"Tess didn't take such drastic measures just to ask the obvious questions." There was no point in mincing words. Sabrina had to know that all was not well on the home front. And he was too tired to play diplomatic word games. "So what answers did you give her?"

"Other than the obvious ones, I have no answers to give her, Mr. Jordan." She put down her untouched coffee and rose to her feet. "I'll show you where Tess is," she offered quietly.

Ramsey felt as if she'd seen right through him, human frailties and all. His control was sliding away, exposing him. He'd never been very good at hiding his feelings and, right now, he was interested in more than Sabrina's motives concerning Tess. He was attracted to a woman he'd been sure he wouldn't like, and very uneasy with his involuntary responses to her. Under the circumstances, those responses didn't seem natural.

As he followed Sabrina from the living room, he watched her walk with grace and straight-backed dignity. This couldn't be easy for her either, yet her control appeared ironclad, unassailable. And somehow that didn't seem natural, either.

Sabrina turned to point out the room where Tess was sleeping. "Tess..." Her voice died. She couldn't break the hold of his gaze as he studied her intently in the brighter light of the hall.

"Tess is in here?" he prompted as he took in every detail of her face. The skin around her eyes was a little puffy and red. Her skin was a little too pale. At some point she had lost control. He ought to have been reassured by that, but instead, he just felt lousy.

"Uh, yes. I'll... be in the kitchen."

He nodded and watched her until she was out of sight. Now if he could just get her out from under his skin...

Collecting the dishes, Sabrina carried them into the kitchen, resisting all temptation to think. To think was to analyze and comprehend. There were some things she wasn't ready to understand—like Ramsey Jordan's effect on her.

A low, rumbling sound warned her she was not alone. Not ready to face him again just yet, she continued to wipe the already clean counter. "Is Tess getting dressed?"

"No. She woke up for a few minutes, then dropped back to sleep in the middle of a sentence. I didn't have the heart to drag her out of bed." He sighed. "Can you recommend a motel?"

Sabrina bit her lip as she stared out the window. "I can recommend several, but I don't think it will do any good." She nodded her head toward the landscape of wind-drifted snow and zero visibility. "Every available bed will have been taken by stranded travelers by now. If the roads aren't closed, they soon will be."

Ramsey reached for the dials of a radio on the counter. "May I?" The radio announcer confirmed Sabrina's opinion. Muttering an expletive, Ramsey leaned toward the window, gauging his chances of making it to his Jackson office, where a spare room was outfitted with bunks for just such an occasion. The wind had clearly picked up speed since he'd arrived, and the drifts were already piled dangerously high.

Frowning, he considered his options. There weren't any. To take on the single-lane road into town would be suicide, even in the Blazer. An employee had driven him here from his office....

"You're welcome to stay here, Mr. Jordan," Sabrina offered. What else could she do? The man looked as if he were contemplating hiking the twenty miles to town on snowshoes.

Seeing his reluctance to accept the inevitable, she picked up the bowl of food that stood cooling on the counter. "You're hungry. I have stew left from dinner. Would you like some?" Her stomach somersaulted. Why had she done that? Making a meal for a man was such an intimate thing. As intimate as offering him a place to stay for the night. Embarrassed at the direction her thoughts were taking, Sabrina lifted the plastic wrap from the bowl.

Ramsey's sigh sounded like a continuation of the wind, restless and frustrated at meeting obstacles to slow its progress. "I guess we're stuck with each other," he said finally.

Gently setting the bowl down again, Sabrina looked at him with deceptive serenity. "Tess didn't tell me how charming you are."

"Charming?" His eyes sparked; her statement had apparently ignited a fuse—a short one. "Miss Haddon, I'm in a place I don't want to be, because my daughter has run away to a woman she had no business meeting—not now. I'm damn tired, bloody furious and frustrated as hell." His hand again found the knotted muscles on the back of his neck, as he softened his voice. "I said I'd try to behave and I will, but charming is more than I can manage right now."

Sabrina's gaze flew to his face. She couldn't blame him, yet she wasn't about to let him blame her, either. "I sympathize with your position, Mr. Jordan, but I won't accept responsibility for it, nor will I be a target for your frustrations."

"Right now, all my frustrations have your name on them."

"Aim them somewhere else, Mr. Jordan." Her voice softened, too, and she took pains to choose and present her words carefully. "Tess showed up on my doorstep, remember? I didn't wake up this morning, expecting to be confronted with my very painful past, or to be cast as a referee in your family disputes."

Without missing a beat, she indicated the bowl of stew and reached into a cupboard for a plate. "I'll heat this for you."

Ramsey watched her careful, precise—busy—movements with interest. Evidently he was to be given a meal, whether he wanted one or not. Then he heard his stomach grumble. "Are you always like this?"

"Like what?" Sabrina slid the plate of food into the microwave and punched the appropriate buttons.

A corner of his mouth slanted as he held out one arm, indicating her board-straight posture. "Starched and pressed, not a ruffle out of place since I talked to you this morning."

Sabrina exhaled in a rush. Did that bother him? She hoped so. Perversely, she thought it only fair that he be as bothered by her as she was by him. "What good would my being upset do?"

"You mean if you let it show that you were upset, don't you?" He walked toward her, not stopping until he was a mere foot away.

Twelve inches of high voltage physical awareness wreaked havoc in her mind. It seemed to Sabrina that volcanoes erupted with less provocation, and it made her angry that, of all the men in the world, it was this one that had such an effect on her. She stared at the wisps of curling brown hair at the base of his neck. Those hairs invited speculation about more personal territory. Her nerve endings took over as he lightly urged her chin upward, compelling her to meet his eyes.

"Miss Haddon..."

The timer buzzed, saving her from having to do anything but turn away from him to open the door of the microwave and pull out the plate. Carrying it to the table, she frowned at the setting for one she had placed just so on the linen cloth. "Do you want this?" she asked briskly, realizing he had neither accepted nor declined her invitation.

"Yes...thank you." He spoke softly as he again focused on her face. "What about you?"

Was that gentleness she detected—as if he were trying to establish a measure of peace between them? "Umm...there's salad left. I'll have some of that."

"In here?"

Looking up, Sabrina found Ramsey searching her refrigerator, as if he did it all the time. As if, in spite of his initial hostility, he felt comfortable in her home, in her presence.

"Here it is," he announced. "Do you need anything else?"

"No. Sit down. I'll pour some coffee." The feeling of intimacy persisted. Her kitchen was shrinking by the second. The luminous gray of the blizzard wrapped itself around her house like a blanket. It was too cozy, too quiet, far too warm—and she didn't have the faintest idea what to do with herself.

With the coffee poured and the food served, she had to sit down across from him: more propriety, when there was nothing proper about any of this; more pretending that everything was progressing in a civilized fashion. Yet at times, Ramsey Jordan struck her as being anything but civilized.

Ramsey eyed the food dubiously. "Who made the dumplings?"

"I did. Why?"

He looked sheepish. "I probably shouldn't say this, but Tess's dumplings are—"

"Like rocks. She told me."

For one misplaced moment, their smiles reached across the table. Sabrina was spellbound by his genuine, honest-to-goodness grin, tender and a little sad, free of sneers and sarcasm. She could almost believe that he'd never insulted her on the phone or been angry when he'd arrived. She caught her breath and stared, feeling his fascination, feeling her own and denying neither. She was simply a woman who—given half a chance—would have liked to get to know the man sitting across from her.

But fate had decreed that she would never have that chance.

For that same timeless moment, Ramsey stared at Sabrina's eyes—were they violet?—and her silky hair, thick and falling past her shoulders. Womanliness radiated from her like an aura.... He definitely liked what he saw.

He brought himself up short. *Violets? Silk? Aura?* What in hell was he doing? What in hell was he thinking? He wasn't sure whether she was a threat to his relationship with Tess or not, but he was damned sure that she presented a threat to him. Every healthy male cell in his body reinforced that conviction. His libido was suffering from deprivation and he was vulnerable. He'd better remember why he was here. "You haven't answered any of my questions," he said tightly.

Narrowing her eyes, Sabrina dropped the piece of lettuce she'd been nibbling. "I told you I have no answers to give."

Ramsey nodded. "Concerning Tess. But what about you?"

"I am none of your business," she said pleasantly.

"I have the right to know about the woman my daughter has just spent the day with."

Sabrina couldn't argue with that, so she didn't try. "I'm a fashion designer with a half interest in a clothing company. I'm considered an upstanding citizen and support several charities. My record is clean—no arrests, not so much as a traffic ticket. With one exception, I've done nothing I regret...."

"Having Tess?"

"No!"

To Ramsey's ear, that simple, vehement utterance had a lot of other words crowding around it—words he really had no right to hear. But there were others he did have a right to hear and things he needed to know. "Giving Tess up?"

"In a way, yes." Sabrina sighed. How many times would she have to go through this in one day—in one lifetime? "Giving Tess up was the best thing for her and me at the time, but I'll still regret it for the rest of my life. My recklessness victimized both of us." Feeling his intent stare all the way to her bones, Sabrina dropped her gaze to her fork as she took a bite of tomato.

"You've been crying." Ramsey had the feeling he was pushing his luck, but he threw in the statement anyway, hoping to catch her unawares.

Unconsciously putting distance between them, Sabrina sat back in her chair as the fork clattered in her salad bowl. "Aren't we supposed to be talking about Tess?"

"Okay, let's talk about Tess." Ramsey sat back as if he, too, suddenly needed distance from the truths she might utter, as if her sharing those truths might in some way bring them closer than they should be. A mutual understanding would enhance the atmosphere of intimacy that neither of them could quite ignore. "How do you feel about Tess showing up?" he asked. "I'd really like to know."

Thrown off balance by his sincere tone, Sabrina responded automatically. Bending her head, she rubbed her eyelids with one thumb and forefinger. "I feel as if I've tripped and fallen into a bizarre dream, and this is last night and I'm still asleep. I've wondered about Tess for years. I have to keep telling myself that today is almost over and my second chance is used up. If you play your cards right, you and Tess will come out of this with a stronger relationship—"

Abruptly Sabrina stopped herself. She wanted to confide in him, wanted to reveal the confusion and uncertainty she felt. Most of all she wanted to tell him how badly she wanted to be a part of Tess's life. But she knew that if she did wear her heart on her sleeve, it would be knocked to the floor and trampled. There was no reason on earth for Ramsey Jordan to care one way or the other about her feelings. Why should he?

"From where you're sitting, that's bad," he stated flatly.

Sabrina lowered her hand and met his gaze head-on. "No. I want Tess to be happy."

"What will make her happy? Having you in her life?"

Clasping her hands now, Sabrina gripped them hard. "If you'd open your eyes, you'd see what she needs. I don't believe she consciously recognizes her actions as a last-ditch effort to get her father back. I'm merely the means to an end. She's hurting. You're the only one who can make it better."

Ramsey looked again at her eyes. "I suspect that you don't cry easily, Sabrina, and that when you do, no one else knows about it. You're hurting, too."

Sabrina. His use of her name startled her. He looked as if it had caught him by surprise, as well. That simple slip of the tongue made it seem as if their relationship had crept into a more substantial dimension without either of them realizing it. Sabrina stood up and began clearing the dishes, rinsing them, filling the sink with soapy water—fussing.

"I'll do that." Ramsey left his seat and came up beside her.

He was close enough to touch—closer than she could handle. "All right. I'll lock up the house." Handing him the dishrag, she quickly left the kitchen. Between them, the Jordans had hit so many nerves that she felt as if every one she possessed was battered and screaming. She was hurting in so many places that she didn't know how to begin to fight the pain. Stopping in the middle of the living room, Sabrina stared into the fireplace.

The fire was dying, and only a few embers glowed among the ashes. Her breathing shuddered, her head and shoulders drooped. She was weary to her soul. Had it been only this morning that she'd been thinking her life lacked excitement?

Ramsey's thoughts remained on Sabrina as he cast a wry glance at her built-in dishwasher, wondering how many dishes she'd washed by hand today. He was beginning to see patterns in her behavior. She was always calm, always in strict control, yet she always found something that needed doing when he drew too close, whether mentally or physically. Did she equate closeness with losing control... or having it snatched away?

The more relevant question was why he should be interested in her behavior patterns. Because of Tess? If he had any sense, he'd convince himself of that pretty damn quick.

His task completed, he headed for the living room, but stopped short in the doorway. The candles were burning low, casting somber shadows upon the walls. The hearth looked empty and cold in the wake of the bright fire that had welcomed him earlier. Sabrina's shoulders were slumped, and he saw her brush a hand across her eyes. His heart went out to her, but he forced himself to call it back. Damn it! He didn't want to witness her pain. It would be easier to believe that she didn't care, and that she'd be glad to see the last of the Jordans. The knowledge that her feelings were beginning to matter to him stuck in his throat like bile.

He felt like a villain who terrorizes women and children. But as she pulled herself up again to stand straight and proud, he thought she couldn't look less terrorized. She bent over a candle to blow it out, and the light from the guttering flame caught a tear as it rolled down her cheek. Hearing a soft sizzle when it fell onto the wick, he cursed softly.

She looked defeated. The thought disturbed him, and his chest tightened. Emotion clogged his throat. *Well, isn't that what you wanted, Jordan—to defeat her before she could sink her claws into Tess?*

Sabrina's hand curved around the candle, the light making her unpolished nails appear translucent. Her neat, pretty hands were trembling.

Sensing Ramsey's presence, she straightened, yet didn't turn to face him. "I'll say good night." Her voice sounded husky and strained. "The bed is already made in the room next to Tess's. The bathroom is across the hall." Extinguishing the rest of the candles, she turned on a lamp and checked the locks. "Will you turn off the lights before you go to bed, please?"

Ramsey stared into thin air as Sabrina vanished into her room. He heard the soft click of her door. Within minutes, the strip of light underneath winked out, and he felt as if Sabrina had thrown an internal switch, too, turning him out of her life, leaving him feeling more alone than he'd ever been before.

Burrowed under the covers of her bed, Sabrina concentrated on taking slow, measured breaths and relaxing her body as she listened to Ramsey moving around the house, switching off lights, double-checking locks, and finally entering the room down the hall.

She'd heard of strange bedfellows, but had not imagined she'd have one of her own. A mirthless smile formed at her whimsy as she rolled to one side, plumping her pillow and pulling it over her head to stifle further thoughts of Ramsey Jordan. It didn't work. She could hear water running into the bathroom sink. And even after all sounds had ended, she could still hear her thoughts.

She liked him; that was an incontrovertible fact. Beneath his contrariness and bursts of anger—and could she really blame him for that?—lurked a genuinely nice man. Remembering his smile, his gentleness, his willingness to admit he was wrong and apologize, she caught her breath. He hadn't wanted to understand her, yet he'd tried to, anyway. Jerking away the pillow, she told herself that after tomorrow she'd never see Tess or him again. She should have been relieved, but she wasn't. It shouldn't have mattered, but it did. And her only thoughts should have been of Treasure, but they weren't.

Sabrina drifted into sleep, visions of a faceless baby mingling with those of a tall man with eyes the color of fine brandy and a smile that intoxicated her.

CHAPTER FOUR

HAD IT REALLY happened? Or was it just an old dream, the players of which now had names and faces?

Sabrina awakened to a morning the color of cold cinders. The empty silence of the house sent shivers racing up her spine; somehow the previous day's happenings seemed as intangible as shadows in darkness.

Ignoring the silence and the sense of solitude, she opened the draperies on her bedroom window. The Tetons had donned a new winter robe that trailed over the valley below. The road was freshly plowed, and a rectangle of exposed concrete on her driveway flawed the crushed-diamond sparkle of the landscape. The parallel lines on the driveway that led away from the house—from her—were a cruel message of farewell engraved in the snow.

She found another message waiting for her in the living room. Propped against the mantel was a folded square of parchment that marked the end of her hopes. She reached for it, but did not read it. Not yet. Not until she had time to adjust to what she already knew, time to accept what must be written inside.

Opening the shutters on the large bay window, she sank onto the cushions of the seat built into its curve, unfolded the sheet and stared at the note for a moment before focusing on the neat, but hurried scrawl.

Miss Haddon—
The roads are passable, but it's supposed to snow
again. We need to fly out while we can. Thanks for
your hospitality.

                                    Ramsey Jordan

"In other words, thanks but no thanks," she muttered to the room at large. Damn him. Couldn't he even
allow her to say goodbye? But what had she expected?
A tearful leave-taking and promises to write? She
crumpled the paper in one hand. Fool that she was,
she'd hoped for...something.

A sigh echoed in her soul, as haunting as a voice in an
empty room. Loneliness had become so familiar to her
that she'd barely noticed its presence...until now. It had
been so long since she'd had someone to love, so long
since she'd belonged to anything but her work, to anyone but herself—so long since she'd loved a child she
didn't know and had never had the chance to like.

Well, she'd had that chance yesterday. It was all she
could ever have. Ramsey Jordan had made it clear that
she was as welcome in their lives as a door-to-door
magazine salesman. She couldn't really blame him. The
initial choice had been hers....

Tossing the crumpled note into the fireplace, she
headed for the kitchen and a cup of tea. Oceans of work
lay ahead; the new designs were waiting to be finished,
the model garments to be made, and specifications still
had to be typed up. If she didn't drown in all that, she
had to go to Denver to oversee a special showing for
buyers. Work was always being touted as a panacea for
all manner of afflictions—grief, desolation, loneliness.
Now was the time to prove whether it really was, or if it
was just another old wives' tale.

In her own style of disorganized efficiency, Sabrina labored through the fading of each day into night. For ten days, she thought nonstop. For ten days she hurt with an intensity she'd never known. She rarely left the house as she pushed herself to finish the new collection. Her work went well, but her thoughts did not. The world had tilted, leaving her suspended somewhere between reality and fantasy.

Reality was a teenaged girl, rather than the baby she'd held in her memory for sixteen years—years of loss and emptiness, of insignificance, compared to what might have been.

Reality was also a crumpled ball of parchment, whose message of finality had pierced her like cold steel.

Her dream of someday learning the fate of her baby had been fulfilled. She told herself it was enough. So why did she answer the phone, anticipating a deep masculine voice, or check her mail for his now-familiar scrawl? *Why him?* It was Tess's voice she wanted to hear, Tess's letter she searched for. All she wanted from Ramsey Jordan was sanction to build a relationship with Tess.

She really was dreaming. It was over. Both shoes had dropped. What more could happen?

Absolutely nothing.

DEAR MS HADDON...

Ramsey tossed his pen onto the desk, frustrated that he couldn't think past the salutation. He'd wasted half the day staring at the sheet of stationery, seeing visions of Sabrina discovering both an empty house and his impersonal, yet cruel note.

He'd done it deliberately in a vain attempt to contradict his everything but impersonal feelings toward her.

For a while he'd even deluded himself into believing that he'd done it to protect Tess.

But he knew he'd done it to protect himself.

He'd expected to feel relief upon leaving her, not let down at the thought of never seeing her again or ashamed for sneaking out of an uncomfortable situation. Knowing that she didn't expect further contact with Tess hadn't eased his guilt. He could have stuck around long enough for her to say goodbye. She'd been entitled to that much.

His conscience rode him hard. Tess's heavy sighs and accusing glares didn't help. Each morning he awoke with the hope that Tess had forgotten about Sabrina or given up on the idea of seeing her again. And then he hoped that he would forget about her, too.

But in spite of his efforts, he couldn't forget the woman who, in the course of one encounter, had reached deep inside him to touch something tender and needing . . . something he'd thought long dead and buried. Something he'd vowed never to feel for a woman again.

Pacing restlessly around his office, Ramsey reached for the telephone each time he came within range, then veered away at the last minute. He had to talk to Sabrina or renege on his promise to Tess. He couldn't do it in a letter and he couldn't do it on the phone. That didn't leave him many options.

He'd heard nothing but "Sabrina this" and "Sabrina that" for ten days, until he'd given Tess a noncommittal "We'll see." Of course, Tess had translated that to mean yes.

Right or wrong, like it or not, he was in this mess for the duration. The trick was going to be in keeping an emotional distance from the most fascinating and irritating woman he had ever met.

Jamming his hands into his pockets, Ramsey stared at the ceiling. He and Tess had gone further than he'd anticipated in working out their problems. He'd been honest with her, and a week-long vacation in the Rockies had gone a long way toward restoring their father-daughter relationship. It would never be quite the same, but then, he and Tess weren't the same, either. She was growing up. And he had to learn how to share more of himself, how to be a family man again—and how to be consistent in both.

Yielding to the inevitable, Ramsey punched a button on the intercom. Seth Jamison, his general manager, answered through the speaker.

"What's up, Ram? I thought you'd already gone home."

"I'm on my way, Seth. Can you put a Lear on the schedule for tomorrow?"

"Who's flying?"

"I am."

"A special run?"

"You might say that," Ramsey answered dryly.

"What are you carrying—people or cargo?"

"Just me, Seth. It's personal."

"It's expensive, Ram," Seth shot back.

"I know." Ramsey knew better than to wish that money was the only thing this trip would cost him. Even thinking about it robbed him of peace of mind. And if he wasn't careful, he would lose a hell of a lot more.

When Ramsey had nothing more to say, Seth sighed. "Okay, Ram. It's your dime. Want me to file a flight plan?"

"I'd appreciate it."

"Well, what am I supposed to do—tell them you're going to never-never land?"

"What? Oh. File it for Jackson, Wyoming."

"Again?"

Ramsey broke the connection without answering. Now that he'd made the decision and set the wheels in motion, his body quickened in anticipation; it was a sensation he experienced every time he thought about Sabrina. Maybe when he saw her again, he'd discover that she was less than he remembered, and he wouldn't react to her anymore. Maybe, with the feeling of opposition removed, the novelty of seeing her would wear off, and Tess's near obsession would take a back seat to the things teenaged girls were supposed to be obsessed with.

Like first love? That, too, was becoming a concern to him. Tess hadn't had a date with a boy her age in weeks—and not for a lack of offers. All she could see was Seth. Her latest gambit was flying lessons. After a lot of thought, he'd agreed to Seth teaching her, hoping that familiarity might breed indifference.

Seth had tried every way he knew how to get out of the lessons, stopping just short of hurting Tess. Ramsey appreciated that and sympathized, but there was no way he himself was going to teach Tess to fly. Every Saturday night would find them in neutral corners, with Tess sulking because of his impatience, while he popped antacid tablets. He knew his limitations.

There ought to be a merit badge for paternal endurance, he thought wryly as he got ready to leave.

AFTER SETTING the last stitch in a garment, Sabrina sat back and pushed her glasses farther down on her nose so that she could rub her eyes. All too often she'd caught herself brooding over things that were best locked away in her own Pandora's Box. Everything she saw, everything that happened, stimulated thoughts of Tess.

And Ramsey.

The sight of a brown Stetson or a sheepskin coat worn by a broad-shouldered tourist particularly disturbed her. Her senses were more fully alert than they had ever been.

Sabrina was at ease with her womanhood and had come to terms with the foolishness of her youth. Her scars were deep, but they hadn't disfigured the face of her dreams. She wanted a man with whom she could share involvement of the mind and body as well as companionship of the heart. She longed for children to nurture and guide and enjoy. In short, she dreamed of having a family...of belonging.

It was just a matter of finding the right time and the right feelings for the right man. Unfortunately, these things never seemed to come simultaneously.

Dreams, indeed. Wasn't she beyond the age of idealizing and expecting...what? A cataclysmic eruption of all-consuming passion? She'd been watching too many old movies and reading too many romances.

Sabrina vowed that the next book she purchased would be a manual on how to build a yacht in her spare time.

Her doorbell rang. Good. She needed a diversion to keep Ramsey Jordan from creeping around in her thoughts.

Aware that her glasses were still perched on the tip of her nose, that her sewing smock was flecked with bits of thread and fabric, a chalk pencil was stuck through her upswept hair and a tape measure draped around her neck, Sabrina opened the door.

This time she stepped back neatly as Ramsey checked the forward motion of his arm. Recognizing the source of her agitation, Sabrina tensed. Anger had been simmering in her since she'd read his oh, so charming note; anger at herself for having expected more from him, and anger at him for having disappointed her. The man disturbed her enough when he was absent. In person he created havoc in her life, both physically and emotionally. None of her rationalizations and denials could change that one inescapable, infuriating fact.

She raised her head and peered at him over the rim of her glasses. "Did you leave something behind?"

He still looked like a sinfully rich dessert.

And he made her heart trip over itself.

The right place. The right time. The wrong man. She *must* remember that.

Ramsey stared at Sabrina. She stiffened and seemed to grow a little taller as she glared at him. She'd obviously been working. Her makeup had worn off, and she looked as if she'd been in a fight with a ragbag and lost.

She looked . . . charming . . . pretty . . . sexy.

His senses came to full attention. He could smell a faint trace of fragrance. Soap? Perfume? Her cheeks were flushed and her eyes were dark, drilling holes through him. He wanted to forget her connection to Tess and think only of her as a woman.

He should have stuck with writing her a letter or calling her on the phone.

Ramsey cleared his throat. "Can we talk?"

Too rattled by his unannounced arrival to worry about good manners, Sabrina spun on her heel and led the way into the living room. She'd had the strongest urge to shut the door in his face, just as he had done to her eleven days ago with his abrupt departure.

She looked like a hag. Why couldn't he have warned her? Why couldn't he have simply called . . . or written? Why was he here?

Following in her wake, Ramsey pushed the outer door shut with a backward nudge of his foot. If he turned his back on her, he thought, she might throw something at him.

Sabrina clenched her fists, trying to banish the thousand imps that were skipping along her nerves. Sensing Ramsey's nearness, she moved away and collided with a chair. "If you're here to reaffirm what was written between the lines of your note, don't bother. Message received."

He pulled off his Stetson, placed it on the same sconce as before, and raked his hand through his hair. "That note was an exercise in self-delusion."

"Oh?"

"I was running scared. I thought Tess would be satisfied after meeting you, that once back with her friends and—" He rubbed the back of his neck. "You've become a real problem."

His glare of resentment was mutilating. On impact with the chair, Sabrina's knees gave way, dropping her inelegantly into a sitting position. Knowing what the admission must have cost him took the punch out of her anger, but her impression that he held her responsible put it back in again.

Sabrina ran her hands along the arms of the chair, curling her fingers over its edges. "Mr. Jordan, Tess is your problem. The fears conjured in your own mind are your problem. I am not. If you hadn't run, you would have found that out and saved yourself a trip." She winced at the hardness in her voice. He was being honest with her, while she was being just plain bitchy.

His wince mirrored her own as he sat down heavily in the chair facing her. "Why aren't you my problem?"

Her fingers dug into the velvet upholstery. "I have no intention of interfering in Tess's life—or yours. You can go home and relax. Problem solved."

She sounded so cold and uncaring, not at all like the warm, sensitive woman he remembered. He should have been pleased to see her in this less flattering light, but all he felt was disappointment. "What you're really saying is that you don't want Tess cluttering up your life. I should have known." The warm brandy of his eyes hardened to the dull sheen of polished agates.

Sabrina's head jerked back at the injustice of his remark. "You wouldn't know cow manure from chocolate ice cream."

The sneer disappeared from his face, and he gave her a slow, lazy smile. Leaning back, he raised one booted foot to rest on the opposite knee. "I'm very familiar with cow...manure. Why don't you tell me about chocolate ice cream?"

Closing her eyes, she lowered her head, her anger gone as quickly as it had come. How did one reveal the longing of half a lifetime? In her mind it had always been something abstract; a wish here, a dream there, if-onlys everywhere. Sabrina felt him watching her... waiting. She tried to shrug off the heat that was spreading through her from the inside out. "It's a treat. Something you ask for, even when you know you can't have it."

"Like Tess?" he asked softly.

Sabrina nodded. "Yes."

"Are you so sure you can't have it that you don't even ask?"

Sabrina raised her head. Was he playing some kind of cruel game? "I'm not a child, Mr. Jordan. I learned to accept that impossible is more than a word. Sometimes it's a fact."

His deep, ragged sigh tore through her as if it were her own. "You said all the right things to Tess, pushed all the right buttons. She wants to see you again. How do you feel about that?"

"Does it matter?" She was afraid to believe it did.

"Damn!" Ramsey slammed his fist against his open palm in frustration. "It's like pulling teeth out of a crocodile to get a straight answer from you. What are you fighting against?"

She spoke without thinking. "False hope, disappointment..." *You.* The thought escaped her subconscious, touching her with the lightness of a breeze. "Telling you feelings I've never shared with anyone."

Rising abruptly from his chair, Ramsey paced in front of the mantel. Shoving his hand into a pocket, he curved his fingers around his keys, gripping them hard. He hadn't given her much reason to expect sensitivity from him. "Okay. Let's agree that I've acted like a case of arrested maturity. I'm not too thrilled with me, either."

She looked so solemn, like a child being told the secrets of the universe. She also looked stunned, as if she hadn't expected to be entrusted with such a profound revelation.

Sabrina was speechless. He was throwing too much at her, too quickly. She was still trying to control her own responses to his presence. The hope he brought her of seeing Tess again confused her so much that she couldn't even *find* the emotional barriers to keep him at a distance, much less put them up.

Ramsey's mouth quirked into something between a smile and a grimace. "Tess took your advice. Instead of sneaking off to see you, she's asking—twenty times a day. I can't come up with one valid reason why not. At least none I'm willing to admit to her."

His state of mind was as chaotic as her own. Sabrina saw it on his face, heard it in the cracking of his voice. She admired him for not trying to hide it under the guise of macho pride. "Can you tell me?" she asked gently.

He studied the toes of his boots. "I'm...feeling a lot of things I don't know how to handle yet. Jealousy, because Tess came to you. Resentment, because she needs something I can't give her and she thinks you can. Our lives fell apart, and I haven't been able to put them back together." Tilting his head, he looked at her accusingly. "One day with you, and she's more normal than she's been in a year."

"And you hate it . . . and me."

"Hell, yes, I hate it. My pride hurts. You, I'm not so sure about." Ramsey forgave himself the lie. He *was* sure. Now he knew how Adam must have felt about the apple. Forbidden fruit was sweet, enticing, and invited a touch, a taste. But why was Sabrina forbidden? The question was driving him crazy, because he couldn't answer it with any kind of logic. Beyond her connection to Tess and the memories that were afflicting him like a timed-release poison, he couldn't find one good reason why he shouldn't allow himself to know her, like her....

Want her.

Sabrina willed her thoughts to drift away from the probing eyes of Ramsey Jordan. He had come here to talk about Tess, yet there was something else driving him that she didn't comprehend. The only thing she could cope with right now was his need to make a decision concerning his daughter. He'd asked for honesty, and that was all she could give him. "You want to know how I feel about seeing Tess again?"

He nodded.

"You won't like it," she warned him.

"I'll live with it. This has to be settled, Miss Haddon."

Again she had the feeling that he was referring to more than Tess. Tess was all that mattered, she told herself firmly. For better or worse, there could be no ambiguity or careful evasions. "Tess is my daughter. She always has been . . . here." Placing her hand on her chest, she rushed on, seeing his jaw clench. "But I'm not her mother. I wouldn't try to be. I care about her. I like her. I'd give the last sixteen years—and the next—to share a few moments of her life." Sabrina shook her head. "I don't know what else to say."

Ramsey studied her through narrowed eyes. Sincerity was apparent in her direct stare, the calmness of her body. If she knew that his real problem was the way he felt about *her*, she'd probably laugh him out of the house. How could it have happened so quickly, this wanting that went far beyond simple lust? "You don't play fair, Sabrina Haddon," he whispered.

His soft voice felt like a caress, stirring, exciting her. Just then she almost hated him for the effect he had on her. "I don't play emotional games, Mr. Jordan. I hope you don't, either. Not with Tess as the stakes."

Ramsey's mouth tightened. This wasn't the first time she'd put him down. He didn't like it. But dammit, she was right. He was playing a game, but it had nothing to do with Tess—and everything to do with defeating the way Sabrina affected him. Would she be able to keep her cool under the same circumstances? Shooting her an annoyed glare, Ramsey sat stiffly back in his chair.

Sabrina let her gaze fall to the ends of the tape measure that dangled from her neck. Picking one up, she began winding it into a tight, neat roll. If he didn't leave soon, she was going to say or do something foolish...like coming apart at the seams.

"You're so bloody together, it's intimidating," he said conversationally. "What do you do? Wrap your feelings in neat little bundles and put them in labeled compartments?"

Together? Startled at his perception of her, Sabrina dropped the tape into her pocket and cocked her head. "Would it help if I told you I feel like Humpty-Dumpty, held together with Band-Aids and school glue?"

He met her nervous smile with a wry one of his own. "Yeah, it would help. I've felt that way since Claire died. Before then, there was hope...a reason to try...." He shook his head and stared at the carpet. "Now there's just loneliness and a sense of failure. The battles don't have any meaning, and the victories seem more like consolation prizes." He knew he shouldn't have been talking to her like that, yet it was so easy, so right. He felt as if he'd known her as long as he'd known himself.

Something wrenched at Sabrina's heart as she listened to him express a kind of despair she knew all too well. He was looking into the past now. She sat quietly, waiting for the ghosts that had passed between them to disappear.

Ramsey focused on her still form. "I don't know why I'm telling you this."

"Maybe because you need to. After I gave Tess up, I felt as if she had died. I wanted to talk to someone about her."

"But?"

There was no one willing to listen, she wanted to scream, but kept silent. This kind of sharing with him was too...poignant, too personal. He'd mentioned the possibility of her seeing Tess again, so complications had to be kept to a minimum. "Is there anything else, Mr. Jordan? About Tess, I mean."

Resting his elbows on his knees, Ramsey clasped his hands between them. About Tess? No. He'd made a decision shortly after he'd arrived. Sabrina could be trusted. She would cut out her heart before she'd hurt Tess.

But another question had been clinging to the edge of his mind, refusing to let go. Compelled to ask, he told himself he needed to know for Tess's sake. Annoyed by the other reasons that were taunting him, he blurted it out without care for form or tact. "What about men?" Twin vertical lines formed between his brows; he watched Sabrina's face pale and her eyes blink, as if she'd been struck by an unexpected blow. "I mean—"

"I know what you mean," she snapped, her words as hard and cold as icicles. "Men—as in lovers, one-night stands, et cetera. Right?"

Ramsey lowered his head, let out his breath and looked up again. "Sorry. Poor choice of words."

Was it? Shivering, Sabrina pulled up her knees and wrapped her arms around them, experiencing again the vivid pain and humiliation of her past.

The people of her hometown had dealt a mortal blow to her youth and naiveté. In the small town, everyone had been like an extended family—at least until she'd returned from a summer spent with friends in Cheyenne, pregnant and alone. She'd immediately been branded "one of them," no longer "one of us," a social pariah who, they feared, would corrupt their daughters and contaminate their sons. Everyone whispered about her, but rarely spoke to her.

The idea that Ramsey might hold the same low opinion of her morals brought back the disillusionment and sense of betrayal with a rush.

It bothered Ramsey to see Sabrina curled up in her chair like a dead leaf. He looked at her, his eyes warm and soothing. Compassion laced his voice. "I didn't mean it the way it sounded. It's natural to assume that an attractive, intelligent woman like you would have a man in her life. I only wondered if Tess's presence would make things awkward for you." *Pretty lame, Jordan.* He hadn't even considered that aspect. Next he'd be trying to convince himself that he didn't want to hold her and kiss the stricken look off her face.

Sabrina believed him because she wanted to. She'd already learned that he spoke his mind and damned the consequences. She was much the same way and had choked on her own feet more than once. She relaxed an inch at a time.

"I really clobbered you with bad memories, didn't I?" It didn't take a genius to figure out when those memories had been created.

"Yes. I . . . overreacted."

Shrugging, Ramsey smiled in commiseration. "I seem to be doing a lot of overreacting myself." He sobered and returned his gaze to his hands. "You haven't answered my question."

"No. Tess won't make things awkward for me." Noting his frown, Sabrina wondered why she hadn't simply told him that there was no man in her life and there hadn't been one for a long time. Though she'd told the truth, its incompleteness left the bitter aftertaste of a lie in her mouth. Yet it was none of his business. . . .

"Anything that touches Tess is my business," he said, as if he'd read her mind. Ramsey wondered if his nose were growing. He'd sunk pretty low, using Tess as an excuse for his curiosity.

"I'm not . . . involved with anyone."

The tightness he hadn't been aware of drained from his body, and he eased back into a sprawl. "Lady, you're one irritating woman."

"Don't call me Lady."

"Don't call me Mr. Jordan," he challenged her, forgetting his determination to keep things impersonal.

Bemused, Sabrina returned his stare. The sound of their laughter surprised her; it was an easy, mellow sound that dispelled the tension like light dispels darkness. She enjoyed the smile that remained on his face after the laughter faded. It was a smile that never failed to captivate her.

Ramsey felt good, comfortable, more relaxed than he had in a long time. Suddenly his smile fell away with the realization that he'd never felt this good. He experienced a jolt, as if he'd flown through an air pocket and been caught in an unexpected updraft. Her lips were parted on an indrawn breath. She looked as stunned as he was over the impact of the moment.

Sabrina knew that they had touched in some indefinable way. Their mutual hostility and defensiveness were gone, as if they had never existed. And her desire to get to know him had intensified to the point where she could hardly bear it. Layer by layer, the attraction she felt for him was building, becoming more of a barrier to her self-control and common sense. She'd seen too much of the inner man, and liked too much of what had been revealed: his openness, painful though it often was; the sensitivity that broke through his resentment and mistrust; and his willingness to forgo his own needs in favor of those of one he loved.

What would it be like to be loved by him?

Sabrina pushed the wayward thought away. Things were getting out of hand. *This,* she told herself firmly, *is a purely physical response to a good-looking man. Generic lust.*

When had she started lying to herself?

Ramsey studied her openly, hungrily, enjoying her tangible presence after being haunted by the nebulous images in his memory. His gaze followed the same path his mind's eye had traveled over the past ten days—over her forget-me-not eyes and forget-me-not body—intelligence shining in the former, pride and grace enhancing the latter. But he didn't like what he was feeling for her, and told himself that she was just another pretty woman, nothing special.

He didn't believe it for a second. Sabrina was everything special. Everything he'd dreamed about once upon a time....

This was insane! He rose in one quick motion, afraid to linger more than he already had. "I'll arrange to bring Tess up here for a weekend as soon as I can. We'll take it from there."

Sabrina stood on legs that felt like Slinkys. She nodded, knowing that her voice would come out in a croak if she tried to use it. She'd be seeing Tess again. And Ramsey would be coming with her.

She should have expected that; his way was logical, and consistent with his need to protect both Tess and himself.

She would be the only one unprotected.

Together, she reminded herself. *You're supposed to be together.* Her control might wander once in a while, but it never left her completely. She'd just have to be more careful.

His reluctance to leave her rooted him to the floor. He touched her cheek—just a simple touch, just this once. It was a mistake. Her skin burned under his fingers, and her sigh blew away every ounce of his resistance. "Somehow," he whispered hoarsely, "I've got to find a way to stop wanting you."

Curiously, Sabrina wasn't surprised by what she heard. She touched the back of the hand that lay on her cheek. "Why?" she asked simply.

Why? Ramsey turned away from her and strode to the door. Her question told him more than he could afford to know about her feelings. For the second time in his life, Ramsey sought escape.

"I'll call you," he growled over his shoulder as he opened the door to breathe in cold, sobering air.

Why. All of a sudden he didn't have any answers.

Sabrina watched him, understanding his need to bolt. She had the same compulsion, but was aware that escape would only work if she could leave herself behind.

Out of the corner of her eye she saw his hat. Plucking it from the sconce, she rushed toward the still-open door. "Don't forget your hat!" she called, but he couldn't hear her over the roar of his car. Absently tracing the design on the band, she walked slowly back into the house.

CHAPTER FIVE

THE BRIGHT NEW HOPES Sabrina had for seeing Tess again turned to a flat gray by the end of the following week.

Ramsey hadn't called.

And if he tried to contact her now, he would receive a message from her answering service. It hadn't occurred to her to tell him that she would be coming to Denver.

"Ms Haddon? It'll take a few minutes to run this down."

Sabrina nodded to the clerk in the air freight office. He'd said the same thing twenty minutes ago, when she'd come in to claim the wardrobe trunk full of sample garments. Tossing her coat onto a chair, she strolled across the reception area with barely controlled patience. Nothing was going right.

Why hadn't Ramsey called?

Why. It was a word that recycled questions over and over again.

She stared out of the window at the activity in the private sector of Denver's Stapleton Airport. The sight of people running around in shirt sleeves intensified her discomfort. If she hadn't been so preoccupied with the Jordans, she would have had the presence of mind to check the weather before leaving Jackson. Her taupe wool trousers, winter-white sweater and wool jacket were fine for the cold weather at home, but the temperature in Denver was a balmy sixty-eight degrees Fahrenheit.

A tall man and woman came into view, the woman chattering excitedly, the man bending his head to listen as they walked toward the building. The woman—no, a girl in her teens—glanced up and stared for a moment before breaking into a run. "Sabrina!"

Stunned and disoriented, Sabrina barely heard either the ecstatic squeal or the sound of the door being jerked open. Dimly she realized that it was Tess who was giving her an enthusiastic hug.

"I knew it was you! What are you doing here? Did you come to see me? Did Daddy call you?"

"I'm here on business...the showing I told you about," Sabrina answered absently, instinctively returning the hug and trying to concentrate on Tess's chatter, while her gaze found Ramsey. He stood outside, hands on hips, body perfectly still, as if he were giving himself time to absorb a shock. She knew how he felt. Tess and he were the last people she'd expected to run into—but the ones she most wanted to see. Prickles of unease skittered over her skin. His expression wasn't discernible through the tinted windows, but she did notice his stiffness, his tension as he opened the door and walked in.

"Miss Haddon." He nodded politely, the effort almost more than he could manage. He was too stunned by her sudden appearance to think clearly or react logically. His eyes developed a will of their own as his gaze roamed over her form, appreciating the way she filled out her sweater. God, she looked good, he thought. Her slacks fitted just right over her full hips and showed off her long legs. Those legs inspired some very stimulating fantasies.

For one brief moment, nothing existed but Sabrina. His blood sizzled and he pulled hard to get enough air in his lungs. His heart goose-stepped in his chest. He clenched his jaw as Tess threw her arms around his neck and planted a kiss on his cheek, erasing everything but the whys and wherefores of Sabrina's presence... here...now, when Tess was sure to be around.

"Daddy, you didn't forget. You called her."

Why are they here? Dazed, Sabrina looked at Ramsey over Tess's shoulder. Every thought stumbled and fell at his expression. His smile looked as if it had been poured into a mold and left to set. His entire manner seemed strained....

Though Ramsey's face didn't soften, his voice did as he ruffled his daughter's hair. "I didn't forget, Tess, but I didn't call her, either. I've been in Dallas all week, remember? I was going to call her this afternoon."

"But..."

"It looks like Miss Haddon came here on her own." Ramsey pinned Sabrina with a probing stare, silently asking a question, wondering if he really wanted to hear her answer.

He hadn't changed his mind. Sabrina's spirits flew out of the dismal trench they'd been wallowing in for the last week and a half. Then she registered the grimness of his tone.

Why was he acting so strangely, so distantly? She had the impression that he was guarding every thought, every feeling, forcibly restraining himself....

"Ms Haddon?" The clerk called from behind the counter. At first impassive, his manner grew increasingly nervous as he glanced at Ramsey. "Your trunk hasn't arrived yet."

Absorbing the information, Sabrina turned to the clerk—Joe, his name tag read. "Why isn't it here? I paid for first-day delivery two days ago," she explained, forcing herself to be patient. "It never arrived at my office. My partner was told it had been loaded on to the wrong delivery truck yesterday, but that I could pick it up this afternoon."

"I...uh..." He flicked another strained glance at Ramsey. "It appears to be lost, ma'am."

It infuriated Sabrina that the clerk kept looking at Ramsey, as if he were the one he had to answer to and she was of no consequence. What did Ramsey have to do with her trunk?

The contents of that trunk represented her entire line for the summer, plus the originals for Cachet's special charity auction in a little over a week. She'd spent days longer than necessary making the prototypes, ripping out and resewing botched seams while she mooned like a lovesick fool over an irascible man whose attitude now bordered on accusation. What was he accusing her of?

Suddenly she was sick of it all: living on the edge of the hope *he'd* given her and which she hadn't asked for; struggling to cope with emotions she had no business feeling for him; always sympathizing with his predicament. What about her own?

And now her trunk was missing. If she thought about it long enough, she was sure she'd be able to blame Ramsey for that, too. It might be unreasonable, but what the heck! If he could be angry at the drop of a hat, surely she was entitled to be unreasonable at the loss of her trunk.

She's losing it. Ramsey was fascinated at the prospect—Sabrina actually letting go of her control? At the same time it annoyed him that it could happen over a mere trunk of clothes, when she'd been so unflappable about everything else.

His fascination didn't override his fury—a fury directed mainly at himself for feeling so let down at finding her here. He recalled Chet telling him that she came to Denver several times a year, but that didn't explain why she was in this particular place at this particular time. Sabrina had made such a point of telling him that she would neither take action on her own nor interfere in their lives. He'd believed her, trusted her, respected her honesty. Finding her here, thinking that she might have tracked them down in spite of what she'd said, felt too much like betrayal. And it was a betrayal he was taking personally, like a hard kick in the gut.

"Sabrina, does the trunk have all your new designs in it?" Tess asked with genuine concern. "That gorgeous red dress and everything?"

Hearing it said aloud threatened what was left of Sabrina's control. The patterns and duplicate sample garments were at the plant, but the originals for the auction were one of a kind, hand-sewn and -finished inside and out—irreplaceable in the time that was left. The showing was scheduled in a little over a week. "I'm afraid so, Tess."

Tess tugged at Ramsey's arm. "Daddy, *do* something. All those neat clothes are *lost*."

Ramsey almost choked on a stifled burst of laughter. Tess wasn't worried about Joe—an apprentice mechanic who was having to work the front desk until he fully recovered from hand surgery. The only thing that seemed to matter was a box full of clothes.

"What's the problem, Joe?" Ramsey let himself in behind the counter. Joe was a good mechanic, but his experience in dealing with the public was limited, and Ramsey knew that Sabrina could corrode steel with a few softly spoken words. He'd hate to think what she could do if she really let fly.

"Well, sir, I think the trunk somehow got loaded on the wrong plane in Jackson. I'm...not...sure which one."

Sir? Sabrina blinked at Ramsey, standing so comfortably behind the counter as if he— Her gaze flew up to the sign on the wall. Ram Air Couriers. Terrific. She'd used this carrier for years. The coincidence staggered her. She didn't know whether to dissolve into the floor or go through the roof.

Taking in Ramsey's jeans, safari shirt and Nikes, she asked herself how she could have possibly known. Aside from Ramsey's casual references to business meetings and constant travel, nothing had been said about the nature of Ramsey's business. And she'd conditioned herself not to seek forbidden information.

"Okay, Joe. I'll get a printout of who went where and make some calls. I don't think anyone could miss a steamer trunk in the cargo. They're practically extinct now." Ramsey squeezed his employee's shoulder in reassurance.

"Yes, sir. I hadn't thought of doing that. I'm sorry, sir."

"Why? Did you lose the shipment?"

"No, sir."

"Then don't sweat it." Favoring Joe with a smile, he began tapping keys on the computer terminal.

Indignant at having been overlooked when Ramsey was passing out aid and comfort, Sabrina summoned the voice she occasionally used on balky fabric sales-men and employees whose favorite phrase was "I can't." "I need that trunk no later than Monday."

"Morning or afternoon?" he asked, distracted by the data on the computer screen.

"Morning."

"Piece of cake." Ramsey glanced up from the screen. Her expression was enough to make the queen of England feel like a peasant.

She wanted him to elaborate, but wouldn't give him the satisfaction of asking. Nodding imperiously, she turned away from him to speak to Tess. "How have you been, Tess?"

Tess had finally picked up on the tension between the adults. "Uh, fine," she said. "Dad's GM is teaching me how to fly." She waved her hand in the direction of the hangar. "We just finished a lesson."

"What fun," Sabrina said weakly as she looked at the small plane just inside the open hangar doors. "Is it safe?" she had to ask. The twin-engine prop seemed . . . insubstantial.

Ramsey frowned at her back. She sounded just like a mother, bringing home to him the strangeness of the relationship between Tess, Sabrina and himself.

"Sure. Daddy says there's more room up there than there is on the freeway." The girl craned her neck to scan the parking lot, her eyes at first bright with antic-ipation, then dimmed with disappointment. "I guess Seth is already gone. I wanted you to meet him, Sa-brina. He's the most—"

"Seth is a fully qualified instructor, Miss Haddon."

"I see." The warning in Ramsey's voice drew clear boundary lines between his territory and her own. And she saw more than that. Tess's expression when she spoke of Seth left no doubt that he was the reason she wanted to be older. Sabrina wanted to know more about this man, but that was not her right, either. Worrying about it was, though—a natural side effect of loving.

She looked at her watch. "Well, I really must go...." Picking up her coat, she kept her gaze averted from Ramsey and smiled at Tess. "Take care...."

"Miss Haddon." Ramsey stopped her at the door.

His hand on her arm was gentle, but unrelenting. To anyone watching, it would have appeared that he was being courteous, preparing to open the door for her. But his expression was as hard as the concrete beneath her feet.

Sabrina glanced down at his hand, silently demanding that he release her.

"We need to know where to contact you when we retrieve your trunk," he said mildly.

Sighing, Sabrina pried her arm out of his grip as unobtrusively as possible. "I'm staying at the Brown Palace."

"Will you be in tonight?"

"Yes."

"Then you can have dinner with me?" It was a challenge fenced in by civility; he was daring her to refuse.

"I..." Sabrina would have refused, but caught Tess's expectant gaze and knew she couldn't. No doubt Tess thought they'd be discussing her and making plans to get together. "All right," Sabrina said. "I'll expect you around seven." It was a puny bid for control, but some was better than none, and it had occurred to her that she'd been outmaneuvered.

With her acceptance given and duly witnessed, Ramsey accompanied her outside. The predatory smugness

on his face confirmed her suspicions. He had outmaneuvered her.

"It was a dirty trick, asking me in front of Tess so I
couldn't refuse."

"You should learn to take what you dish out."

"What?"

"We'll talk about it tonight." Ramsey wanted to believe the innocence she projected, but he had to be sure
that she was what she appeared to be—for Tess's sake.
For his own, he wanted to use that mistrust as a ten-foot
pole, to keep some distance between them. Though he'd
been trying to do just that all along, every time he saw
Sabrina, the pole seemed to become shorter. This time
she'd made it easy for him by showing up so conve-
niently—so blatantly. Had she engineered it?

"We can talk now, Ramsey." She slipped back into
using his first name, deliberately reminding him of their
last meeting and of how well they'd communicated,
letting him know that she was open to the same honesty they'd shared before. Without that, there was no
point in seeing either him or Tess again. She swallowed
painfully.

"No," he said through gritted teeth. "Not now." As
she tilted her head in question, he exhaled and his
mouth twitched in a parody of a smile. "I'm a little too
close to being angry, Sabrina."

"That bad, huh?" He didn't answer. Perplexed, she
walked beside him in silence. His other bursts of temper had been generalized, unfocused, radiating from a
multitude of sources. Those she'd been able to cope
with, knowing that she wasn't one of the sources and
aware that underneath his frustration he recognized that
she was as much a victim of circumstance as he was—
if not more so.

This time she was very definitely the target of his anger, and he was acting as if he expected her to know exactly why. What had he said? *It seems Miss Haddon came here on her own.* She'd heard disappointment in his voice—a kind of fatalistic acceptance, as if he had been aware of the worst that could happen, yet had not wanted to believe it actually would....

Oh, no. Her step faltered as the answer came to her. He thought that she'd tracked them down when he hadn't called. What else could he think? Even she had been staggered by running into him and Tess like that. No wonder he'd been so cold and distant. At their previous meeting, he'd displayed an astounding amount of trust in her. He'd talked to her as if he'd known her for a very long time, and he must have felt horribly betrayed at finding her in his office. In his place, she might have come to the same conclusion.

Unconsciously she speeded up her steps, her heels hitting the pavement a little harder; the sound resembled that of a drumbeat heralding battle. She would have liked to think that, in his place, she'd at least ask questions first and shoot later.

She stopped just short of colliding with the company van that had been left at the airport for her and looked up at him. "You're so ready to judge me, Ramsey...so willing to think the worst. Even criminals are given the benefit of the doubt."

"Sabrina, I'm trying bloody hard not to judge." He glanced toward the building. "Tess is waiting for me. We'll take care of this tonight." Opening the door to the van, he cupped her elbow to help her in, relieved that she didn't resist, also relieved that she'd stopped looking at him with an expression of such innocence; it made him want to drop the subject altogether.

Sabrina climbed into the van and sat down sideways, facing him so that he couldn't shut the door, confronting him with her eyes on a level with his, her throat tight with the effort to keep her voice steady and calm. "I want to settle this now, Ramsey," she said.

Ramsey glared at her, not fighting anger now, but in its unrelenting grip. She was so close, her gaze steady and open; too close—just a kissing distance away—and he wanted to kiss her almost as much as he wanted to throttle her. "We agreed that I'd call you to set up a meeting," he said evenly, keeping his emotions firmly in check.

"We did." Sabrina nodded slightly.

His mouth tightened. "Dammit, what am I supposed to think?"

"Exactly what you did, under the circumstances. And I suppose that under the circumstances the burden of proof falls on me."

"This isn't a trial, Sabrina. Contrary to what you're probably thinking, I do understand—"

"No, you don't."

She said it so calmly that Ramsey almost missed it. "I know how much you want to see Tess. When I didn't call—" Then her words caught up with him. "What do you mean, I don't understand? I damn sure thought I did."

When he said nothing more, Sabrina made her explanation, knowing he needed one, knowing that if he didn't accept it, she would never see him again—and that would be her decision, not his. "I came to Denver on business. I had no idea that you and Tess were here—or that you are Ram Air Couriers."

Rubbing the back of his neck, Ramsey grimaced at the knots of tension he could feel in his muscles. "You didn't say anything about coming to Denver."

"I'm not accustomed to reporting my movements to anyone." Sabrina realized he might not identify with that. Being a family man, he would have a built-in responsibility to make others aware of his comings and goings. "Don't take my word for it, Ramsey. Check your company records under Cachet Fashions. I've used your service for years, and always in late October."

Swinging her legs around, Sabrina grasped the door and pulled it shut as Ramsey stepped back. "Think about it. If you still don't believe me, then there's no point in any further contact between us." When he didn't reply, she put the van into gear and drove out of the parking lot. Catching a last glimpse of him as she turned on to Smith Road, Sabrina wondered if she'd just issued an ultimatum or passed sentence on herself.

Hands in his pockets, Ramsey stood in the parking lot, watching her go, fighting himself—and losing, in the face of a creeping certainty that he'd made a jackass of himself . . . again.

IF DENVER WAS considered the Queen City of the plains, the Brown Palace Hotel was surely the grand duchess: imposing, regal, her Mexican onyx walls a swirl of rich color, the brass and iron railings mellow with age, the nine-story atrium roof of stained glass bringing in sunshine and a feeling of warmth. The Brown carried her age well, like a friendly, welcoming dowager who was at her most lively when she had guests and family to coddle—and perhaps more history to witness.

The spontaneous greetings of the staff, many third and fourth generation, always made Sabrina feel as if she was coming home for a visit. Everyone from the doorman to the in-house historian treated her like a favored daughter returning to the nest. During her stay they would pamper her and make her feel comfortable in her surroundings. Right now she needed that—badly.

As the waitress serving tea in the mahogany- and glass-enclosed lobby waved at her, Sabrina sent her bags up to her suite and sat down at one of the small Italian marble tables that were scattered among burgundy leather sofas and chairs. The waitress appeared at her side. "Miss Haddon, when I heard you were coming, I saved you some scones. They've been popular today."

Sabrina sighed and visibly relaxed. The continuity soothed her. Tea at the Brown was one of her favorite rituals. "Thank you, Theresa. Scones and a pot of tea are just what I need." What she really needed was distraction, nourishment and a long bath. Maybe then she would be able to approach thoughts of Ramsey and Tess with more enlightenment and less confusion. Maybe after a half hour or so of seeing familiar people and chatting with them, she wouldn't feel as if she'd been tipped out of the life she knew into one of chaotic emotions and uncontrollable situations.

The minute she was alone in her suite, though, her tension returned. Ramsey stepped to the forefront of her mind. Trying to push him back, she wandered the rooms, reacquainting herself with their appointments, smiling at the personal touches that had been provided for her. A monogrammed terry cloth robe hung in the closet of the art deco dressing room. The radio was tuned in to her favorite station. An arrangement of her favorite flowers sat on the desk in the parlor.

She was invariably touched by the personal care given by the hotel, yet at the same time was made achingly aware that she was alone, not just in this suite, but in the world—a world where everyone else seemed to have binding ties, with family, lovers, children...lasting ties, sealed by commitment.

With jerky, impatient movements, Sabrina raided both her luggage and the suite for props to create an atmosphere guaranteed to induce tranquillity. Soon, a decadent amount of milk bath was frothing in a tubful of steaming water. She tossed her clothes into a pile and donned transistor earphones tuned to a symphony by Rachmaninoff. Then she lit a single candle, which cast a mellow glow onto the tiled walls. Once immersed in the silky water, Sabrina shut her eyes, determined to relax if it killed her.

All that effort was a dead bust. The clutter in her mind overwhelmed her, closed in on her from all sides, nagged at her like a junk drawer that needed cleaning out. She wouldn't be able to unwind until she sorted through it all.

The matter of the trunk could be shoved into a corner. For the moment there was nothing more she could do, and she had absolute confidence that Ramsey would find it. In all the years she'd been shipping with Ram Air Couriers, nothing had been lost. The law of averages had simply caught up with her.

Her mouth curved upward. Tess had been happy to see her. The feeling was mutual. Only a few short weeks ago, there had been no promise in her life, nothing to look forward to but more of the same. Tess's appearance had brought her some very special moments. Ramsey's second visit had promised so much more. Her smile slipped into the bubbles that were rising to her chin. Ramsey had been neither happy to see her nor pleasantly surprised. Ramsey had a nasty habit of sneaking into every thought. Granted, he and Tess were a package deal. The problem was that she had far too many thoughts of Ramsey that had nothing to do with Tess. . . .

Not long after she'd climbed out of the tub, Sabrina found herself standing in front of the mirror, dressed in shantung pants and silk charmeuse camisole of smoky violet with a sheer kimono jacket that had been hand-painted in shades of violet and gray on a cream background. Holding a mascara brush, her hand paused in midair. Now why had she chosen an ensemble suitable for an intimate, purely social evening? And why in heaven's name was she bothering? Wishful thinking? Since when? She wasn't even sure what she was wishing for.

Yes, she was. . . .

Sweeping up her hair into a loose cluster of curls, Sabrina slipped on a pair of sandals with two-inch heels and gave one last glance at her reflection. Ready. Nonetheless she nearly jumped out of her skin at the sharp rap on her door. Anticipation surged, propelling her toward the sitting room. At the threshold to the small foyer, she hesitated, reluctant to find only disappointment, in the form of a waiter delivering the wine she'd ordered from room service. At the second knock, she took her courage firmly in hand and pulled open the door. Her gaze touched the middle of a broad chest, traveled upward, then down again.

Ramsey stood in the corridor, wearing a tailored three-piece suit that boldly stated "executive material" and emphasized his muscular fitness—and an elegance she hadn't associated with him before. Her temperature shot up ten degrees. Desire plucked at her nerve ends. Her senses stretched and purred with pleasure.

She really didn't want to think about their problems right now, but he had that look of brooding intensity on his face—a look that said he was caught between a rock and a hard place and couldn't find anywhere to settle. His posture was stiff, as if a move in any direction might be the one to do him in.

He cleared his throat. "I made reservations for eight." After his first glimpse of Sabrina, Ramsey fixed his attention on one of the amethyst teardrops hanging from her ears. That one brief look had made him hungry—hungry for her. He took a deep breath. Her perfume teased him, lightly touching his senses before drifting away, leaving behind a subtle come-hither invitation, inspiring a desire to touch and taste and breathe her. He reminded himself why he was here and focused again on the earring.

She smiled—barely—and had to work at sounding natural. "Good. That gives us time to talk." Loosing her grip on the door, she stepped back. "Come in, Ramsey. I won't bite if you won't."

As soon as he entered the sitting room and heard the door click shut, Ramsey turned to face her. If Sabrina had been close to falling apart earlier, she had it all together now. Everything about her was calm and relaxed as she strolled over to the sofa and sat down, gesturing for him to do the same. He chose to pace the width of the room.

"I ordered some wine."

Ramsey nodded and loosened his tie.

"Did you check your records?" she asked, suddenly impatient with the conversational preliminaries.

"No." Ramsey stared glumly at the wall.

Sabrina looked down at her hands. "I see."

"I took your word for it."

Sabrina couldn't have been more shocked if he'd zapped her with two hundred and twenty volts. Her head jerked up, her eyes widened, and she wasn't quite sure if she was breathing. "Just like that? Why?"

"Damned if I know." He joined her on the sofa and turned his head to look at her. "No, that's not true. I've been looking for excuses not to trust you. When I saw you, I overreacted. I was ready to judge and sentence you without a word being said, and I apologize for that."

"It's an unusual situation, Ramsey. Your daughter is involved, and I'm a relative stranger. You have a right to be wary of my motives." Sabrina very badly wanted to reach out to him, not because he'd accepted what she'd told him at face value, but because he hadn't watered down his apology with excuses or qualifications. She had to respect his lack of conceit and obvious sincerity.

Ramsey had no explanation for believing her except that he'd wanted to. It had felt right. The tension drained out of his body in a rush. After hours of fighting his instincts, he felt good again. A corner of his mouth lifted in a lopsided grin. "You really don't know where we live?"

Sabrina shrugged. "I thought maybe Cheyenne."

"Didn't Tess—?"

"No, and I didn't ask."

"Why not?"

"Because I would have been tempted to do what you thought I'd done," she admitted.

Ramsey shook his head. "Sabrina, you're one—"

"Irritating woman. I know. And you, Ramsey Jordan are—"

"Paranoid?" He stretched out his legs in front of him and sighed. As he looked at her, again, his body tightened in a different way. She was close enough to touch. Close enough to... "Tess and I were in Cheyenne to bury Bill. We live in the mountains outside Denver," he explained.

Sabrina exhaled slowly. "Is your revelation the ultimate gesture of trust, or did you tell me because I already know enough to find out the rest?"

A corner of his mouth twitched, and mischief sparked in his eyes. "Yes."

A frown pleated her forehead. "What kind of answer is that?"

"The only kind you deserve."

Remembering her past reluctance to give him anything but the most generalized answers, Sabrina touched her tongue to her forefinger and drew a figure one in the air. "Touché." Her grin slipped as she stared at him. On the brink of a profound discovery, she was afraid to move, lest the knowledge escape her grasp. What she felt for Ramsey was more than simple liking, more than physical attraction....

With Ramsey Jordan, she experienced the meaning of affinity.

Ramsey's smile faded into a look of concentration as he watched her tongue delicately lick the tip of her finger. It seemed the most natural thing in the world to capture her hand on the downward stroke, caressing the still-damp pad of her finger with his thumb. "No more scoring off each other, okay?" he said softly. It was both a question and a promise.

Sabrina's eyes were drawn to the circular motion of his thumb. Her breath snagged in her throat, and a weak, trembly feeling invaded her limbs. A husky whisper was all she could manage as she dragged back her gaze to his face. "Okay." Heat rushed through her when he replaced the gentle massage with the warm touch of his lips. She'd never realized how sensitive fingers could be.

She knew she should pull away. She was enjoying this far too much. Her heart beat in an erotic, stirring rhythm as he shifted to wrap his other hand around her neck, urging her forward to meet his kiss. The embers that had lain banked since his last visit to her glowed more brightly, flaring into passion.

This is insane . . . impossible. Since he had come into her life, she'd repeated the words as many times as there were hours. But "impossible" was merely a word, its meaning nothing but mere words. Underneath her pragmatic surface, she had discovered a card-carrying idealist who was glorying in her own femininity.

She had to accept her feelings for Ramsey, explore their possibilities—or forever live with yet another what-if.

Cradling his face, she stroked his cheeks with her thumbs. His groan rose over her doubts, and he enfolded her into his arms, as if he was afraid to let her go.

Her hands found a haven in his soft, wavy hair. Sparks showered inside her, igniting her nerve ends as his tongue skimmed lightly over her lips, then plunged deeply into her mouth. She gasped, and her body burned with awareness of each place where they touched. She felt her breasts swelling in anticipation of the next stroke of his hands. . . .

A discreet tap on the door was followed by another, equally discreet, yet more insistent in volume. Sabrina was inclined to ignore the signals, but Ramsey pulled away from the kiss with a jerk, a startled expression on his face that made her think of things like back seats, and policemen's flashlights illuminating hands that were sneaking onto forbidden flesh.

Realizing that he had reacted with all the aplomb of a guilty adolescent, Ramsey smiled ruefully as he rested his forehead against hers and dragged air into his lungs. "The wine you ordered?" he asked hoarsely.

"Yes, darn it."

Her vehemence caught him by surprise. Did the woman never conceal an emotion, never leave anything to be read between the lines? Open books were so enticing; invitations to read more until the end was reached. Only with Sabrina he couldn't think of endings at all, just beginnings. He'd known he was in trouble the minute he'd stepped into her suite.

Closing his eyes, Ramsey sighed and lifted his head. "I think we'd better skip the wine and go right on to dinner."

"Yes. Dinner." Sabrina whispered the word as if it were foreign to her and there was only one kind of hunger.

Ramsey enveloped her hands in his own, lingering over the feel of their strength and softness, lingering again to press a kiss into each of her palms.

Abruptly, he pulled back and started fumbling with his tie, giving it all his attention. "Dinner," he said firmly, rising on legs that felt about as substantial as unset Jell-O....

CHAPTER SIX

THE SOFT WHISPERS and discreet service of the elegant restaurant compelled patrons to check their cares at the door along with their coats. The private booths muffled conversations, and the overall ambience encouraged a sense of pleasure and well-being.

When Ramsey had reserved a table here, clearing up misunderstandings and setting ground rules were what he'd had in mind. His thoughts had been on apology, not on total seduction of the senses. He'd planned on a pleasant, getting-to-know-you kind of evening. He hadn't counted on falling under the spell of forget-me-not-blue eyes and an atmosphere of romance. And he definitely hadn't expected the kind of wanting that went beyond a mere physical ache.

With old-world charm, the waiter deftly performed his ritual, then seemed to fade away. Candlelight drifted around the table in random bursts of golden light, obscuring the harsh disillusionments of the past in shadow. Music whispered in the air, muting the voices of cynicism and doubt, stirring the rhythms of his body, whispering secrets, secrets he would allow himself to hear tonight, but would try to forget tomorrow, when time and reality had meaning again.

Reality? the voice of experience asked scornfully. *You're a glutton for punishment, Jordan. Remember Claire?*

Ramsey clenched his fists. Claire—the perfect lover, the perfect wife, the perfect mother. But not all three at the same time. Each title had replaced the previous one, the last finally taking over completely. Somewhere along the way they'd stopped sharing themselves, had stopped sharing a life.

And your hopes and dreams disappeared faster than you could find new ones, the voice whispered snidely. *Remember who Sabrina is. Remember how and why you met her.*

But all he could remember was what had happened when he'd met her. He'd wanted her on sight. That quickly, that absolutely. Her first smile had captivated him; her laughter had invited so much. His resistance had been broken by the sound of her pain. He'd known her loneliness equaled his own. Yet when Sabrina was near, loneliness didn't exist, had never existed. When she was near, loneliness seemed unnecessary, use-less. . . curable.

None of it should have happened, yet it had. None of *this* should be happening, he thought, not now, not ever. He should be making fast tracks out of here. But what he knew he should do and what he wanted were two entirely different things. All it took was one look at her to forget the past, ignore the future and live only for one private moment, a moment in which no one else belonged and nothing else mattered.

Sabrina knew exactly when Ramsey had withdrawn into his thoughts. She'd looked up while the waiter was opening the wine to find Ramsey watching them without really seeing anything but the images in his mind. He'd clearly been listening to an inner voice that had taken him to a place where she wasn't welcome.

She retreated into her own silence, and her heart cried out at the emptiness of it all. It shouldn't have bothered her, she knew. She was accustomed to solitude. But this was different. Ramsey and Tess had made it different. Carefully laying down her fork, Sabrina clenched her hands. Why did it have to be Ramsey who made her yearn so strongly for someone to fill the empty spots in her life?

Why not Ramsey? He had everything she was drawn to in a man: sensitivity, strength, and the ability to laugh at himself. He didn't try to cover his feelings with a false layer of charm, a too-easy smile and a glib tongue. His charm was real and honest. She smiled wryly. His looks didn't hurt, either. He was one hundred percent male and knew it, but didn't waste time thinking about it.

"I think the standard question is, 'Do I have dirt on my nose?'" he asked solemnly.

Sabrina welcomed the sound of his voice and greeted him with a smile, as if they'd just met after a long separation. "Was I staring?"

"You were."

"I'm sorry. I was thinking."

"Do you ever stop?" he asked, not joking now.

She knew what he was asking. She could tell him that she never entered into anything blindly, never lost control, never acted impulsively or bought anything without asking the price, accepting it. Not anymore. She could tell him all that, but she wouldn't, and so she gave him a quiet, discouraging, "No."

Ramsey understood. Her eyes showed more than she knew. There were some pretty desolate landscapes inside him, too—vulnerable, delicately balanced places that he wasn't willing to let anyone see and maybe destroy altogether. Moving into more neutral territory, he cut into his prime rib. "Why Jackson, Sabrina? Don't you get tired of commuting?"

"Once in a while I do. I worked here in Denver for several years and just couldn't seem to settle in. I'm a small-town girl. Jackson gives me silence and incredible scenery. If I want company, the town is always full of interesting people." She smiled wistfully. "Every day the Tetons have a different personality, different colors and patterns. Sometimes I throw my sketch pads in the car and drive up into the mountains or even Yellowstone."

"You could have moved into the Rockies—Evergreen or Dillon."

Sabrina shook her head. "Too close. My partner and I are both take-charge managers. The only difference is that she can't design a paper bag, and when I'm in the middle of putting together a collection, I get cranky. Marty makes everyone think she's doing them a favor when she chews them out. If I lived outside of Denver, I'd be at the plant every day, driving everyone nuts."

So, she gets cranky. Ramsey smiled as he filed the information away. The nuances of her personality were as important to him as the obvious traits. He'd known from the first that there was more to Sabrina than she allowed the world to see, and much more—much more—that he wanted to see. Giving up on the food he couldn't taste anyway, he laid down his fork and feasted on her instead. "Each of you stick to what you do best and then you put it all together."

"Mmm." Sabrina sipped her wine. "What about you, Ramsey? You're in a tough business, yet you've managed to make it grow. Why haven't you gone public?"

"Issue stock? It didn't seem necessary until recently." He sat back in his chair, his expression thoughtful. "But you're right. I've created a monster. Independents from all over the country are trying to join up, form a nationwide network of air charter and freight services. I've been playing around with the idea of affiliating with them, if the paperwork looks good."

"Sort of like FTD?" At his nod, Sabrina tilted her head. "You'd have a wider range of services and clients, be more competitive, yet you'd still have control of your own operation. It sounds like it's worth looking into."

"It's an option. If I decide to do it, the work load will increase, though." Seeing her frown, Ramsey knew she was thinking of Tess. Suddenly it seemed important to reassure her, to ease her worry. "I'm also thinking about making Seth a partner."

Sabrina frowned even more at the mention of the man Tess was so fascinated with. "I had the impression that he was a young man."

Ramsey's mouth twitched. "Very young...two years younger than you are." He'd expected the standard flip remark about never mentioning a lady's age. Instead, she seemed to become even more troubled. "He's been with me since he was Tess's age, working part-time behind the counter. Seth knows the business as well as I do."

Running her finger around the rim of her wineglass, Sabrina stared at the tablecloth. "Tess is...fond of him."

"Tess thinks she's in love with him," Ramsey corrected her.

Sabrina's gaze flew up to his. "*Thinks,* Ramsey?" she said sharply. Labelling Tess's experience a "crush" or "puppy love" discounted her feelings. Sabrina couldn't dismiss those so easily; she knew how emotions could leave permanent scars on a young girl's heart.

Sighing, he placed his napkin next to his plate. "That sounded callous. Believe me, I'm not insensitive to Tess's feelings. *Thinks* or *is* doesn't make any difference to a sixteen-year-old. First love is magic, and it's painful. If it were anyone but Seth, I'd be damn worried."

Encouraged by Ramsey's willingness to discuss the subject, Sabrina asked the questions that had nagged at her since she'd realized what Tess was going through. "And Seth? Does he know? Is he sensitive to her feelings?"

"Tess isn't long on subtlety, Sabrina. She runs on impulse, as you well know. I haven't asked him, but I can't imagine Seth is unaware of the situation. And yes, he's up to handling it . . . thank God." Ramsey smiled. "Feel better about it now?"

She nodded. "Thank you, Ramsey. I've been . . . concerned."

Concerned? Ramsey was willing to bet that she'd been worried sick. He'd seen her anxiety earlier in the afternoon, when Tess had mentioned Seth. Given the disastrous results of Sabrina's first experience with love, he couldn't imagine her not being worried about Tess's.

His smiled faded. Funny, he'd never once thought of the relationship that had produced Tess as anything but a first experience. And he hadn't once questioned the fact that she was really concerned about Tess and not putting on an act. Both assumptions on his part were blatant reminders of just how much he believed in Sabrina. Funny, but the knowledge didn't make him uneasy. The truth was, he felt damn good about it. Funny . . .

Clearing his throat, he changed the subject. "There's something I can't figure out," he said casually.

She watched his smile fade, then come back, a little lopsided and strained. His eyes were sparkling. "Uh-oh," Sabrina murmured into her glass.

He went on as if she hadn't made a sound. "What is a practical, logical businesswoman like you doing at the Brown—in a suite—when Denver is full of less...impressive hotels?"

Sabrina's eyes narrowed at the seemingly innocent question. Why did she get the impression that he was asking so much more? Unable to figure out what that might be, she decided it was her imagination. "When Cachet really started paying off, I acted on impulse and booked this suite as a present to myself." She shrugged her shoulders. "I've stayed there during my fall trip ever since."

So, the lady is impulsive. The idea pleased Ramsey and confirmed his suspicion that there were a lot of interesting things going on beneath her smooth, calm surface. The lady wasn't always controlled. "You're a closet hedonist," he stated with mock disgust.

"Only once a year," she reminded him.

As he raised his glass, Ramsey's mouth stretched in a pleased grin. "Here's to hedonism...once a year."

Bemused by that grin, Sabrina clinked her glass against his and finished her wine. Right then, she could visualize him with the sun sparkling on his teeth, doing a macho commercial for a macho cologne with a macho name. A slight giggle escaped her as she imagined him opening a thirty-dollar-a-bottle scent, wrinkling his nose and blurting out, "This smells like a dead cat!" right into the cameras.

Arrested by the sound of her amusement, Ramsey stared at her and slowly lowered his glass to the table. "What's so funny?"

His voice startled her. His obvious fascination sent excitement skittering over her nerves. She felt ridiculously self-conscious. "Nothing. Just a bit of whimsy."

His brows arched. "You? The logical lady? I don't believe it."

"Oh, I have odd moments of madness." When he picked up the bottle, she shook her head and placed her hand over her glass. "I've had my limit."

"What happens if you go over your limit?" Ramsey wondered if there was a wine anywhere to compare with the taste of her kiss, the bouquet of her skin, the clarity of her eyes....

"More madness," she answered as he pulled the glass from under her hand.

Grinning wickedly, he filled the glass and slid it back to her. "Drink up. If two glasses take you on flights of fantasy, I can't wait to see what happens after three." He wiggled his eyebrows suggestively.

Sabrina's eyes widened in surprise. "You're flirting." The realization was headier than the most potent of spirits. She'd never indulged in that kind of male-female game before; she'd always kept her relationships straightforward so there would be no cause for misunderstanding. That had scared off some men and challenged others. Neither response had impressed her.

"Yes, I am," Ramsey stated gravely.

Sabrina stared back, seduced. His seriousness went through her like hot, liquid silk, pooling in the most intimate places of her body.

Sabrina's obvious discomfort, the self-conscious way she dipped her head to avoid his gaze and the little catch in her breath told Ramsey even more about her. She was willing to indulge her senses by treating herself to luxuries, but she was scared to death of indulging her emotions. "Try it, Sabrina. It's harmless," he said softly.

She felt reckless and excited and more than a little mad. Knowing she was losing her grip on caution and common sense, she tried very hard to remember why she needed them. She picked up her fork and took a bite of food. "Our dinner is cold," she said, noticing that their plates were still almost full. "Do you suppose it was good?"

"Didn't you taste it?"

"No."

"Neither did I." His eyes followed the path of her tongue gliding over her lips, which were delectably glossy in the candlelight. He wanted to touch her. The table between them might as well have been the Great Wall of China. Either the restaurant owners had installed a blast furnace in the last few seconds, or he was running a dangerously high fever. He'd only had one glass of wine, yet his head felt as if it were twenty feet above his body. He knew for a fact that they were in a building full of people, but his body didn't seem to give a damn.

Sabrina couldn't stop staring at him even when she said a soft "No thank you," to the waiter's query about dessert. For once in her life, she was immune to the lure of lemon soufflé or Dobosh Torte. And as they left the restaurant, she wondered why Ramsey had wrapped her coat around her, when all she really needed for warmth was the touch of his gaze, the closeness of his body.

The warm night, full of stars and a silver moon, further conspired against common sense. Their silent drive back to her hotel sustained the feeling of being insulated from the outside world. Outside her door, the very air seemed charged with anticipation, vibrant with promise, intense with need.

Ramsey moved closer and raised his hand, his knuckles brushing her cheek, his head dipping to reach hers, his mouth parting slightly...

A group of people walked by, their quiet conversation sounding like the shouts of the cheering section at a Bronco game. Sabrina blinked, Ramsey stared at the floor and then looked up at her, his mouth quirking. "This is too much like a front porch with parents peeking out the window."

"Would you like to come in for a glass of brandy?" she asked him, refusing to think rationally, not wanting to think at all. There was a feeling in the air of promises not yet kept, and she wanted—needed—to know exactly what those promises were.

Nodding, Ramsey followed her into the suite, watching her every move as she turned on a single lamp and dropped her coat onto a chair. The magic was still there, beckoning from corners, whispering enticements into his ear, reminding him of dreams he'd once believed in.

Dreams, Jordan? You'd have been better off with cold meat and potatoes. The worst that can happen is indigestion, the voice advised, but Ramsey was too busy to listen. His hand reached out as he walked toward her, his body aching with a desperate need to touch her, press against her, be surrounded by her. He could still taste her on his tongue, feel the heat of her mouth, hear the sigh of her breath mingling with his.

Gossamer shadows followed the lines of his face, veiling the tightness of his jaw, darkening the creases on either side of his mouth, intensifying the fires that burned invitingly in his eyes. Her gaze bound to his, Sabrina felt desire race through her veins, intoxicating her, the force of it frightening her a little. When had she ever felt so much from a simple touch?

Gently taking her hand from his, she drew a shaky breath. "Brandy," she said huskily and moved away from him.

"Sabrina." Enthralled by need and desire—an emotion stronger than any he had ever known, Ramsey caught her arm and drew her back to him. His other hand cradled her chin, and he lost himself in the bewitching depths of her eyes.

Her lips parted to begin a word. Ramsey lowered his head to take her mouth with teasing nibbles before she could utter a sound and break the spell. Raising his head, he searched her expression as she drifted closer, wrapping her arms around his waist, exploring the shallow valley of his spine with a gentle skimming of fingertips. He found the pins in her hair and pulled them out, one by one, until a cascade of shining black curls fell down her back.

Sabrina's restraint melted into nothing. Everywhere he touched, each brush of his long, hard body against hers sent a sizzling charge of excitement through her. Sacrificing thought for pleasure, she unbuttoned his vest and slid her hands under his shirt. With the release of her hair she tipped back her head, parting her lips, fitting her hips to his, catching her breath at the heat and hardness of him pressing against her stomach.

Ramsey breathed deeply as he stroked her sides with his palms, enjoying the feel of silk and the soft fullness of woman beneath. Her jacket drove him crazy, tantalizing him with misty glimpses of her form underneath sheer fabric. Hooking his thumbs over its edges, he grazed the tips of her breasts as he eased the jacket aside. Through the camisole he felt her swell and harden at his light caress. When his thumbs returned to touch and circle, his shudder answered her own.

He was a starving man. Her parted lips and half-closed eyes were an invitation to a feast. He accepted with a growl. He nibbled her lips lightly with his teeth, savoring her with his tongue, and deepened the kiss to enjoy the textures of her mouth. A groan ripped through him as she not only received his passion, but gave of her own in return. Her hands stroked him—here gently like a ripple in the air, there with a firm, kneading pressure, driving him closer to the edge of control, farther into a pleasure he'd never felt before.

Need gripped him. For Sabrina. Only Sabrina.

Ramsey lifted her camisole and opened the front catch of her bra to fill his hands with the weight of her breasts. She arched her back as he bent his head, opening his mouth over one nipple while his fingers teased the other.

Pure sensation shot through Sabrina like sunlight through crystal, scintillating, intensifying until every nuance of air and fragrance and light felt like an extension of Ramsey's touch.

Trailing his mouth over her skin, Ramsey straightened, enfolding her in his arms, holding her tightly, desperately...as if he were fighting her and wanting her, and the conflict was tearing him apart.

Somehow I have to find a way to stop wanting you. The memory of him saying that in a voice tight with strain matched the desperation with which he held her now. Reality flashed through her mind so quickly that she almost missed it. Reality. Tess. Claire. A hidden torment she sensed in him, yet couldn't name. All were unresolved issues standing between them like electrified fences. It was too soon, too fast, too consuming. She was being reckless—losing control. Once she had squandered a moment without care or thought, and a corner of her heart had turned to stone, forever engraved with the price she had paid.

With a small whimper, Sabrina eased out of the kiss she didn't want to end and rested her head on his shoulder. "Ramsey."

"Hush, Sabrina."

"Ramsey, I need to think. We both do." Her voice was husky; was it regret, pain or loss? he wondered.

He stilled, absorbing what he'd heard, looking at her in stunned disbelief. "Now?" he croaked.

Sabrina pressed her hand to his mouth. "I'm sorry, Ramsey."

Lowering his hands to her bottom, he pressed her against his hips, imprinting on her his need and urgency. "Sabrina, there's a time for thinking, and this isn't it."

"Later would be worse." She disengaged herself from his arms nearly crying out at the cold that suddenly surrounded her. Her strapless bra had fallen to the floor. She looked down at her breasts, still naked and swollen, still needing his touch, still responding to the memory of his mouth.

"Later we'd have something to think about," he said softly. "Something special."

Regarding him with a clear, steady gaze, Sabrina adjusted her camisole and backed away from him. "Yes. Later we would think about what a heck of a good time we had, rushing into something you didn't really want and I regretted." She groped for the right words. "I had something special once, Ramsey, and I lost it because I wasn't equipped to handle the responsibility.''

"You're a grown woman, Sabrina," he said roughly.

"And I still have limits. The only difference now is that I know what they are and make it a point to stay within them."

"Are you telling me that because of some boy with more glands than sense, you can't handle sex?"

"No. I'm telling you that I can't handle hit-and-run sex."

"Now, that term is a real passion killer." Sarcasm dripped from his voice. "Is that what you think I wanted?"

Her own frustration goading her temper, Sabrina glared up at him. "Why not? You don't want to trust me and you don't want to like me. Life would be a lot easier for you if Tess hadn't found me. You said yourself that you had to find a way to stop. . . ." Her voice wavered. Striving for calm, she picked up her bra and tossed it onto a cushioned bench by the door. "What better way to get rid of a craving than to satisfy it? What better weapon to use against me than a moral one? Or maybe you don't know what you want and decided to try a little bit of everything until you found it."

Out of the corner of her eye she saw Ramsey stiffen and jerk, as if he'd been unexpectedly attacked. Why had she said that? She didn't really believe him capable of such calculated cruelty. It was simply easier to see him as the villain than recognize her own weakness. She didn't feel strong, in control or even particularly rational when it came to Ramsey, and it scared her to death. And in spite of what she believed him to be, a part of her was terrified that she was wrong about him, that she couldn't trust her instincts.

Johnny might have tossed her away like a pair of dirty socks, but she'd survived and even been grateful after the shock wore off. Better that than a shotgun marriage to a man who exercised his masculinity instead of his heart, and never knew the difference. She hadn't loved him. Not really. Not like...

Stricken, she raised her eyes to Ramsey, then quickly looked away again.

Ramsey felt as if he'd received another kick in the gut, only it had been harder this time, hurting more and knocking the wind out of him. *Let her believe it, Jordan, and then go home and try to convince yourself it's the truth. It'll save wear and tear on both of you.*

Shut up! Ramsey's snarl vibrated through his mind.

What's the problem, Jordan? You know all about illusions. Deep down inside, aren't you wondering if she's using you?

Ramsey frowned as Sabrina's gaze approached him, then shied away like a spooked animal. His anger vaporized, escaping on a long, expelled breath. There was something... vulnerable in her expression and the way she'd wrapped her arms around herself—as if she were trying to keep something in—that made him want to hold her. Just hold her.

Get the hell out of here, Jordan. You're under the influence of candlelight and wine. Anything you say or do can and will be used against you.

Ramsey's sigh fell over the room like a dark cloud as he walked to the door, watching Sabrina lower her arms to her sides as she did the same. He crooked a finger under her chin, lifting her face. Broodingly he looked into her eyes and ran his thumb across her lower lip, giving her a gentle, wistful smile. "You're wrong, Sabrina. I do know what I wanted."

"What?" The word touched his finger like a kiss.

He answered in a whisper so low that Sabrina didn't hear it until he'd already left, quietly shutting the door behind himself.

"I wanted chocolate ice cream."

CHAPTER SEVEN

SABRINA STROLLED along Denver's Sixteenth Street Mall, her thoughts drifting with the gauzy white clouds that were scattered like scarves on a sky-blue background. Tree limbs reached upward, worshiping the Indian summer sun; joggers and walkers wearing track shorts, designer sweatsuits or simple cutoffs passed her by on their way to fitness and an oxygen high.

She'd had her high last night, in Ramsey's arms. When it was over, she'd crashed into a dark, troubled sleep that had left her aching in every cubic inch of her body, as if she'd done too much all at once, and it had caught up with her. In the last three weeks she had performed too many feats of emotional gymnastics, wrestled with problems that outweighed her experience and tried to outrun the feelings that had already overtaken her.

Only three weeks? That wasn't very long. But that was all it had taken for caution and common sense to be replaced by the urge to be reckless, to live a moment at a time...to fall in love.

Love. She didn't even try to find another word. Lying to herself wouldn't change a thing. All she could do now was face her feelings, accept them and handle them. She was having a hard time finding the practical Sabrina, the one who analyzed her emotions for hazards and potentials, wrapped them into neat little bundles and stored them in compartments in order of importance. Now they no longer fit into such limited spaces, and kept spilling over into others, upsetting her sense of order, rearranging her perceptions and overwhelming her control.

In Ramsey's arms she'd had no choice but to succumb to the dictates of her physical and emotional chemistry and admit the truth. In his arms she'd become achingly aware of the deficiencies in her life. She had friends—good friends—to share an hour or a day with, but she needed someone to share the moments and the years. She needed Ramsey.

Ramsey wanted chocolate ice cream—dessert—a treat with no real substance, no staying power, only a sweet taste and bitter consequences.

An elegant storefront of beautifully finished wood and mullioned windows caught her eye. The name caught her imagination. Fantasy. Cupping her hands around her eyes, she peered inside, wondering what merchandise it had to offer. With a sad smile, she turned away and headed back to the hotel.

The store was empty. No fantasies for sale.

Her head was throbbing and her knees were weak as she fumbled with her room keys. She hadn't eaten more than four bites at dinner last night, and she'd been walking around the mall and Larimer Square for the better part of two hours. As she finally managed to slip the key into the lock, her phone rang.

Lunging through the entry way, Sabrina fell into the chair by the window and grabbed the telephone, before another strident ring exploded in her head. "Hello?"

"Sabrina? Did I get you out of the shower or something?"

"Mmph." Breathing deeply and letting it out slowly, Sabrina tried to talk around the beating of the heart in her throat.

"Oh gosh, I'm sorry. I'll call back—"

"No, Tess. It's all right. I was just coming in from—"

"It's eight o'clock in the morning. Coming in from where?"

"Walking." Her pulse slowing and her heart settling back in her chest, Sabrina registered the unlikelihood of any sane person phoning for an idle chat so early in the morning. Especially Tess, who had confessed to never surfacing for air on the weekend until lunchtime. "What are you up to, Tess?"

"A party. It's Daddy's birthday. Can you come?"

"Is it a surprise?"

"Yeah. He'd find some dumb excuse not to do it, if he knew. Please say yes, Sabrina."

Sabrina closed her eyes, swallowing a quick, unqualified yes. Unwisely, she wanted to see Tess and her environment. Foolishly, she wanted to see Ramsey. Prudently, she searched for a good excuse, but her mind was as empty as her stomach. "Tess, birthdays are for family and close friends. I think I might be more of a surprise than Ramsey would appreciate."

"So you're calling him Ramsey now."

"It is his name."

"Yesterday it was Mr. Jordan." Tess's voice grew lower, making the name into a angry growl. "Daddy said you weren't fighting anymore."

"We never were."

"Sure you were. Yesterday…well, you were polite to each other, but you fought with your eyes. Every look dripped poison."

"Come on, Tess. Looks don't drip poison."

"Those did," Tess said sagely. "Will you come to the party? Seth Jamison will be here, and I want you to meet him. He's single, sexy and terrific."

"Just what I need."

"Doesn't everyone? It's too bad he's married to his plane."

"Do I hear disappointment in that observation?"

"Resignation," Tess corrected her. "He's every woman's dream, except for that dumb airplane."

"I seem to remember that you spend an hour or two every Saturday alone with him in that dumb airplane."

A sigh of pure disgust came through the wire. "He spends the whole time worrying that I'll chip the paint. He can be a real creep about it."

"Right. A terrific, single and sexy creep," Sabrina said teasingly, though her heart wasn't in the banter. She'd heard unrequited young love in Tess's voice, and knew how badly it hurt at any age.

"Yeah. It doesn't make sense, does it?"

"No, Tess. It never does."

"I wish you'd come, Sabrina. I'll be cooking hamburgers on the grill outside," Tess added hopefully, as if hamburgers had to be a deciding factor.

"It sounds wonderful, love, but I really can't. I'm sorry." Sabrina closed her eyes, wishing that she could spend the day with Tess, wishing that she could help Ramsey celebrate his birthday, wishing that "impossible" wasn't sometimes a fact.

"If you change your mind . . ."

"I won't, Tess, but thanks for asking me."

After saying goodbye, Sabrina leaned back her head and stared at the ceiling, trying to fight off the germs of depression that were insidiously infecting her system.

The day was young and threatened a slow and painful aging. A crutch of self-indulgence was called for, just this once. She dialed room service, ordering coffee to stimulate, juice to fortify, a sweet roll—hot, with lots of butter—to cheer, and out of guilt, oatmeal to nourish herself.

Now she knew she was at a crisis point. Her love of calories only overcame her willpower when she was faced with a big problem. And this one was big, all right: six feet, four inches' and two hundred pounds' worth of problem that would be there for a long time to come, blocking her view of other men, other chances to love.

The situation had more than the common garden variety of complications. There was Tess and through her a shared past, spent apart, yet bound together. At this point, Ramsey couldn't see that blood ties were no threat to the more enduring ones of the heart. And there was another complication, one that Sabrina couldn't put her finger on. She sensed something inside him, an aching of the spirit, as if the ashes of lost dreams still smoldered inside him.

Sighing, Sabrina tried to detach herself from her problems and look at them objectively. It was a black and white world, after all. Seeing no alternatives, she expected to be hurt both by Tess and Ramsey. *Double jeopardy,* she thought. *Face it. Accept it. Handle it.*

Grimacing at the cheery voice and lighthearted knock announcing the arrival of her breakfast, Sabrina called out her permission to enter.

The kitchen had either given her the wrong order or hadn't heard her right. The oatmeal was missing, and in its place was a second roll. She was too hungry to care. Apologizing to her hips and thighs for the abuse, she promised to take better care of them in the future.

Sitting by the window, she drank a second cup of coffee and picked at the crumbs on her plate. It was a perfect day for a family gathering or birthday cook-out—a bad day to be away from home, with no appointments scheduled or meetings to attend. Restless and out of sorts, she opened the Sunday paper, searching for a good sale or an interesting diversion. Maybe she'd bleach her hair, buy a new hat or find that book on yacht building.

A rap on the door distracted Sabrina from her musings. She kept silent, wishing the intruder gone. Hearing an impatient shifting in the corridor, she thought of the maid, trying to do her job, and sighed. "Come in."

"Haven't you heard that women are beaten and raped just as often in luxury hotels as in back alleys?" Ramsey kicked the door shut and stormed across the room, the canopy of his brows lowered in a scowl. "I could have been Jack the Ripper."

"You could have been the maid." Irritation sharpened her voice as she saw him raise his eyes to the ceiling. "Ramsey, do you always come into a room armed with thunder and lightning bolts?"

Like storm clouds over a bleak landscape, his brows descended even lower before he abruptly turned away from her, muttering under his breath as he paced to the far end of the room. "Normally, no. But then, there's nothing normal about any of this."

Sabrina's irritation became anger. She didn't need this. The edges of her emotions were tattered enough. "Of course, you're the only one suffering because of it. Tess and I are having a ball."

"Damn it. I didn't say that." He swung around to face her. "And Tess *is* having a ball. She thinks you're the greatest thing since stereo. *You're* easy to talk to. *You're* understanding. *You* design terrific clothes. And *you're* lots better than any of the women our friends have been pushing at me. *You* don't treat her like a mosquito or ask dumb questions about me."

Before Sabrina could mold her thoughts around what he was revealing, Ramsey continued his tirade.

"In fact, Tess is why I'm here. I overheard her conversation with you this morning. She turned that to her advantage and enlisted me to change your mind."

Sabrina coated her smile with false sweetness. "Are you going to accomplish that by charming me with sarcasm? Will you ask me nicely between yells?"

His mouth thinned into a tight line. "She wants you to come. It'll make her happy."

"Is she so spoiled that you'll do anything to make her happy, no matter what?"

"You know bloody well she's not spoiled. This is her party—"

"Wrong. It's your birthday and your party, Ramsey. Tess will survive, and no doubt you'll celebrate even more."

"What in the hell has gotten into you?" He'd never seen her like this, wired for anger and spitting fire.

"Oh nothing much. Just a lousy mood that's deteriorating fast."

"Well, don't take it out on me."

"Why not you? You're the one who's acting as if you need a cross and garlic around your neck to keep me away."

Belligerence radiated from Ramsey in waves. Fists on hips, he glared at her. "What do you expect? For me to welcome you into the family bosom?"

Fury propelled Sabrina out of her chair. Her fists clenched at her sides, she advanced on him. "No, thanks. Anyone in your family would need combat pay. Or are you this inconsistent only with me? You try so hard not to trust me or like me." She took the final step that brought her close enough to touch him. "Then you talk to me as if I were a real person with real feelings. And now something new has been added, hasn't it, Ramsey? What was last night all about? More self-delusion?"

The muscles in his arms bunched under the rolled-up sleeves of his shirt and he stalked across the room. "Forget last night."

"Give me one good reason why I should." Sabrina glared at his back, painting an imaginary target on the sleeveless brown sweater he wore over his shirt.

"It was a mistake. We lost control. It's over. Drop it."

"Sure, Ramsey. Two glasses of wine, a few kisses and touches and—bingo!—consenting adults turn into mindless idiots, out of control."

"You were consenting? You sure fooled me."

"Do you expect every woman who responds to you to automatically invite you into her bedroom? Sorry. My invitations are qualified."

"Well, that's clear as mud."

Sabrina raised her arm in a wide arc. "Look at you. You're tied up in knots over what's happening between us. If I'd gone to bed with you last night, your conscience would have kicked me out this morning."

"My conscience?" Ramsey exploded as he pushed away from the wall to step toward her. "Sabrina, I made a pass. Two years between women is a long time. You just happened to be there, with candlelight and dinner for two, when it caught up with me. Why in hell should my conscience bother me for that?" Stopping in the middle of the room, he shoved his hands into his pockets and looked away.

"Why, indeed?" she countered, her temper at a steady rolling boil. The hunted expression on his face told her she'd scored a direct hit. By implying that he'd been using her, he'd meant to divert rather than insult. There was no way she'd let him get away with it.

Her smile made him nervous. When her voice came out quiet, its tone at once inquisitive and faintly bored, he knew she was going to say things he didn't want to hear, ask questions he wasn't ready to answer.

"Ramsey, you're talking about physical therapy. You can find practitioners under every street lamp. If that's too commercial for your tastes, you can always *use*—" noting his wince, she smiled in satisfaction "—one of the women your friends are sending your way. After the obligatory rituals of dating are observed, I'm sure you'll be accommodated." Tilting her head to one side, Sabrina looked at him consideringly. "With all the options available, I can't help but wonder why I was blessed with your attentions. After all, with anyone else, you wouldn't feel as if you were consorting with the enemy."

"Damn, you're frustrating!"

"Why?"

"Because we're fighting!" he yelled. "And when people fight, they don't talk as if they ate dictionaries for breakfast. They don't spout logic and stick to the subject."

Sabrina threw up her hands in disgust. "Well, if I'm exposed to you long enough, I'm sure I'll get the hang of it." Storming over to the sofa, she flopped down indignantly. "If we don't stick to the subject, how can we settle anything?" She eyed him suspiciously. "Or is that what you were counting on?"

"There's nothing to settle." Ramsey felt cornered in a room full of corners. No windows. No doors. Just corners.

"The heck there isn't. Ramsey, if I'm frustrating you're downright obtuse."

"I'm sharp enough to know what's happening," Ramsey said regretfully. He'd rather be in blissful ignorance of it all.

"I'm dying to hear your version of what's happening."

"Too damned much, too damned fast." Raking his hands through his hair, Ramsey spotted the bottle of brandy they hadn't gotten around to last night. "You know, Sabrina, you're more trouble than a ten-car pileup on the freeway."

Sabrina's eyes narrowed as she rose to intercept him. "You know, Ramsey," she said sweetly, "there are times when I can't understand why I like you." Picking up the brandy, she tried to unscrew the cap. Feeling the bottle being tugged out of her hand, she looked down to see him open it with one easy twist. Wrapping her hand around its neck, she stalked over to the table to splash some brandy into her empty coffee cup. She gulped it down as if she drank hard liquor every day before lunch.

She glared at him through watering eyes and swallowed her gasp. "You say I'm trouble. Ramsey, you don't know what the word means until you discover you're falling in love with a stubborn, bad-tempered, opinionated jackass." Raising her eyes to the ceiling, she slapped her forehead. "What am I saying?" A hiccup jerked her body. She took a deep breath, holding it in as she looked away.

Ramsey stiffened and inhaled sharply. Her words were the last thing he wanted to hear, the worst possible thing she could have said, yet they felt good, right. Too good. More than right. They sounded like desire—not of the body, but of the soul, the heart, the spirit—a desire that he was feeling, too, to become something other than a man to whom emptiness had become a natural state of being.

"Your face is getting red," he observed, refraining from saying more. For all her strength, she seemed so fragile right now, and he was afraid he'd say the wrong thing. Removing the cup from her hand, he drank the remaining liquid, wheezing as the shock of it burned down his throat. "I take it back, Sabrina. You're more than trouble. You're downright dangerous."

With a fresh gasp, Sabrina exhaled. "To whom? You or myself?"

Taking hold of her arm, Ramsey backed her into a chair. "You...me...both of us. What in the hell am I supposed to do with the confession you just made?"

A dimple flashed in her cheek as a corner of her mouth lifted in self-disgust. There really ought to be a cure for foot-in-mouth disease. "As far as I'm concerned, you can stuff it and mount it in a trophy case." She glared at him. "But I give you fair warning, Ramsey. Make another pass at me, and I'll assume I mean more to you than your doubts. I won't say no, and you'll be getting more than a willing body. You'll be getting me."

A new scowl drew his brows together. "You can't go around issuing that kind of invitation to a man you hardly know. Are you crazy? You're setting yourself up to be used."

"Not by you," she stated simply, like a child proclaiming her belief in Santa Claus. "You're not going to use my feelings just to satisfy an urge."

"How do you know?" Ramsey swallowed as he watched her shift back in her chair. He had no more anger to override his hormones. Instead of turning him off, her honesty had had the opposite effect. It had activated his senses to receive every nuance of her.

Sabrina shrugged helplessly. "I trust you." It didn't matter what she told him now. Not really. Not when she'd already offered him . . . everything.

The import of her words hit Ramsey broadside and left his mind gasping. His legs felt as if they had turned to air. He dropped like a rock into a chair. *Damn*. People fell in love all the time, but it didn't mean that trust was part of the package. She had just handed it all to him. And it was getting harder to justify the reasons why he couldn't accept, harder to remember that what was given could also be taken away, harder to care about cost. *Damn*. "Do you have to be so bloody honest?"

Sabrina shrugged. "It saves time."

He shook his head as if to clear it. "I don't want to save time. For crying out loud, Sabrina, not everyone can solve problems faster than a speeding bullet."

"Who asked you to? I told you how I feel. I don't expect you to do the same."

"Thanks a lot. I really appreciate that, since I don't know how I feel." He sat forward in his chair. "How can I be around you without—?" Falling silent, he shook his head again.

"That's easy." Sabrina marched to the door, jerking it open. "You don't have to be around me at all. Go home, Ramsey, and don't come back."

His hands flattened on the door, pushing it shut. She tried to step away, but she was between him and the door. His arms were on either side of her, fencing her in.

"It's the easiest way out," she said, her voice leaving a trail of sadness in its wake.

"It's a cop-out, Sabrina. And it's too late for casual goodbyes. Tess won't forget. And, contrary to what I said earlier, I can't forget."

Sabrina turned and leaned against the solid wood. She needed the reassurance of seeing him to convince herself that he was still here, that he hadn't walked out, that he'd said what she'd never expected him to say. Looking into his eyes, she saw that he was as surprised by his own candor as she was.

Ramsey's gaze followed the lines of her face, probing deeply, searching for answers. "Could you forget, Sabrina? Would it be easy for you to dismiss the feelings, without exploring them to see where they lead?"

"No. As you said, it's too late." Too late to say goodbye without feeling unfinished inside.

Ramsey stared at his feet. "Dammit, Sabrina. This is a unique situation with a lot of prejudices and fears attached to it. Who knows if they're valid? Anything between you and me automatically involves Tess." He raised his head. "Right now she's just a visitor in your life. I'm the one responsible for her, and I almost blew it once already. I won't let her down again."

"I know. Ramsey . . ." Sabrina put her hands behind her back, pressing them against the door. He was so close. Every instinct she had urged her to reach for him, touch him, hold him. And be held by him. Suddenly he seemed much stronger than she was, more certain of the course they should follow. She was afraid that this time no one would betray her but herself. This could so easily end with bitter farewells and haunting memories.

Ramsey cradled her cheek, caressing the sensitive skin beneath her eye with his thumb, as if he were wiping away the tears she wouldn't allow to fall. The gesture awed her with its tenderness. She turned her head, speaking into the strength and gentleness of his hand. "Why, Ramsey?"

His mouth quirked in self-derision. "As in why have I stopped running?" At her nod, he took a deep breath. "Because I tried to shove my emotions into a closet once too often, and when I opened the door, they all came down on top of me. I can't escape anymore. It's happened. We'll all have to see it through."

"Like a trip to the dentist, necessary but potentially painful."

Turning away from her, Ramsey stared out the window. "What do you want me to say? That I'm no more anxious for you to walk out of my life than you are for Tess to disappear from yours?"

Sabrina frowned, knowing there was something wrong with the way he said it—a statement disguised as a question. It was as if experience had given him information that she didn't have access to. But it was something he refused to acknowledge openly and that she couldn't pursue. Because the moment was becoming too heavy for comfort, she smiled, drawing on her sense of humor to ease the tension. "Well, it's only fair. Don't you think one good confession deserves another?"

Ramsey felt her hand touch his arm and saw her grin from ear to ear. He smiled back as he tugged on her ponytail. "You are not a restful woman, Sabrina."

"When I'm ninety-three, I'll be restful. Right now, I'd rather be exciting."

Exciting. A tame description for how she affected him. The idea didn't disturb him as much as it had before. His smile twitched, a prelude to his answering chuckle.

"Does this mean we're not fighting anymore?" she asked as she traced his bottom lip with her forefinger. "I could use a break from hostility."

"Are you using feminine wiles on me?" Ramsey couldn't help but admire her resiliency, her refusal to give in to tears, anger or defeat.

Her fingers smoothed over his mouth, and she enjoyed the feeling of his warm breath puffing against her palm. "Whatever works. Since I've told you all my secrets, I see no point in fighting my instincts."

Closing his eyes, Ramsey battled the hardening of his body and the softening of his resolve not to touch her. All he wanted to do was seal the truce with his mouth on hers, sign formless messages of peace on her skin, her body until they both surrendered . . . unconditionally. Instead, he clamped his fingers around her wrist to draw her hand away from his mouth. Impatient with himself and the fantasy pictures that were playing in his mind, he glanced at his watch. "It's getting late. Tess will be expecting us."

It took Sabrina a minute to remember the birthday party. Before she could talk herself out of it, she reaffirmed her earlier decision. "Ramsey, the glitter won't wear off Tess's day if I'm not there. You're the one she needs."

"Sabrina, I'm not asking for Tess. This time is for me."

Sabrina's eyes widened. Her heart beat a little faster and her skin tingled with pleasure at his admission. "Can you give me a minute to change?"

Ramsey's gaze traveled down her body, something he'd been avoiding since his arrival. Her rose-colored jogging suit flowed over her, emphasizing every little dip and hollow, right down to the dimples on her tush. If she didn't change, he doubted he'd make it through the day with his good intentions intact. He nodded.

"Fifteen minutes," she promised on her way to the bedroom.

"I'll call Tess to tell her we're on our way." Lifting the receiver, he paused. "Sabrina?"

Sabrina stopped at the door, but didn't turn back to him. His voice hinted at uncertainty and warning....

Seeing her stiffen her back and square her shoulders, he wondered why he felt the need to say anything. Sabrina would give all she could and take what was offered, and if it wasn't enough, she wouldn't hesitate to let him know. He was as sure of that as he was sure that his warning was for himself, not for her. "No promises, Sabrina. It has to be a day at a time...."

Turning her head in profile to him, Sabrina nodded. "A moment at a time, Ramsey," she agreed. "Until I need more or you want less."

CHAPTER EIGHT

TWO SEASONS COEXISTED brilliantly, as one lingered with unseasonable warmth, and the other prepared to take its place in nature's cycle. Flowers swayed amid fallen leaves. Snow glistened on the highest peaks of the Rocky Mountains, while the plains were still carpeted in rich green. Home owners tackled assorted tasks, mowing lawns, weather-stripping windows, washing cars and stacking firewood on their patios.

As they drove toward the mountains, Sabrina tried to concentrate on the scenery, but her gaze kept straying to Ramsey. As he shifted gears, sunlight poured over the dark hairs on his arm, making them gleam like the bronze and copper metallic threads she used to embroider special garments. The muscles in his leg flexed, shading the fabric covering them as he worked the pedals. Her skin grew warm as she imagined how those legs would feel against her own, bare and moving in primal rhythms. Her body felt heavy, her head incredibly buoyant.

The only sound that had filled the car since they'd left her hotel was the changing timbre of the powerful engine. The silence seemed charged both with positive and negative forces of excitement and self-consciousness. It was as if they were on their first date and awkward with the urgency to discover everything at once, before they lost the ability to view the magic of discovery through innocent eyes and open minds.

While Sabrina was lost in her own thoughts, Ramsey tried to concentrate on driving, wishing there was enough outbound traffic to occupy his mind—and keep thoughts of Sabrina from filling in the blanks.

She was falling in love. With him. He'd seen her confidence. She believed in love, even though her first experience had cost her more than a young girl could possibly afford. And her unattached state hinted at other hurts, more disappointments.

Sometimes when he looked at her, listened to her, he felt as if he were seeing himself reflected in the mirror of his soul. He, too, had lost his faith in dreams and the power of love....

The city disappeared from his rearview mirror as they drove through the foothills and penetrated the mountain range. Ramsey turned onto a two-lane private road and downshifted on the steep ascent. His arm brushed Sabrina's. Heat and awareness shot through him. He heard her breathing falter. He thought of pulling off the road and carrying her into the woods. The ground was soft with leaves; the air was barely cool. Her skin was as hot as his....

What had possessed him to invite this kind of torture for an entire day? His memories of last night were too fresh, his desire for her was too strong, his need too consuming. Every touch set off chain reactions.

So keep your hands in your pockets, Jordan.

His arm brushed hers again as he turned onto a smaller road, making him regret bringing the small car rather than Tess's Blazer or his own Wagoneer. And it made him aware of how completely Sabrina was invading his space.

A part of him hoped that she would fill the emptiness inside him with magic and dreams and joy. He'd forgotten about joy.

Sabrina's spirits sank to her feet as Ramsey steered his Ferrari onto a road blocked by security gates. He hadn't mentioned that the fence-enclosed land they'd been driving past for the last few blocks belonged to him. She couldn't quite reconcile Ramsey the successful businessman with this down-to-earth, volatile person. But then his Ferrari had surprised her, too. She'd expected a station wagon or maybe a Jeep.

The winding road on the other side of the gate probably led to a mansion, filled with guests dressed in clothes that cost many dollars per thread. She wasn't worried about her own clothing. Her slate-blue linen trousers, matching lacy knit sweater and hand-painted silk scarf were both fashionable and flattering. Ordinarily, being thrust into a high society crowd didn't bother her, but today she didn't feel up to exchanging the double-edged repartee that was common at such gatherings.

After pushing a series of buttons on the dashboard, Ramsey drove through the opening gates. "That was a pretty heavy sigh," he commented. "What's wrong?"

"Ramsey, how many people are you expecting today?"

Glancing sharply at her, Ramsey caught Sabrina biting her lower lip. She sounded tense and uncertain. It was hard to imagine her being socially shy. Hell, he couldn't imagine her being any kind of shy. "Don't let the fence and gates fool you. They came with the house. I still forget to activate the system half the time."

"You haven't answered my question."

"Oh. Well, my GM, Seth Jamison, and his Uncle Hap will be here. Hap is my chief mechanic. Tess told me this morning that Lenny Harris, a mechanic and part-time pilot based in Casper, flew in to help me celebrate the big four-oh. You'll have to get used to Lenny. She knows more raunchy jokes than a submarine crew."

"Did you say she?"

"Yep. Lenny's the best aircraft mechanic I've ever seen. And if you tell Hap I said that, I'll strangle you. They fight enough as it is."

"Why?"

"Hap is a diehard chauvinist. He took exception when Lenny chose her grease gun over his marriage proposal. I figure one of these days they'll both decide to compromise."

"Obviously you're not a chauvinist."

"Don't you believe it." Ramsey stopped the car and rested a forearm on the steering wheel. "I have my share of macho prejudices, but I can be practical, too. It's good business to employ the best."

Sabrina couldn't resist teasing him. "Is business and practicality why she flew in from Casper for your birthday?"

Ramsey stared at her and rubbed his knuckles along her cheek. "Hey. These people are friends, family almost. They've been with me from the beginning when all I had was three airplanes, a prefabricated shed at the county airport and more ambition than money." Sliding his hand around to the back of her neck, he massaged the tension out of her muscles. "Don't you like parties?"

Sabrina gave a small sound of pleasure like a purr and rotated her head. "Not big, high-style affairs. They're what I hate about being in business. Social war games. I have to post sentries around my thoughts.''

"To keep them in,'' Ramsey guessed.

"Mmm. I'm not very good at lying, even to those who consider it an accepted art form.''

Ramsey silently agreed with her. Moreover, he was willing to bet that there were some thoughts she didn't succeed in keeping in. They would be evident to anyone who bothered to look beyond the polite smile and slightly unfocused look of rapt attention that one learned to cultivate during social war games. It was the only way to escape being either bored to death by the friendlies or picked clean by the vultures.

His gaze locked with hers as it always did, as if they were both part of a gear structure made to mesh on contact. Her eyes were so clear. She had as many empty places as he did, only hers were wide open, welcoming, waiting to be filled. His own were closed—tombs for his former self, his youth, his innocence, his trust—sealed by time. Until Sabrina had pried them open and peeked through the cracks.

Deep inside, he hoped that she would open the doors, letting in air and sun. And then he hoped the brightness wouldn't blind him.

Suddenly the car seemed too confined. Ramsey maneuvered his big body out of the driver's seat and took a long pull of air as he walked around to the passenger side.

Sabrina waited for him to help her out of the low-slung vehicle. There was no sense in arousing his macho prejudices. Taking his hand, she stepped out, her legs wobbling a bit from sitting for the last hour. Ramsey steadied her, holding her arms. Their toes touched; her breasts brushed his chest. She stared at him as if nothing else was worth looking at.

The scent of his cologne mingled appealingly with that of his cashmere sweater and the dried-in-the-sun fragrance of his shirt. Hearing a waterfall, she thought it was inside her, pure sensation flowing warmly, clearly, powerfully. He released her gradually, letting the length of his hands slide over her arms until nothing touched her but his fingertips. Hearing voices in the near distance, she turned away from him and caught her breath.

The mansion she'd expected didn't exist. In its place stood a sprawling, multileveled house nestled into a fold of the mountain. Like its owner, the house—built of mellow, weathered wood and shining glass—had clean lines and a friendly face. The land around it had a wild, natural look, with aspens and evergreens growing free, untamed by gardeners' shears. A small waterfall gushed from a crevice in the rock a short distance away, splashing into—

"A genuine babbling brook. I don't believe it, Ramsey. It's wonderful."

A handsome man in his late twenties approached, cutting off Ramsey's answer. "Hey, Ram. It's about time. Tess wouldn't feed us until you—" His voice and stride faltered when he saw Sabrina, but he recovered quickly. "Haven't you taught her it's impolite to starve a guest?"

Tess ran up behind him. "Seth, it's only one o'clock. Besides, it's good for you. Keeps you humble."

"Honey, I don't need humility. I need food." His blue eyes traveled from Tess to Sabrina and back again.

Tess moved to Sabrina's side. "Sabrina Haddon, *this* is Seth Jamison."

Curiosity became open speculation as Seth saw both women standing together. "It's nice to know she has some manners. Hello, Sabrina Haddon."

To cover her sudden nervousness, Sabrina extended her hand and said the first thing that came to mind. "Tess tells me you're married to your airplane."

Studying her anxious expression, Seth winked outrageously. "Actually, it's only an affair. I have my eye on a fan-jet."

"All because of a little chipped paint," Tess said in mock disgust.

Terrific, single and sexy. Sabrina agreed with Tess's summation. No wonder she had a crush on him. He had a slow, easy way about him—in his walk, his smile, his eyes—that seduced a woman's attention.

They all walked around the house to a large, terraced deck that followed the slope of the mountain. Ramsey introduced Sabrina to Hap Jamison and the brass cuspidor he took with him when he went visitin'. The slight bulge in his cheek testified to the legitimacy of such a prop. His eyes, as mischievous as his nephew's, twinkled as, with a courtly bow, he requested her company for the meal.

A plump, matronly woman in baggy jeans carried a large bowl of salad out of the house. Sabrina had to stop herself from gaping when the woman set down the bowl, giving Sabrina a full view of the slogan emblazoned on the front of her T-shirt: Mechanics Don't Die—We Just Clean Our Fingernails.

"I'm Lenore Harris. You'd better help that old goat hanging on your arm to a chair. He might overexert himself, spitting in that damn fancy can of his."

Sabrina watched the by-play between Hap and Lenore, then shifted her gaze to see Tess giving Seth directions on how to light the fire in the grill. It pleased her to find that Ramsey lived as he acted—casually, openly and without pretension. Delighted with Ramsey's friends, his home and the world in general, she relaxed and looked forward to the rest of the afternoon.

IT WAS LIKE being part of a Norman Rockwell painting.

Sabrina wrapped her hands around her coffee mug, smiling at the argument between Lenore and Hap that was growing louder by the minute. She didn't know what a solenoid was, but it sounded impressive. Ramsey chuckled as he sprawled in the chair next to her, his feet propped on the glass tabletop, his eyelids half closed, a glass of lemonade held on his chest.

A few feet away, Tess and Seth indulged in a good-natured battle over a Scrabble board. Sabrina cringed inside at the brilliant light of first love that she saw glowing in Tess's eyes. Monitoring Seth's reactions to Tess's coquetry, Sabrina found him displaying nothing more than an affectionate indulgence that clearly said, "I care about you—like a sister."

A squirrel missing one of its front legs perched on the table, eating the bits of food Ramsey had arranged for it in a little pile. The creature was more familiar with the humans than with those of its own kind who could neither accept nor tolerate anything less than the fittest of the species. It was a miracle that the squirrel had survived at all. The Jordans made sure it never went hungry for food or soothing words. Tess had told her the squirrel was a member of the family....

Insight struck her like a flash of lightning; it came and went before she fully registered its happening. *This,* she thought, *is what belonging feels like*. Spirits integrating; their patterns sometimes clashing, but the colors always harmonizing. At odd moments like this, she did feel as if she belonged, and she wondered what it would be like to really be Tess's mother... and Ramsey's wife. How would it feel to end the day by saying good-night to Tess and walking arm in arm with Ramsey into the master bedroom?

"I won," Tess announced smugly as she perched on the arm of a chair.

"Only because I let you. Since I skunked you at cribbage last week, I thought you needed some consolation." After replacing the game pieces in the box, Seth joined them at the table, his gaze once again making the journey from Sabrina to Tess.

Abruptly, Ramsey sat up. "How about a walk, Sabrina?"

"I don't think I can move yet. Hamburgers and potato salad never tasted so good."

"They must have. You ate enough."

"Mmm. I know. I ate almost as much as you did," she said placidly.

Seth shook his head in disgust. "At your advanced age, Ram, you should know better than to comment on a lady's capacity for food. Especially such an attractive woman. In fact, Sabrina is as pretty as Tess," he said, looking at the two of them.

Tess beamed at the compliment. "That's because—"

"Tess, would you mind making some more lemonade?" Ramsey emptied the pitcher into his glass.

Annoyance again flawed Sabrina's day. Both Lenore and Seth had been sending curious, comparing glances from Tess to herself, as if she were a puzzle piece they couldn't fit into a particular space. At least Lenore accepted her at face value and kept her suspicions to herself. The bad moments came whenever Seth would join her for a few minutes of conversation that was liberally spiked with veiled inquisition.

It further irritated Sabrina how Ramsey parried every thrust of Seth's curiosity with ham-handed feints and terse monosyllables, blocking her own replies. If he didn't want his friends to know who she was, he shouldn't have brought her here. Did he think the subject was any less awkward for her?

Narrowing her eyes, Sabrina took a sip of coffee. "You know, Seth, I've often wondered why people beat around the bush when the sidewalk is just a few inches away."

Recovering quickly from his surprise, Seth accompanied his answer with a wry smile. "Because the damn fools are afraid of going the wrong way."

Sabrina defiantly ignored Ramsey's warning frown. "If you're afraid of getting lost, ask directions."

Ramsey sighed, clearly surrendering to the inevitable, and waited...for whatever came next. With Sabrina he never knew.

Seth's eyes held admiration as he raised his glass in a salute to her. "Okay. You and Tess look too much alike not to be related. Since Tess is adopted, I figure you're either long-lost sisters, cousins or whatever."

"We're not sisters or cousins. Try the whatever."

Seth nodded in understanding. "Then you are the reason Ram made not one, but two mad flights to Jackson after Tess ran away."

"No," Sabrina said dryly. "Tess was the reason. He was afraid I'd fatten her up and throw her in my oven for Sunday dinner."

Ramsey got to his feet in one, easy motion, pulling her up beside him. "I wasn't far wrong. She cut me up into mincemeat instead." He stared thoughtfully at Sabrina. "I'll be hanged if I can see the resemblance."

Crunching a piece of ice from his glass, Seth eyed Sabrina appreciatively. "Ram, if I were in your place, I don't think I would, either."

"What in the hell does that mean?"

Seth fished out the last cube and popped it into his mouth. "It means that you'll always see Tess as your little girl, no matter how grown-up she is."

"And?"

"And you see Sabrina as a desirable woman." With that, Seth winked at her, then turned to add his voice to a heated discussion on magnetos between Lenny and Hap.

Ramsey broodingly scanned Sabrina's features from forehead to chin and farther, lingering at points of interest along the way. Desirable? Sure . . . like dawn after a nightmare, or fresh, sweet rain pouring into the mouth of a thirsty man cast adrift on the ocean. Like those things, Sabrina was both desirable and necessary. Ramsey braked the thought. He glared at Seth, who was watching him with a look of commiseration. Seth had a knack for seeing a lot and perceiving even more; it was an asset in business, but an aggravation at times like these.

Feeling Sabrina's hand squirming in his grasp, he looked down at her and felt new growth rising from the site of his emotional burnout. His fingers tightened around hers as he led her away from the house, his hold on her gentle, yet firmly insistent.

The touch of his hand and the intimate caress of his eyes combined to nettle Sabrina. Ramsey had gone out of his way all afternoon to avoid touching her. Now he was all but admitting that he found her desirable. Add to that his attempts to avoid any references about her connection to Tess, and Sabrina was totally confused. He'd insisted that she come today. He hadn't kept his hands in his pockets before they'd arrived. Of course, with Tess there, Sabrina didn't expect him to make any public announcements, but he'd evaded even the most innocent and natural contact with her....

She was so wrapped up in her indignation that his tug on her hand pulled her off balance, and she had no choice but to follow him. "I told you. I don't want to go for a walk."

"Come on, Sabrina. It's my birthday. Humor me."

"I'm fresh out of humor," she muttered as they arrived at the waterfall. "Would you settle for a card? Or maybe another glass of lemonade?" Freeing herself, she executed a dignified flounce to a smooth-topped boulder, but on eyeing its hard surface, she changed her mind about sitting down. Since Ramsey had dragged her out for a walk, she decided that she might as well walk. She veered away from the pool to stroll along the edge of the brook.

Frowning, Ramsey caught up with her in two strides and planted himself in front of her. "For someone who didn't want to walk, you're sure doing a lot of it." He raised his hands toward her shoulders, then stopped himself, remembering how hard it was to stop once he started touching her, and he rested his splayed fingers on his hips instead.

Disappointment stabbed Sabrina. Being upset with him didn't seem to matter in the least. She wanted the reassurance of his touch, needed it, craved it. That need told her more than she wanted to know at the moment. She was no longer falling in love with Ramsey.

She had already fallen.

His earlier words came back to reprimand her impulsive emotions. *Too damned much. Too damned fast.*

And probably futile. Love didn't grow easier with age. The feeling just had more depth, more meaning, more permanence. She was well and truly caught by a man who had enough reservations about her to build a mountain between them.

"Sabrina, what's wrong with you? I'm the only one around here who has a reason to be upset."

"Spoken in true arrogant fashion, Ramsey. Why do you have a corner on the market?"

Ramsey raised his eyes to the sky. "Why? she asks. I spend the afternoon trying to save her from awkward questions, and she blows it. No wonder chivalry is dead. It was probably beaten over the head with a blunt woman."

"Is that what you were doing?" she asked in a whisper. "Protecting me . . . my feelings?"

"I thought I was." He kicked a rock, plunking it into the shallow water.

"Oh. That didn't occur to me. I thought . . ." The truth of what he'd told her felt like spring after a long winter. How long had it been since someone—anyone—had tried to protect her? How long since anyone had seen beneath her strength and self-reliance? How long since she had stopped hoping that someone would see—and hear and care?

"Don't say it, Sabrina," Ramsey warned her bleakly. "I can fill in all the blanks except for the one after 'Why?'"

She reached out to touch his arm, but drew back at the memory of how he'd shied away from physical contact. He held out his hand in silent invitation. She responded instantly, lacing her fingers with his, feeling the rightness of their flesh uniting.

"Why, Sabrina? And don't tell me it was the practical thing to do."

"Well, it was. The truth was already half-formed in their minds, Ramsey. The faster a mystery is solved, the less attention it receives. Being the subject of speculation and gossip makes me claustrophobic." She squeezed his hand in a subtle gesture of reassurance to accompany her words. "I'm not ashamed of it."

"No, not anymore," he said quietly.

"Not anymore," Sabrina agreed with a catch of sadness.

"Sabrina, I don't give a bloody damn what they think. I'm all grown up and I make up my own mind about my relationships...." His brows drew together as his voice trailed away. Shaking his head, he sighed as he saw the question in her eyes. "It hit me with all the finesse of an avalanche. I'm buried up to my neck in a relationship with you."

"Do you think you'll be able to ignore all those emotions, Ramsey?" Sabrina needed to know now, before Ramsey and Tess became so much a part of her that losing them would mean losing a vital part of herself. It was frightening to know how much power they had over her, yet she couldn't escape it.

"No. They're growing by the minute, Sabrina. All I can do now is figure out what I should do with them."

Looking into his eyes, she saw that her power over Ramsey was just as great, just as frustrating, just as absolute as his power over her. She couldn't help but feel a little smug at his admission. "Why not try doing what comes naturally?" she suggested.

His eyebrows arched expressively. "Here? Now?"

"That's not what I meant, and you know it," she chided him.

"You sure?"

"No."

Groaning, Ramsey pulled her into his arms, roughly, desperately, and took her mouth with a hunger that seemed to feed on itself, growing, multiplying, magnifying with every second, every thought, every heartbeat. Her mouth opened as if she could do nothing else, and her response matched his, thrust for thrust, stroke for stroke. His arms tightened, as if he would lose her if he didn't hold her close enough.

Sabrina stood on tiptoe, wanting to make him so much a part of herself that not even air could separate them. It was impossible to distinguish between the sounds of rushing water in the stream and her rushing blood, the breeze that was whipping through the trees and their breathing. She didn't know who was fire and who was fuel. Then it didn't matter, because they both became flame—intense, hot, climbing higher than the mountains....

"Hey, Ram..." Seth's voice warned of intrusion, reminding Ramsey of the existence of a world beyond the aspen grove and people other than Sabrina. With a last sip at her mouth, he drew his head away and reluctantly loosened his embrace, his body shuddering in violent withdrawal from the taste and heat and fragrance that was Sabrina.

His mouth quirked at the exaggerated noise Seth made as he entered the grove. "I swear I'm going to open a branch on the moon and send Seth there," he muttered darkly.

Sabrina stepped back, feeling cold away from Ramsey's fire. "It's not far enough. How about Pluto?"

"I heard that." Seth stopped more than an arm's distance away from them. "Ram, I'm sorry, but—"

"Daddy—" Tess appeared behind Seth, her gaze fastening on the way her father held Sabrina. She looked at their faces: their flushed skin, slumbrous eyes and swollen lips. Her own face paled. "You had a phone call. You're to call right back."

Seth grimaced, his eyes apologizing for not giving them more warning.

Grateful that Tess had only seen Ramsey's arm around her waist as they stood side by side, Sabrina moved away from him as casually as she could. She sensed suspicion in Tess's manner, saw it in her stricken expression and heard it in her stammered words. Problems. Complications. For a few minutes, she and Ramsey had forgotten that, in this case, one plus one equaled a volatile three. The reminder tainted her dreams.

CHAPTER NINE

LENNY AND HAP were still arguing the finer points of aviation mechanics, their differing opinions punctuated by snorts of disgust and glaring silences. Seth poured himself a glass of lemonade. The three-legged squirrel he and Tess had named Ralph hopped about, gorging itself on every crumb in sight. Everything seemed normal, as if he and Sabrina had never gone for a walk, as if he hadn't given in to an emotion stronger than any he'd known.

As if nothing had happened at all.

Ramsey picked up the cordless phone from the patio table and dialed the number Tess had written down. Over Tess's head, his glance collided with Sabrina's, as it had several times on the walk back from the aspen grove. He knew she was blaming herself for Tess finding them that way and worrying about how much Tess had seen; how much she could discern from their faces, their breathing, their sudden uneasiness. Hell, he was wondering the same thing, feeling the same guilt....

Smooth move, Jordan. He was lucky that Tess hadn't come sooner...or later. A few more minutes—and she might have found both of them reduced to a pile of smoldering ash.

He winced, remembering how Sabrina had had the presence of mind to casually move in front of him, purposely shielding his lower body from view. A view that would have left nothing to his daughter's imagination....

He dismissed all thought of it when the manager of his Aspen office finally answered the phone. Distracted by the undercurrents seething around him, Ramsey had to think a minute before remembering the man's name. "Yeah, Steve. Ramsey Jordan. What's up?"

As he listened, Ramsey's face drained of color. Turning from the others, he walked away and fired short, to-the-point questions into the receiver. The answers he heard cut all the way to his soul.

"Who's down, Steve?"

Lenny abruptly stopped talking. For the first time that day, Hap missed his cuspidor, and Sabrina watched him exchange a wordless, troubled look with Seth. Tess's head jerked up to stare at her father's back. He was pacing across the lower level of the deck, grim-faced, just as if he'd descended into a pit, she reflected sadly.

She looked at Seth, a query in her eyes. He moved closer to her, speaking softly, his tone dismal. "It sounds like we've got a plane down near Independence Pass. They haven't found it yet."

The cordless phone dangling from his fingers, Ramsey stared into space for a moment before climbing back to the upper deck. "Hap, I need a plane checked out ASAP. I'll be flying to Aspen as soon as I can make some calls." He walked toward the house without stopping. "Seth, I need you inside."

"I'll go, Ram. You just got back from Dallas...."

Choices. Inside the patio doors, Ramsey paused to look back at Tess and Sabrina. He resented Seth's offer, resented Tess's silent plea to stay. And he resented

Sabrina for tempting him even further, just by being. The compassion in her eyes should have made him feel better, but it didn't.

He was confronted by choices that beguiled, that ripped him in two, that mattered. He wondered if they would have mattered a month ago, when his inner vision was still cluttered by selfish debris?

"I can handle it, Ram," Seth argued quietly. "You have enough problems here."

Moving toward his study, Ramsey put his problems in order of importance. Sure, Seth could handle the chaos in Aspen, probably with more equanimity than he himself was capable of right now. But the chaos in Aspen involved *his* company and, more importantly, the life of a pilot working for him. The man was his responsibility, not Seth's. As the most immediate problem, it had to take priority. The troubles here would still be waiting for him when he came back.

"I can get things started, and you can fly in tomorrow," Seth continued. "Just slow down a minute and think about it, Ram."

That was the problem. He *was* thinking about it. Rubbing the back of his neck, Ramsey entered his study and went straight to the safe, knowing that he had copies of all important documents here, as well as at the office. As a result, he reflected, he'd spent the last few years working his life away, stopping only to eat, sleep and otherwise go through the motions.

"Ram, sit down!" Seth commanded in exasperation.

Ramsey dropped the papers into his briefcase and sank into a chair. "It's Bob Jansen," he said bleakly. "Did you know we were in Nam together?"

Seth nodded. "Have they picked up anything from his ELT?"

"No. Either his Emergency Locater Transmitter is out, or..." Ramsey didn't need to finish his sentence. The possibilities ranged all the way from mechanical failure to total destruction. "Judging from Bob's last radio contact, it seems like he had a heart attack. Every minute it takes to find him is another strike against his survival...if it's not already too late. Don't offer again, Seth. It's my place to be there. I have to talk to Carol and the kids. *Damn!*" His fist crashed onto the desk.

"A heart attack? But he's—"

"My age. And he just passed his physical." Ramsey dragged both hands down his face. "They're already searching. I need you to take care of things here. Call the insurance people first thing in the morning. Hell, you know what to do." Recovering from the initial shock and anger, Ramsey snapped shut his briefcase and sat back in his chair. "All of a sudden I'm tired. My ambition was bigger than my capabilities. This business is too much for one man to run." He fixed Seth with a steady look. "How would you like a partnership?"

Startled, Seth blinked several times. "What's that got to do with—?"

"Nothing. I was going to bring it up tomorrow, but I won't be here. I know you think we should affiliate with that nationwide network of carriers. This way you'll have a voice in the decisions we have to make." Ramsey tried to smile, but he succeeded only marginally. "And Tess won't have to worry that you might accept one of those offers you've been getting. All I need is for her to blame me because you took another job and left us."

Seth's eyes widened. "You know how she feels?" He checked his arms and legs, felt his body. "And I'm still in one piece?"

It felt good to change the subject, just for a minute, until Ramsey could adjust to the prospect of losing an old friend. There were definite drawbacks to knowing his employees and liking them. But he wouldn't have it any other way. "I know Tess's feelings for you are as real to her as what I felt for Claire at the same age. I know you're not encouraging it." His eyes narrowed. "Are you?"

"She's a kid, Ram. I have a sister older than Tess."

Ramsey nodded. "Remember that. If I catch you looking at her below the neck, you *won't* be in one piece." Sighing, Ramsey stood up. "I'd better pack and get out of here. You can give me an answer when I come back."

Sabrina, Tess and Lenore were leaning over the rail that surrounded the bottom level of the deck, watching a deer wander through the trees. As soon as Seth reached them, Tess centered all her attention on him.

"What happened?" she asked and listened as he told them. "I'm going with him," she declared when he was done.

"Not this time, Tess. The search could take a while, and Carol will have enough to cope with."

"I'm not a dumb kid, Seth. I can help."

Seth rested his hands on Tess's shoulders. "Tess, the best way you can help is to make your dad a thermos of coffee and not argue with him right now."

In spite of the tears that were running down her face, Tess stood a little straighter and looked at Seth with regal dignity. "He doesn't want me to go, does he? He never does."

"Tess..."

She shook her head and ran into the house.

Seth started to follow her, but Sabrina caught his arm. "Let her be, Seth." Her voice trembled with grief—for Ramsey, for Tess, for the pilot who had crashed in the mountains—and for herself, because she couldn't help any of them.

Sagging against the rail, Seth ran his hand over his face. "I didn't handle that too well."

Lenny spoke up for the first time. "You sure as hell didn't. That girl is like a piece of cracked glass. One wrong word, and she's going to fall apart."

Sabrina winced on a sharply indrawn breath and turned away, knowing that she had contributed to Tess's problems. It had been foolish to believe that the situation could be controlled, played out gradually so that everyone—herself included—would be able to adjust and accept it.

She was in control of nothing. The realization panicked her. Registering a warmth on her arm, Sabrina looked down to see Lenny's hand there, offering comfort and sympathy. The woman's brown eyes, too, were warm and understanding.

"For what it's worth, I don't think it would matter who Ram took up with. Tess is acting like a lot of kids do. They react first and think later—sometimes much later."

Sabrina's eyes misted at Lenny's gesture; she hated herself for displaying her vulnerability to virtual strangers. Only they didn't seem like strangers. They acted like friends, friends who saw too much. After being dissected, scrutinized, criticized and condemned so many years ago, Sabrina had made it a point to establish and maintain her privacy. She abhorred the idea of her life being an open book that anyone could read.

Ramsey and Tess walked down to them, arm in arm, saving her from having to reply.

"You're just in time," Lenny said. "I'm supposed to take off in less than two hours."

"Can you stay, Lenny?" Ramsey asked. "Our housekeeper is on vacation. I need someone to stay with Tess."

"No can do, Ram. That new flu bug has bitten half my crew. If I stay, we'll have to shut down the Casper office."

"Great."

Sabrina bit her lip in an effort to keep quiet. Suddenly she felt like an outsider and wanted to melt into the background. Tess hadn't spoken to her since the aspen grove, and Ramsey was looking everywhere but at her. The world had become lonely again.

"Why don't you ask Sabrina?" Seth asked. "Something tells me she wouldn't mind staying with Tess."

"Sabrina is here on business, Seth," Ramsey said, a hunted expression on his face as he impatiently glanced at his watch.

"You can always call a baby-sitter or put me in a day-care center," Tess said bitterly.

Hearing the hurt that was threaded through Tess's sarcasm, Sabrina broke her noninterference rule. "I'd like to stay with Tess. After school, she can come to my office. I always need an extra pair of hands when I'm putting together a showing." She gave Tess an uncertain smile. "That is, if you'd like..."

His hand tearing through his hair, Ramsey pivoted away from them. Sabrina had jumped into the opportunity fast enough. So much for her promise to let him take the lead. Tess came first with her and probably was the reason behind all her actions. He was just a convenient means to an end.

Probably.

His conscience reminded him that he'd been ready to ask her to stay. She loved Tess. He should be grateful—Tess needed a woman who cared in her life. But memory held him back—a memory that was like an ever-present ache, one that he could live with—until something happened to trigger an inflammation.

"You mean I can help you with the show?" Tess asked, her tone wary, as if she didn't really believe she would be included in anything important.

The tightness on Sabrina's face softened, he noted. "If it's all right with your father, you can do more than that. Remember the design you liked so much?"

"The red one?"

Sabrina nodded. "I need another model. That gown would look lovely on you."

"Me? Radical."

Ramsey glanced back at them over his shoulder. Tess had lit up like a neon sign in Vegas. Jackpot. Sabrina had hit Tess right in her obsession—clothes. He couldn't compete with that. He wasn't even sure he needed to. "Yeah. Radical. I guess it's settled, then." His mouth twisted. Settled, whether he liked it or not. "Seth can drive you to your hotel to pack and pick up your car."

Regretting her impulsiveness, Sabrina nodded miserably. His attitude puzzled her. She could understand his anxiety over the fate of his pilot, and he was justified in being unhappy about the way she'd maneuvered him into letting her stay with Tess. But, as before, she sensed something else bothering, tormenting, haunting him. There were times when she clearly saw a question in his eyes.

If only she knew what it was.

"Daddy, can I go to the airport with you?"

Ramsey pulled his daughter close in a hug of relief. "No, Little Bit." His voice cracked. "But thanks for offering."

Relieved? Why, Sabrina wondered, was he showing relief at Tess's normal act of caring? Were Ramsey's suspicions and defensiveness rooted in insecurity... fear of being pushed aside? By herself? Surely he didn't still see her as a threat to... what? And why? Never mind the whys and wherefores, she knew she'd really put her foot in it this time. She looked up at him, apology and pleading in her eyes. Couldn't he understand how impoverished her life had been until she'd met Tess and himself—how desperately she wanted to make up for it while she had the chance?

As desperately as he'd held her in the aspen grove.

Ramsey felt Sabrina's gaze like a hand extended to him. Her eyes promised more than the half-empty life he'd been settling for until now. He knew then that he'd changed and could no longer settle for anything less than life, emotion, commitment, risks—all of it... life as he'd once dreamed it should be, before one bitter experience too many had dulled his expectations. He wanted life as it was meant to be.

More than anything, he wanted to join his life with hers, to trust her with more than his daughter. He wanted to trust her with himself. And love her without reservations.

Ramsey clenched his jaw. Love. A four-letter word, a curse or a blessing, depending on how you looked at it. But, once said—even in the privacy of his mind—it became as irrefutable as the air he needed to breathe, as solid as the mountains.

And as treacherous.

"Ramsey, if you object..." Sabrina didn't recognize her own voice. It was uncertain, full of tremors, devoid of spirit. What was happening to her? She'd cracked the toughest nuts, stood up to the strongest opposition, withstood the harshest of criticisms, survived the worst disappointments. Yet here she was, cowering in the face of one man's displeasure.

Ramsey cleared his throat. "I don't know how long I'll be gone. Tess goes to a private school in Denver. If you can take her in the mornings, either Seth or Hap will pick her up and bring her to your office in the afternoon."

"All right." He sounded businesslike, impersonal, as if she were simply someone he'd hired for a temporary position, someone he didn't expect to be around any longer than it took to do the job.

"Tess has plans to spend the night with a girlfriend Friday. Weeknight dates are out, and she has an eleven o'clock curfew on weekends. If she does have a date, she's to let you know exactly where she'll be, and I always insist on the boy coming to the door for her. I draw the line at boys with pastel hair or who wear leather and chains. And no motorcycles."

Sabrina rigidly controlled her expression, keeping her hurt and confusion from showing. She knew she was not as successful at getting rid of the thickness in her voice. "What about phone numbers...where you can be reached...emergency numbers?"

"They're all on my desk in the study. Call them first, then Seth. I won't always be near a telephone. He can reach me by radio, if nothing else."

Sabrina took a step backward; his tone was freezing her from the inside out. She felt as if she were taking the rap for someone else, for an unspecified crime. "Tess and I will be fine, Ramsey," she said stiffly. She saw his gaze move to Tess, saw his reluctance to leave her again so soon after his last trip, saw his anxiety equally divided between his daughter and a pilot who was stranded—injured, maybe worse—at an altitude that was never free from snow and hostile conditions. Her own frosty tone melted. "Don't worry, Ramsey. I'll take very good care of her for you."

Her reassurance undid him. He'd been thumping his chest again, trying to prove... what? That he was in control, for once? It was all he could do not to grab her, wrap her in his arms, and absorb some of her heat and softness to take with him. He stared at her and sighed. "I know you will, Sabrina. I..." Glancing at his watch, he cursed under his breath. "I have to go. Seth will keep tabs, in case you need anything."

Before she could answer, he left her. She remained where she was, watching as he spoke to Lenny and Seth and gave Tess a bear hug and a kiss on the nose. Halfway around the side of the house, he turned back.

"We found your trunk. It will be delivered to your office tomorrow morning."

Sabrina took another step backward.

Ramsey could have kicked himself into next year for causing the stricken look on Sabrina's face. How could she know that his suspicions of her were based on another woman's actions? Surely she would tell him the truth. All he had to do was ask her. But by asking, he'd have to relive all the old pain. In her answer he might have to hear all the old truths and feel more pain, pain he wasn't sure he could survive.

Better that than taking it out on her. He halted with the idea of going back to explain. What could he say in a minute or less? That he was being torn apart by the past? That even though Claire was dead the memory of their problems refused to die? That fear of those problems being repeated lurked behind every word he heard Sabrina say, every loving look he saw her give Tess, every reminder she gave him of how important Tess was to her?

No, he'd have to leave it until he came back. By then, maybe he'd be able to see his problems for what they were: either as molehills or volcanoes.

Sabrina watched him pause, then go on his way. Looking up at the sky, she wished the sun hadn't disappeared behind a cloud. It had been such a beautiful day. . . .

CHAPTER TEN

TAPPING A PENCIL against her clipboard, Sabrina paced in front of the runway stage. Even when she was busy, she didn't know what to do with herself. Her nerves were in guarded condition. Misery clung to her like a leech, draining her of energy, patience and her usual optimism. She wanted to jump out of her skin and grow a new one that Ramsey had never stared at with need and admiration, never stroked with passion and desire. She was learning how provocative memories could be, almost as provocative as the moments in which they were created.

Coping with Tess had consumed her days for the past week. Coping with her own emotions had consumed her nights, filling them with dreams that seemed more impossible with every passing thought.

Sabrina knew the reasons for Tess's mercurial behavior. To a girl of Tess's age, Sabrina's world was exciting, glamorous. She hadn't counted on the hard work of a crash course in modeling and the discipline that was required to put those lessons to use. Tess was haggling over the price of knowing Sabrina and participating in her life. While they shared a genuine liking of one another, their love for Ramsey was tearing them apart. A new reserve in Tess's manner was keeping the fibers of affinity from being strengthened.

Right now, Tess is just a visitor in your life. Ramsey's words. Words that hurt all the more because this visit promised to be a short one. *Only on loan.* Her own words—and the interest charged threatened to bankrupt her in every way that mattered. *Only my mother called me Treasure.* Tess's words. *Only my mother...* Those, more than any others, stabbed Sabrina with hard, cold thrusts of anguish.

Since that bright, lovely afternoon when she and Ramsey had begun to face the demons of chance in their situation, Tess had made a point of talking about Claire and Ramsey, as if Claire were still alive, and Ramsey's 'symbiotic other.' Sabrina wanted to resent Claire, but couldn't. The woman had filled her role as Tess's mother and Ramsey's wife too well.

But if that was true, a voice asked, then what had caused Ramsey to develop that streak of bitter cynicism? With every story Tess told about her parents' idyllic marriage, Sabrina heard the question spoken a little louder. Sometimes she thought Tess protested too much to be convincing. At other times, Tess's voice would trail off, as if she knew that something was wrong with the picture she was painting, but wasn't quite sure what.

Sabrina shook her shoulders, trying to dislodge the little devil who was whispering in her ear. He taunted her with Tess's vulnerability, confronted her with the choice she might have to make between father and daughter. In the choosing, she could lose them both, as well as a large part of herself. She hadn't been so plagued with self-doubt or felt this helpless to control her own life since she'd learned of her pregnancy and lost Johnny, all on the same day.

"Tess, glide a little more. Straighten your spine. Be sure to pivot so that your skirts float around you."

Sabrina flinched as she heard the no-nonsense voice of Janet Temple, head of Denver's newest model agency. Janet was doing her a favor by coaching Tess. Little did the other woman know that Sabrina hadn't done her any favors by introducing her to Seth, when he'd brought Tess in earlier. Interest had sparked instantly between the two. Tess had overheard them making a date. . . .

Tess stopped at the front of the runway to stare belligerently at Janet's elegantly suited form. "First you tell me to glide. Then you want me to prance. But only a little, mind you. We don't want to look like a drum major in a parade. You tell me to sway, do this with my hips, do that with my shoulders." Jerking her body in an exaggerated display as she spoke, Tess threw up her hands. "I don't have enough joints to do all that. This whole thing is dumb."

Sabrina's nerves finally snapped. The pencil in her hand broke in two. Tess had crossed the line of acceptable behavior, leaving Sabrina no choice now but to do more than speak in gentle, warning tones. She'd known it was coming, had tried to avoid a confrontation, but she hadn't known enough about teenagers to second-guess Tess's reactions. Tenuous bonds such as theirs were so easily broken. "That's enough, Tess. If you think it's dumb, I'm sure we can reassign your garments."

Opening her mouth, Tess prudently shut it again.

"We're finished for today. Wait for me in my office." It lacked the impact of sending her to her room, but it was the best Sabrina could do at the moment. She turned away to join her partner, who was sitting at the back of the showroom.

"Fine," Tess muttered flatly as she stomped away.

Martine Jensen eyed Sabrina sympathetically over her wire-rimmed half glasses. "I was wondering how long you'd hold out before letting her have it. You've been acting like you're walking barefoot on hot gravel."

Sabrina pushed her glasses to the top of her head and glanced back at the empty stage. "She's having a hard time right now."

"She's been a witch with a capital *B* and something tells me she knows better. She also knows she can get away with it where you're concerned." Marty sighed as she saw Sabrina glance back at the stage. "Why don't you and I treat ourselves to an expensive meal after you drop Tess off at her girlfriend's? We can get drunk on calories and good wine."

"I can't."

"Of course you can. After everything you've been through in the last month, you deserve a good toot."

"Tess's friend has a touch of the flu. The slumber party has been postponed till tomorrow night," Sabrina said wearily.

Marty arched her brows. "Don't tell me you're disillusioned with motherhood already."

Rubbing the bridge of her nose, Sabrina grimaced. "I haven't even considered practicing motherhood. I'd be ecstatic to have friendship."

"I had the impression you two were really hitting it off."

"We were. Until she found Ramsey and me in a position just short of compromising. She didn't need subtitles to tell her what was going on." Sabrina's gaze dropped to the pencil pieces she was nervously twiddling between her fingers. "We still get along, but the openness is missing."

Marty blew upward to dislodge a wayward gray curl from her forehead. "In other words, Tess wants you to herself and she wants Daddy to herself, but the twain had darn well better not meet. The minute she thinks she's losing her place between you, she feels threatened. That's normal."

"Yes, it is, but that doesn't make it easier to deal with. It's bad enough that she's adopted and I'm...who I am. I let her go once. I'm sure she thinks it would be easy for me to do so again." Drinking the last of her coffee from a Styrofoam cup, Sabrina shuddered at its cold bitterness.

"Or she's afraid you're using her to establish yourself with Ramsey."

"Yes. I gather that more than one woman has tried it since Claire died."

"You could always give up on Ramsey," Marty suggested dryly.

"No. I can't."

Marty stared at Sabrina in disbelief. "Are you telling me that after only a month it's too late? Sabrina, you amaze me."

"Yes. Way too late. Mind-boggling, isn't it?" Sabrina raised her feet to the seat next to her.

"You could lose Tess."

"I lost Tess before I ever had her."

"You're her parent, too."

"Only in the mythical land of 'If Only.' I was her mother for nine months. After that I became something else. The best I can hope for is the role of stepmother, and you know what the fairy tales say about them."

Marty reached over to still the nervous flutterings of Sabrina's hands. "You're in for a bad fall, Sabrina." Ever the realist, ever the friend, Sabrina reflected.

"I've fallen before, Marty. I'm a survivor." The words came out with such force that Sabrina wondered whom she was trying to convince—Marty or herself.

Sighing loudly, Marty removed the pencil from Sabrina's hand. "Okay. So when do I meet Ramsey?"

Sabrina shrugged. "I don't know. He was upset with me when he left." The memory had been festering inside her, tearing at her nerves, destroying her peace of mind, puncturing the bubbles of hope that had risen in her when he'd made his declaration: *I'm up to my neck in a relationship with you.*

How presumptuous to build so many dreams on such a small foundation.

"Just how often does he go on business trips?"

Marty's query sliced cleanly through Sabrina's introspection. She wouldn't have tolerated anyone else delving into her private life, but Marty was exempt. She'd given Sabrina a chance all those years ago. Recognizing raw talent, Marty had helped her to develop it, enabling her to carve her own niche in the world. She had been a friend, a mother and a teacher—whatever Sabrina had needed. Marty had cared.

"Often."

Too often, according to Tess. This one couldn't be helped. He'd had no choice. But what about all the other times he was absent even when he was home? Why had work become the driving force in his life, when he had people who loved him and depended on him for more than financial security?

"Mmm-hmm. Is he a workaholic? Like you?"

"Not like me. I do it because there's nothing else . . . no one else."

"Maybe that's why he does it, too."

"He has Tess. Until two years ago he had Claire. This has been going on longer than that." It was the only thing that made sense, yet it didn't. He'd spoken of missing his wife, of loneliness, of grief, and Tess had reinforced the happy home image.

"Sabrina, the more you tell me—or don't tell me— the more I'm convinced this man you've invested your heart in is a luxury you can't afford. You'd be better off buying on the futures market."

Sabrina smiled wistfully. "Oddly enough, that's what I'm doing." Swinging her legs off the chair seat, she gathered her clipboard, briefcase and purse into a neat pile. "Marty, Ramsey is an intense man who doesn't do anything halfway, certainly not when his loyalty or love or obligation is involved." Her thoughts stumbled over the realization that those words might be the key to Ramsey's puzzling behavior.

Had Ramsey's marriage become more obligation than need? More loyalty than love? More convenience than fulfillment?

"That's what I said about Stu once upon a time. What in the hell is intense about watching wrestling on the tube three nights a week, and falling asleep in his chair the other four?"

"I'd love the opportunity to find out." Standing, Sabrina threw her empty cup into the waste can. "Tess is waiting. I'd better go see what I can come up with to keep us occupied tonight."

"Clean house," Marty said. "It's good busywork. Empties the mind and airs it out. If she hates doing it, it might even work off some of her anger."

"Did it work for your kids?"

"Sometimes."

"Well, the dust is getting a little thick." Walking away from the table, Sabrina called over her shoulder, "Thanks, Marty. See you later."

"Sabrina?"

Startled by the voice coming from directly in front of her, Sabrina jumped as she bumped into Tess. "Tess, you scared me."

Tess stared down at the floor. "I'm sorry, Sabrina...about everything. I apologized to Ms Temple, too."

Sabrina reached out to squeeze her arm. "We're both jumpy, living in each other's pockets like this. Ramsey will probably come back just as we're getting used to each other."

"I guess. I wish he'd call, though."

"He's out with the search party, Tess," Sabrina reminded her, as she had every day since Ramsey had left. A storm had blown in, hampering the search, grounding airplanes and helicopters. Ramsey had gone out with a few hardy souls on snowshoes and cross-country skis. His radio messages went to his Aspen office and were passed on to Seth, who called with whatever news he had. Unfortunately, there had been precious little news, and none of it was encouraging.

"I hope he's all right. It can be pretty nasty up there."

Sabrina shared the same anxieties. "Come on, Tess. Let's go clean house," she said with tinny brightness.

"You're kidding. We have a housekeeper."

"She's on vacation, remember?" Over Tess's groan, she heard Marty chuckle and break into a lively rendition of "Hi ho, Hi ho, It's off to work we go...." Sabrina sighed with relief as Tess's arguments grew sillier and sillier. They'd stumbled over another bad moment and managed to keep their balance. She looked heavenward and silently asked for a lull between problems.

"WELL, I GUESS we'd better start," Sabrina said for the third time.

Tess eyed the cleaning materials around them as if they were instruments of torture. "I've just been waiting for you."

"Me? I have enough trouble motivating myself for this."

"You're the adult. You're supposed to set an example."

Glaring at her in mock indignation, Sabrina swept her arm toward the massive oak shelf unit occupying the whole of a twelve-foot wall. "Right. As the adult, I'll let you dust and polish while I vacuum."

"No fair. A good commander never asks his men to do a job he isn't willing to do himself."

"Where on earth did you hear that?"

"TV," Tess said smugly, as if television were the final authority on everything.

"Oh. That explains it." Sabrina bent to unwind the vacuum cleaner cord. "Television is fantasy. Fact is, commanders pull rank, and age has its privileges."

"In other words, you hate housework as much as I do."

"That's about it. Tell you what. I'll split the bathrooms with you."

Placing her hands on her hips, Tess looked at Sabrina suspiciously. "How do two people split three bathrooms? One for you and two for me? You're not old enough for that much privilege. And who's going to do the windows?"

"The windows?" Sabrina sank to the edge of the coffee table, her eyes sweeping the huge expanse of glass on the south side of the house. "Tess, I don't do windows for anyone." She got up and pulled aside the draperies. "Besides, we can't wash them in the dark. How would we know if they're clean?"

Giggling, Tess put the squeegee back into the broom closet. "You're right. Anyway, if we do too good a job, Sarge will think we don't need her. I wouldn't want to hurt her feelings."

"Sarge? Oh, you mean your housekeeper, Mrs. Sargent. From what you've told me, it would take a tank running over her to hurt her feelings."

"Yeah, but she actually *likes* housework."

"How peculiar." Shaking her head, Sabrina turned on the vacuum cleaner and started pushing it over the nutmeg-colored plush carpet.

"Weird," Tess agreed, shouting over the noise on her way to the bathrooms.

Her smile still in place, Sabrina peeked under the cushions of the large sectional sofa to see if they needed cleaning. All she found was a quarter, two nickels and seven pennies. Sliding the cushions back, she smoothed her hand over the plaid upholstery, enjoying the texture of the weave. She liked the way Ramsey and Tess had decorated their home with warm colors and an emphasis on comfort. The diagonally-panelled walls on either side of the stone fireplace were ideal for setting off the Navajo rugs that were displayed against them, and a large piece of fiber art in the room's colors of oatmeal, rust, navy blue and brown was the perfect adornment for an off-white textured wall.

Passing the shelf unit, she read the titles of the books scattered among Indian pottery and brass figures. The selection was eclectic: romances next to classics, science fiction leaning against *War and Peace*, Ian Fleming on top of Ansel Adams, and aviation magazines mixed with fix-it books. Holding pride of place in the center space was a framed watercolor portrait of Tess.

It was a home to be lived in . . . enjoyed.

So why didn't Ramsey stay home more and enjoy it? she wondered. Tess had told her that they'd bought the property some months after Claire had died, so it didn't hold painful memories—

"I'll do all the bathrooms if you'll do the kitchen," Tess shouted from the hallway.

Nodding absently, Sabrina hoped Mrs. Sargent was well paid, even if she did like housework. . . .

Two hours later Sabrina propped her elbows on the coffee table to lick the pizza sauce off her fingers, silently thanking Marty for her suggestion. She and Tess had worked together with no outbursts, save those of silliness. She grinned as she pictured the pouty feminine lips and sultry eyes that Tess had painted on a bathroom mirror with washable tempera paint.

Tess's artistic talent was evident in the partial face, right down to the Fu Manchu mustache drooping under an invisible nose. Sabrina had stared at it thoughtfully and stopped Tess from washing it off. She couldn't help but feel pride that Tess's talent might have come from her, that creativity was one more thing they had in common.

"That was good." Tess leaned back against the sofa, loudly slurping the last drop of soda pop through her straw.

"When you offered to cook dinner, I had no idea you meant junk food."

"The pizza had meat and veggies in the sauce." Tess defended her choice good-naturedly. "You sound just like a mother." Her voice faded, as she looked away quickly.

Sabrina closed her eyes for a moment. If only she could be. If only it weren't too late for useless wishing. "I'll take that as a compliment, Tess," she said quietly.

Tess didn't raise her head. "Sabrina? What was my... what was *he* like?"

Gripping her napkin, Sabrina fought a rush of sadness and regret. She'd known Tess would eventually ask, but she hadn't been able to plan her answer. She smiled sadly. "He was everything a first love should be—handsome, charming, experienced. He sent me flowers. Unfortunately, in my case, love was blind. Because he was older, I saw him as a mature man. He wasn't. At nineteen, he was still looking for his place in the world. When I told him I was pregnant, I think he was more scared than I was. He was cocky with his new independence and didn't want to give it up."

"What a rat," Tess said vehemently. "It was his fault, too."

"*Too* being the operative word, Tess. I knew the facts of life, but didn't think they applied to me. I took a lot for granted." Sabrina tossed her napkin onto her paper plate and began gathering the remains of their meal. "What I saw in him and what he was were two different things. He really was nice, only young and groping at life like the rest of us."

In the telling, the residue of bitterness and hurt dissolved, leaving Sabrina with a gentler memory. She pitied Johnny because he would never know Tess. Had he questioned her fate? she wondered. Would he care if he knew it? "Your eyes are like his, Tess."

Tess stared at the far wall. "I'm glad he was nice. I asked Dad once if I came from bad people. When I did something wrong, I'd wonder. Dad said that you were perfectly normal, and like normal people, you'd made a mistake."

"What do you think, Tess?" Sabrina had to ask.

"I think he was right." Tess looked up. "Have you ever seen him again? Do you know where he is?"

"No." Panic wound through Sabrina. "Tess, you're not thinking of looking for him, are you?"

"No. It's not important. I just wanted to know. None of it really changes anything, does it?" Tess spoke as if she were repeating a lesson she'd just learned. "I'm still me. Besides, what if I met him and was disappointed? It would be like asking for trouble, wouldn't it?"

Sabrina carefully placed a knife on top of the stack of dishes. "Yes, it would. You have a father who loves you." *And me. I love you too.* Sabrina was afraid to say that, though. She was afraid of rejection, afraid it would destroy her.

"Yeah. What more do I need?" Tess's gaze held Sabrina's. "And you'll be around, too, won't you?" The question sounded like an accusation.

Sabrina sensed that Tess was asking herself whether she really wanted her around, after what she'd witnessed last Sunday. Sabrina arranged her words carefully. "I hope so. If I am, I'll help you all I can, but there are some dragons you'll have to slay on your own."

"Is that the same as 'solve your own problems'?" Tess asked with a long-suffering air.

"It means there are some problems that can be solved only if you want them to be. Otherwise they grow so formidable in your mind that they defeat you."

Tess tilted her head. "Why did you stay with me?"

"I wanted to spend time with you. I've worried about you for years. This time I thought I'd do it in person." Sabrina knew where Tess was leading the conversation, hating the knowledge that Tess was also afraid to voice her fears, afraid to hear Sabrina's answers. "Tess, what is it you really want to know?"

"I..." Flushing, Tess stuttered, but recovered quickly. "Okay. Are you here to make points with Daddy?"

Short, dry laughter rasped in Sabrina's throat. At least on this she didn't have to worry about her reply. "In case you hadn't noticed, Ramsey was less than thrilled with my offer to stay. I knew what his reaction would be when I made it. The only points I wanted to make were with you."

"Yeah." Tess grinned. "I thought he was going to have a major cow." She didn't bother to hide her satisfied expression as she picked up the dishes and headed for the kitchen. "I think I'll go to bed. If Seth calls, wake me up. I want to talk him into giving me a flying lesson tomorrow."

Sabrina had been waiting for that. Seth had canceled the lesson because of the extra work generated by the plane crash—another reason why Tess had been so temperamental earlier. "I wouldn't count on it, Tess. He's so busy right now."

"He's not too busy to take Ms Temple out," Tess retorted, then bit her lip. "Sabrina? Do you think she likes him?"

"Seth is an easy man to like," Sabrina said carefully.

"She's older than he is. At least three years. Shouldn't that matter?"

"Janet and Seth are—" Sabrina swallowed the words "mature adults" just in time, words guaranteed to alienate Tess "—independent and well established in their lives, Tess. They know where they're going and what they want when they get there—"

Tess's body language interrupted Sabrina more effectively than any shout. Her stance was rigid, and her arms were crossed over her chest like a closed gate. Tess didn't want to hear what she was saying. This was one of those moments when there was no right thing to say, and every sentence sounded like a platitude.

"Of course, you know what I'm talking about," Sabrina continued, as if she hadn't been interrupted and hadn't changed her mind about what she wanted to say. "Of course, you know you want Seth. I can see that and I don't blame you a bit. He is terrific. But Tess, when you're shopping for clothes, do you buy the first thing you see?" Stifling a grin at Tess's surprise and confusion, Sabrina pressed on. "Or do you look at everything first, just to be sure there isn't something better that you didn't know about?"

"Huh?" Tess dropped to the arm of a chair. "Sabrina, what does Seth have to do with shopping for clothes? I mean...you can't shop for a man. It's not the same thing."

"Well, no. Not exactly, although the principle is the same," Sabrina said thoughtfully. "Take Cinderella, for instance. The prince looked all the girls over—including her—and couldn't find what he wanted. It's sort of like finding a blouse the color you like, but it's too small, and then you find a skirt that fits, but you're not crazy about the fabric. Anyway, he just wasn't going to bend an inch when it came to the image he had of the ideal woman. When Cinderella showed up matching that image, he knew he was in love.''

Sabrina warmed to her analogy as she saw the rapt attention on Tess's face. "The thing is, Tess, he went out to find her and couldn't believe that the ordinary girl cleaning house was the same one who'd been at the ball. He had to have proof. I've always wondered what would have happened if her feet had grown and the slipper didn't fit anymore. Or what if her feet had grown after they were married? Can you imagine being stuck with a man who insisted on glass slippers, when she hadn't worn them enough to know if they'd give her blisters?''

"Yeah. I see what you mean,'' Tess said. "She hooked up with the first guy she'd seen. And the prince chose Cinderella, just because she looked like what he wanted. She could have turned out to be a real nerd. Or... if she'd just waited around for a while, Cinderella might have met a king who didn't care if she went barefoot.''

"I hadn't thought about that, Tess, but you're right. In any case, each of them knew what they wanted, and grabbed at the first person who appeared to be the right one. They were in such a hurry that they didn't bother to check out the possibilities.''

Tess bent over to pick up a fallen napkin. "I don't think Ms Temple is what Seth is looking for. Besides, he and I have known each other for years. That's important. We know all about each other,'' she said firmly as she stood up. "Well, I'm going to bed. We'll be up all night at Jenny's party tomorrow. 'Night, Sabrina . . . and don't forget to wake me up if Seth calls,'' she said over her shoulder as she disappeared into the kitchen.

And that settles that Sabrina thought wryly. Lowering herself to lie on her side, she propped her head on one hand while drawing designs in the thick pile of the carpet with the other. She should have known. At Tess's age she, too, had seen only surfaces and had been guided only by emotion. She hadn't expected failure or heartbreak, either. And if she was to be completely honest with herself, she'd admit that she was doing it again. She might be older than Tess, but apparently she wasn't a heck of a lot wiser.

Disgusted with herself, Sabrina clenched her fists. She knew there wasn't really such a thing as ''happily ever after,'' yet here she sat, acting like a vapid ingenue, waiting for her hero to grace her with his presence. Next her brains would turn to mush, just because he smiled at her. . . .

When the sky turns green! Slapping her open palm against the floor, she gave an unladylike snort as she qualified her own assertion. Not even then!

Restlessness scraped its razor edge along her nerves. She hated being suspended between problem and solution with no control over either one. She hated the idea that *her* future, *her* happiness depended on anyone but herself. Worst of all, she hated knowing that her love for one Jordan could be jeopardized by her love for the other. Why did everything have to be broken down into equal parts of either-or?

Sabrina rolled onto her back and closed her eyes, then jumped as the phone rang. Racing to answer it, she picked it up on the second ring. ''Hello,'' she croaked.

''Sabrina?''

Her shoulders sagged. It wasn't Ramsey. "Yes. Hi, Seth."

"Are you hanging in there?"

"Hanging on is more like it."

"Well, don't lose your grip." There was a jubilant grin in Seth's voice. "They found the plane yesterday."

"And the pilot? Is he—?"

"By some miracle, he's alive. He didn't have a heart attack, but a mild stroke. He had enough mobility when he regained consciousness to practice some good survival techniques. With time and specialized therapy, the doctors think he'll be okay."

"I'm so glad, Seth." Yesterday. They had found him yesterday. "And Ramsey? How are his hands?"

"Huh?"

"You know, Seth, those things you use to dial a telephone."

"Sabrina, he's had a lot to do, not to mention that he hasn't had more than token naps since Sunday."

"All right, Seth." Of course Ramsey was tired. They all were. "When will he be coming home?"

"He should be back in three or four days.... Are you okay?"

"I'm fine."

"Any problems?"

"No. Seth, tell Ramsey that it would be nice if he called his daughter between naps. She's been worrying about him tramping around in a blizzard."

"Sabrina, that's not fair. He couldn't—"

"It's not fair for him to leave us hanging, when all he had to do was place a three-minute phone call."

"Uh-oh. I take it he's not going to come home to peace and harmony."

Is he ever home long enough to notice? Sabrina shook her head at her caustic thoughts. Lately she was all sharp-edged, brittle emotion, taking temperamental swipes at everyone.

"How is Tess?" Seth asked when she didn't say anything.

"As jumpy as a Mexican bean, but fine. I have strict orders to wake her if you called."

"Uh..." Seth paused. "I have some other calls to make. Would you mind...?"

"I'll make your apologies, Seth, but you'll have to call her in the morning. She's determined to change your mind about her lesson tomorrow."

"Oh, boy," he muttered. "You have no mercy, Sabrina."

"None," she agreed. "Thanks for calling. I'll talk to you tomorrow." Sabrina hung up the phone very carefully, resisting the urge to pitch it across the room.

She just wasn't used to refitting her life around others, she told herself as she checked locks, turned out lights and went to bed. She needed to be alone for a while, sort herself out.

Tomorrow. The word flashed like a neon sign, advertising sanctuary from a tilted world. Tomorrow Tess would be away for the night. Tomorrow night she would enjoy the peace and familiarity of her own company, and maybe she'd stop sounding like Little Orphan Annie, ready to burst into song.

Maybe tomorrow she'd recognize herself again.

CHAPTER ELEVEN

MOONBEAMS BROKE through the trees and lay in scattered shards on the road, the patterns of light holding Sabrina's gaze in hypnotic thrall as she drove the near-deserted highway to Ramsey's house. The van hummed a well-tuned lullaby, its tires providing a steady roll and thump rhythm over the seams in the paved surface. Aside from the patches of moon glow that went blurring past, there was nothing to see but varying shades of night.

From a distance she heard the short blast of a horn. The flashing lights of a car several lengths behind her jerked her out of her sleepy trance. Alerted, she turned the wheel just in time to avoid colliding with the rock face on her right. Widening her eyes in an effort to stay awake, Sabrina opened her window to wave a grateful acknowledgement to her unknown companion. The cold slap of mountain air on her face revived her, making her shudder with more than the chill. A close call...the perfect end to a day that had proved Murphy's Law was more than an amusing theory.

Tess had grown moody and uncommunicative after Seth phoned to do his own dirty work. As the morning progressed with no further news, Tess withdrew even more, ignoring Sabrina's attempts to talk to her. After being oppressed by Tess's silence, deafened by the stereo and waylaid by a flat tire on the way into Denver, Sabrina had been relieved to drop her off at the party.

When she'd arrived at her office to take care of last-minute details with Marty, all she had found was a note propped against the telephone on her desk. Stu, Marty's husband, was sick with the flu, and Marty was feeling lousy herself. She'd gone home to administer hot toddies and tender loving care. She apologized for leaving Sabrina to work alone on a Saturday, but everything was under control.

Marty had neglected to tell that to the caterer. He'd wanted to change both colors and menu for Monday night's showing. It took Sabrina half an hour and her last drop of patience to convince him she wanted class, not flamboyance, at a showing of Cachet Fashions. She hung up, wondering why the former owner of the catering firm had chosen this year to retire and sell his business to a twit.

Deciding to escape before more disaster could nip at her heels, Sabrina had made a desperate grab for her purse and briefcase—and collided with Janet Temple on her way out the door.

"Sabrina, where are you going in such a rush?"

"Home, where I can lock out the rest of humanity for a while."

"Oh." The agency owner-cum-former model tugged at her fashionably baggy sweater and tucked a stray lock of hair behind her ear. "I've been trying to call you."

Sabrina wrested a smile from her diminishing store of goodwill. "Janet, I'd love to have a chat with you—tomorrow, next week—anytime but now. I'm sorry. It's been a stinker of a week, and I'm desperate for an unoccupied cranny and absolute silence."

"Uh-oh."

Not liking the sound of that, Sabrina studied Janet's expression. It was harried, apologetic. It could only mean one thing—another problem. "I don't really want to know, Janet, but you'd better tell me, anyway." She dropped her things back onto her desk and all but fell into her chair. "What is it? War? Famine? Pestilence?"

"Flu." Janet stepped into the office to deposit a stack of folders in front of Sabrina. "Three of the models for Monday's showing. We have to choose substitutes and alter the designs to fit them."

Sabrina was grateful for Janet's succinct reply, and the "we" inspired even more gratitude. She was in no condition to make command decisions without a steadying hand. Janet looked disgustingly steady. "I don't suppose—" Sabrina indicated the files under her hand "—any of these have the same measurements as the girls we lost?"

Janet shook her head. "Sorry. If you designed for standard sizes . . ."

Sighing, Sabrina opened the top file. "Silly me. I don't know why I asked," she mumbled as she focused on images and statistics.

In record time, she and Janet had chosen and called in the models for an emergency sewing session. After gallons of coffee and energy-giving sweets they had adjusted the garments, and with groans of relief, migrated for home, long, tiring hours after dark.

Oblivious to the fact that winter had finally caught up with Denver, and fat snowflakes were drifting onto the windshield, Sabrina berated herself for not staying in town for the night. She hadn't even considered it an option. Rationalizations, puny and transparent, staggered forth to make a stand. She was settled into the

Jordan home. There she could enjoy the peace she craved, sans well-meaning friends, desk clerks or late-night carousers in hotel corridors. Then the truth broke through her weak reasoning.

Ramsey might call. If he wasn't going to come home for several days yet, a call would be...nice.

"Phooey." Sabrina cursed as she braked her car. She'd nearly missed the entrance. Making a sharp turn, she drove through the open gates. She was as bad as Ramsey, habitually forgetting to turn on the security system. Reaching under the dash for the remote control that Tess had given her, she entered the code that would lock the twelve-foot iron gates behind her. Once all was secure, she faced forward to capture a view she never tired of.

Dark and silent in repose, the house blended with the land in a perfect mating, nestling in the crook of the mountainside like a lover seeking warmth and intimacy. Even in her exhaustion, she appreciated the grace and harmony of the scene. Ramsey and Tess belonged here.

And she wanted to belong with them—so much.

Her legs trembled with weakness as she climbed out of the van. The only strength she could find within herself was her love for Ramsey and for Tess. And it was strong. Stronger than she was, taking her over, compelling her to blindly follow a course that made nonsense of her own rules of caution and control. She was playing too close to the edge, flirting with emotional devastation for the sake of a few moments of the passion she'd mocked not so long ago.

But the ground kept shifting, and it was growing harder to keep her balance.

Sabrina stabbed the key into the lock of the front door, angry because, of all the men in the world, Ramsey had been the one to clarify her dreams, angry because only Ramsey would be enough to satisfy them. And, she was afraid that enough was, in fact, too much to hope for....

Scolding herself for having thoughts at odds with modern feminist attitudes, Sabrina shut the door with a swing of her hips, jumping as it slammed into the frame. She was becoming too fanciful, too much the dreamer and too little the pragmatist.

Not bothering to turn on the lights, she headed for her bedroom, banging her purse against the wall as she rounded a corner—and gasped in fright.

A figure moved down the hallway, dark as a shadow, large—too large to be Tess. She swerved to avoid a collision, her momentum sending her crashing into the opposite wall. Strong hands gripped her from behind, and her only thoughts were of the security gates, carelessly left open, of the isolation of the place, the wealth of valuable pottery and equipment in the house, and how alone she was.

Her blood surged with adrenaline, rushing energy into every vein and artery. Anger canceled out fear. Resolve overrode caution. She'd been functioning on Automatic for hours. Instincts developed in self-defense classes took over. Darn it, she'd had enough. She wasn't about to be a passive victim to circumstance, fate or some crazy bent on mayhem.

"Bloody hell!"

Concentrating fiercely on her plan of defense, she jerked her left arm forward, then back, her elbow connecting with a hard midsection and moving up again, so that she could position her first and third fingers just under his eyes. Her palm pressed his nose upward, forcing him to work at breathing through his mouth. She found his foot with her heel and ground it into his instep. Then she reached for him with vicious intent, her fingers encountering loose, soft cotton before closing around her objective. She twisted her hand slightly and paused, as her brain caught up with her reflexes.

She knew that voice. Loose, soft cotton? The chest behind her was bare. The skin smelled faintly of Pierre Cardin. Did burglars brush with Crest before going to work?

His hand pried hers away from his face. "Sabrina...it's me, Ramsey. Everything is all right. Please...let...go."

She did know that voice. It was soothing, beloved...and pained. She jerked away.

"Ouch! For crying out loud, Sabrina. Why did you have to grab me *there*?" Ramsey clutched the offended portion of his body. Fortunately the offense was minor.

Sabrina stumbled against the wall again and stayed there, using it to support her. "I thought you were a burglar. My instructor said—"

"Self-defense classes, right? I should have known. I made Tess take them, too," he mumbled as he limped toward the room a few feet down the hall.

"What are you doing here?" Her voice wavered. Energy and strength were leaving her as quickly as they had come. Only a few seconds—a minute at most—had passed since she'd run into him, but it seemed as if the one-sided struggle had lasted for hours.

Light flared in the hallway, blinding her. She raised her hand to shield her eyes and could just make out his form—a tall figure with broad shoulders, and muscular arms bent to prop hands on narrow hips. He wasn't wearing nearly enough clothes.

His only garment—a well-worn pair of pajama bottoms—defied gravity by resting very low on his hips, leaving little to the imagination. She jerked her gaze upward to stare owlishly at his face. It was a mistake. He looked so irresistible with his hair tousled and a little damp—obviously he'd taken a shower not long before. He looked sleepy with his eyelids half lowered, as if he'd just dozed off and suddenly been awakened. His skin was ruddy from being outside for the last week, and a little pink from a recent shave. He looked so sexy. . . .

And they were so alone.

"What are you doing here?" she repeated.

He reached up absently to rub his hair. "I make the mortgage payments. My bed is here." *You were here, and I couldn't wait to come home to you,* he added silently.

Seeing the message in his eyes, she forgot everything but the two of them. She focused on him, tall and bare-chested, the incarnation of her fantasies, impossibly sensuous. Dark hair—not too much, not too little—curled over his wide chest. He was muscular, but not bulky, the lines of his body powerful, symmetrical, like those in a perfectly executed drawing. His legs were long and firmly muscled. The ridges of his stomach muscles flowed into his waistband, along with a line of dark silky hair. And his bare feet were large, strong like the rest of him and lightly sprinkled with hair. A bruise was forming on his instep.

Her gaze flew up again, colliding with his. "Are you all right?" she asked, speaking on one level while feeling on another.

He smiled and briefly closed his eyes, shaking his head at the same time, amused in spite of himself. "My foot will never be the same. I'm seeing spots on the inside of my eyeballs. You've given me a pug nose and damn near emasculated me, but I'm fine...just fine...except for a terminal case of mangled pride." He stared at her, absorbing all the details about her he'd missed before, absorbing her impact on himself, absorbing the certainty of the feelings he had for her. "Sabrina, you are an incredible lady."

Sabrina stared back at him and felt the approval in his eyes. It was like a warm blanket covering her shivering body. She was cold, yet inside she was hot. Her bones felt like overcooked linguine. Her head felt so light....

Something was wrong. Sabrina's distress communicated itself to Ramsey through her silence, the tremors shaking her and the panting breaths she was taking. In one long stride, he crossed to her and took her shoulders in a gentle grip. His gut clenched. "Sabrina? What's wrong? Did I hurt you?"

"I'm going to be sick."

Grimacing as he put his weight onto his sore foot, he guided her into his bedroom. Easing her to the side of the bed, he pushed her head between her knees, then grabbed his grandmother's quilt from the rack in the corner. He toppled the antique as he jerked the quilt off the rail.

Sabrina hadn't moved. He wrapped the quilt around her and tore through his mental file on first aid. Head between knees for nausea, feet up for shock. How in the hell was he supposed to do both? Panic clawed at him. What if he had hurt her? He couldn't have. It was the other way around. Maybe she was sick. There was a flu epidemic. Dammit, Seth had told him about Tess's change in plans and that Sabrina would probably stay in town. Why hadn't she, instead of making the long drive so late at night?

Kneeling in front of her, he took her wrist in his hand. Though a little slow, her pulse was strong. Her breathing was more controlled as she slowly took in air through her nose, and let it out through her mouth. "Sabrina, are you hurt? Tell me."

"I'm . . . not . . . hurt," she said between breaths.

"What's wrong?" He drew the quilt closer around her.

She smiled weakly. "Too little sleep, not enough food, too much work. I'll be fine as soon as I have some tea."

"I . . ." He raked one hand through his hair, not wanting to leave her, yet knowing tea would help her. "Lie down. I'll make you some."

"I'm fine. Really," she said more firmly, the child-like quality leaving her voice. "I need a hot shower. Can you make eggs?"

"What?"

"Eggs. Toast. Soup. Anything. I'm so hungry. And I need a hot shower." She stood up slowly, found herself steady and took a step around him. What she really needed was to be alone so she could decide what to do. She wasn't sure she could handle what would come next.

Sabrina walked toward the bathroom. She could have gone for tea herself, but she didn't trust her strength to take her through the motions of preparing something to eat. She could have used another shower, but she couldn't face entering a darkened room. Here there was light and the comfort of Ramsey's things scattered about. For those few moments in the hall, she'd been truly frightened—frightened of danger, of being at the mercy of someone else, of not being strong enough to take care of herself, of being hurt.

Now a different kind of panic began stirring in her, inspired, oddly enough, by the same fears.

Relieved to see her color returning to normal, the steadiness of her walk and the stubborn line of her mouth, Ramsey stood up. Only her eyes disturbed him. They were too wide, too calm—dark blue water glazed with ice. There was no warmth, no animation—nothing. He reached out to her, feeling as if she were somewhere else and that he had to pull her back.

She didn't see him. The bathroom door clicked shut.

CHAPTER TWELVE

DROPLETS OF WATER sprayed from the shower head, touching Sabrina with warmth before rolling off her body to scatter on the floor. She stared down at the tiles, expecting to see pieces of herself floating in the water as it ran into the drain.

Was this what it felt like to fall off a cloud? she wondered. Depression shrouded her, thick and muggy as the steamy air. Shutting off the faucets, she reached for a towel, paying little attention to actually drying herself. With the bath sheet wrapped around her, she sank to the edge of the tub.

What grand illusion had made her believe she could keep in control of herself, her emotions or the situation? In the hallway, she had looked at Ramsey and found what she had never expected to see: a calm certainty, as if he'd considered, evaluated and approved of what was happening between them. He cared for her and wanted her, and would move mountains or climb over them to achieve his goal. He had made up his mind.

In that instant she'd seen herself from the inside out, and had found bruises on her psyche that she thought had healed long ago. The truth of the matter was, though she'd been honest with Ramsey about her feelings, she hadn't been honest with herself about anything at all. The very idea of losing control struck her with panic.

Ramsey—her feelings for him—made her lose control, yet she feared that losing Ramsey would mean an agonizing death by inches.

Either way, she would most certainly lose. She didn't really believe that love conquered anything. Her honesty had been a weapon wielded by her subconscious to drive him away, as it had driven away others. That was, what she'd wanted. She hadn't intended to hope or dream—hopes and dreams held too long would become a part of her. Expecting the worst was easier, safer, simpler. And she couldn't stand to lose any more of herself than she already had.

Still, she'd done it again: repeated the past, paid lip service to reality, then blithely floated away on a sea of fantasy. She had wanted Ramsey to prove that it would all work out, that "happily ever after" did exist. Now she was afraid to believe it would last.

She could drown.

"Help." Startled by the whispered plea, Sabrina covered her mouth with her hand.

"Sabrina?"

Ramsey's call through the closed door alerted her to the immediacy of her dilemma and the urgency of her desire. Trying to gather her thoughts into a rational whole, she answered him in a voice that creaked, she thought, like an unoiled hinge. "Yes." She'd never felt less rational.

"Sabrina, I brought your nightgown and robe."

Releasing the lock, Sabrina opened the door far enough to stick an arm through. "Thank you."

"I brought you something to eat."

"I'll be right out." Food. She would eat and then retreat to her own room. It was the practical thing to do.

Ramsey stood at the bedroom window, his hand braced on the sash, his chin resting on his arm as he watched her reflection in the glass. Noting the way she pulled the belt of her robe tighter than was necessary and twisted the ends around her clenched fists, the smile he'd intended gave way to a pained grimace. He stayed where he was, sensing that she wouldn't look at him, even if he turned around.

A bed tray lay on top of the mattress, giving Sabrina a focal point. She sat on the edge of the bed with one leg bent in front of her and one foot on the floor, staring at the tray as if she'd never seen sandwiches, fruit, milk and tea before.

"PB and J," Ramsey said, identifying the contents of the sandwich. "Tess insists it's loaded with instant energy."

Sabrina lifted a corner of bread to see what PB and J was. "Oh. Peanut butter. I like it, too." She took a bite, then another, not tasting a thing. Tess. No matter what happened, Tess would still love Ramsey, still be his daughter. The same didn't hold true for Sabrina. Tess didn't love her, and if she wasn't careful, Tess would hate her instead. She'd be hurt. Ramsey would be hurt—and so would Tess. There was too much potential for hurt and not enough for happiness.

Enough, in this case, was too much to hope for.

She ate mechanically and sipped the hot, spicy tea, not noticing when it burned her tongue. Questions, misgivings and fear ran amok in her mind. She wouldn't have thought herself capable of putting on such an act, deceiving both herself and Ramsey. All that positive thinking, confidence and honesty—an act so well per-

formed that she'd fooled herself. She reached for another bite of food, but found an empty plate. Helpless,
she stared at the tray, wondering what to do next.

Walls of silence closed in on them, threatening to
crush any hope of mutual understanding. Sabrina was
different—and so was the occasion—from what Ramsey had imagined. Where was her store of three-dollar
words, well chosen to let him know how she felt about
the way he'd said goodbye, the fact that he hadn't
called, or the way he'd surprised her in the hall?

His first impulse upon seeing her again had been to
pick her up, swirl her around and tell her how much
he'd missed her. He'd wanted to share with her the joy
he had felt at finding his pilot alive, and then talk—
really talk—about the two of them and where they were
going. But one look at her face had changed all that;
he'd felt lost. Being unable to share with her was too
much like a bad trip into the past.

"You think too much, Sabrina," Ramsey said quietly, transferring his gaze from her reflection to her
face.

"Someone has to do it," she said, quoting Tess's favorite catchall phrase as she left the bed.

"Meaning, I don't?" He watched her smooth out her
expression. Her hands curled into fists as she backed up
a step and put them behind her. He could almost think
she was scared.

Sabrina?

"All I've done is think, since meeting you," he said
gruffly.

"What about Tess? Have you thought about her?"

"In relation to what?"

"Your absences. Ramsey, you're gone so much that
when you do have to leave, she resents it, no matter

what your reasons are. She ran away from you, thinking your frequent trips were an excuse to get away from her.''

"You're jerking my chain on purpose, Sabrina. Why? You know that I'm working on the problem. Tess knows it. A few months will see it taken care of in a way we can live with.''

She backed up another step. "I'm glad to hear it. Just . . . please . . . be sure to take care of Tess. And yourself, Ramsey. Take care of yourself.''

A sigh came from the deepest part of him. She was inching toward the hallway . . . away from him. In another minute she'd be out the door. "That sounds like goodbye, like you're shutting doors on me . . . giving up.'' He felt as if she'd already slammed the door in his face. Once he'd wished she'd do just that, let him off the hook, make it easy for him to walk away and forget her.

There ought to be a way to recall faulty wishes, he thought wryly.

Sabrina stopped, aware for the first time of her backward progress. She hadn't consciously decided to leave him, but she realized that the thought had slowly, painfully been awakening within her. She stared past him, blind to the stars that shone beyond the windows; she saw only the absence of color and light, and the blackness was like a loss. . . . "Isn't that what you wanted?'' she whispered.

Ramsey's eyes narrowed. "You're not shutting me out, are you? You're trying to close yourself in.''

"I . . . no . . . yes.'' Plucking the quilt off the bed, Sabrina began folding it, neatly, precisely, finding comfort in putting something in order. "It's safer, isn't it? Putting up barriers, I mean. It keeps you uncommitted, uninvolved, un . . . everything.''

"It's empty, Sabrina. It's not real."

"Yes. That too." Pausing in her task, Sabrina's eyes blurred over the thousands of tiny squares depicting a landscape. Had this been the maker's home, loved so much that she had captured it in cloth for future generations to enjoy? Home. She had thought it was a house, but it wasn't. Not really.

"Things will work out," Ramsey said forcefully, but splinters of doubt left a trail of unspoken "ifs" to contradict him.

"Are you asking me to have blind faith in that?" She smoothed the age-softened fabric.

"Sabrina, will you stop…fidgeting and talk to me?" His gaze clung to her, searching for a way to reach her, to understand what had changed her attitude from "Full speed ahead and damn the torpedoes" to "don't rock the boat." "Are you afraid of being hurt?"

"I…" A tightness in her forehead became a throbbing pressure. Distressed at being too long ignored, doubts nagged her and grew in volume, insisting on being heard. She lifted her hand to massage the painful area between her brows, then lowered it again. "I've always gone after what I wanted. Sometimes it hasn't worked out, and I've had to leave a dream behind. I'm afraid this one can't survive reality. It's just not safe to hold on to it any longer."

"I guess we all have our own ideas of safety. What's yours, Sabrina? Making more money than you can spend? Outfitting other women so they can please their men, while you go home alone? Not taking chances, then wondering why life dismissed you? All of the above?"

"What do you offer in return, Ramsey? A harsher dismissal, a deeper loneliness?" She shook her head. It hurt as much to utter the words as it did to think them. "I'm selfish. If I give a hundred percent, I want that much back—love for love, trust for trust . . . an equal partner." She tilted her head at the strangeness of seeing him so still, not moving about as he usually did, animated by his emotions. She missed seeing his thoughts come alive on his face; she missed being touched by him and coming alive in his arms. "But then, you never said anything about love. I did. You'd think I'd stop going down one-way streets the wrong way."

Everything she said beckoned to him with the promise of things he'd never really had: love, an equal partner. He'd left his dreams behind under a pile of bitterness. The deficiencies of the past glared at him, making him reluctant to believe they wouldn't follow him into the future. Doubts were contagious. She had caught his, and now he was catching hers. "It takes time to work problems out, Sabrina."

"Time has a cruel way of running out before we have a chance to use it all. I'm not willing to spend mine dodging No Trespassing signs, Ramsey."

"Run that by me again?"

Walking deeply in her thoughts, she picked up the tray and set it on the dresser. An hour ago, she'd been afraid to look at her fears or even acknowledge that she had any. Now she was talking about them, analyzing them as she went along, discovering their sources. She was becoming familiar with herself again. Because of Ramsey. He'd always been easy to talk to, confide in . . . because for all his ranting and raving, he really did hear.

She moistened her lips. "You and Tess are a warm, cozy unit. I've been invited in and shown a list of conditions to follow. One mistake and I'm out, evicted because the price is non-involvement and I can't pay it.''

"What conditions?" A chill crawled over him. Why had he asked? He already knew. Those conditions had been designed to keep Sabrina a safe distance away. They were conditions he wouldn't have imposed if she'd been anyone else—if she weren't connected to Tess.

If he didn't connect her to Claire.

But Sabrina wasn't Claire. She was different... special. Maybe.

Watch it, Jordan, your insecurities are showing.

The backs of her knees bumped the edge of the cedar chest at the foot of the bed. She'd seen the expressions that were crossing Ramsey's face, and she knew he was arguing with himself. Over her. She took a deep breath. She'd started this. Now she'd have to finish it.

"Rule number one: don't, under any circumstances, interfere. As you saw last Sunday, I can't keep my word. I can't be objective and detached where Tess is concerned.''

"I'm her parent, Sabrina. I'm responsible for her."

"I know. That brings us to rule number two. Claire was—still is—her mother. Tess has made it very clear that she won't tolerate me within a thought's breadth of the position. That's a tough one, when every cell in my body remembers that for nine months I was her mother. I wanted to be her mother. I still do. It was easy to pretend otherwise, until she came to me full of tears and need. Right there are two boundaries I'll try to cross, and you and Tess will find a way to lock me out."

"Tess is hostile to every woman I show an interest in. I thought about that a lot while I was in Aspen.'' Pushing away from the window, Ramsey jerked open a drawer, closing his hand around the first pajama top he found. He didn't notice that it was the wrong one. Yanking the shirt over his arms, he fastened the buttons in the wrong holes. "She's sixteen, Sabrina. In two years she'll be going to college, living her own life. What am I supposed to do? Live for her phone calls and our Sunday dinners together? What do I do in between, besides regret losing you?"

"I don't want to risk hurting her, or losing whatever feeling she might have for me."

"That's it, isn't it? It's all been reduced to a choice. You choose Tess." Raking his fingers through his hair as he heard the bitterness in his voice, he moved toward Sabrina, stopping halfway. "Ah, hell. I sound like a little kid, bent out of shape because his best friend is playing with someone else." He went the rest of the way and grasped her shoulders. "Tess will get over it, Sabrina. After a while she'll see that you aren't threatening her or taking anything away...."

Frowning at the uneven joining of his shirt, he lowered his hands and ripped it open. "Why am I trying to talk you out of this? The last thing I want is to fight for equal time in my own family again."

Sabrina's attention snagged his last word. "Again? What do you mean, again?" She watched him fumble, as if to shove his hands into his pockets, only to find he had none. He resumed his place by the window, gripping both sides of the frame, his back to her. A bottomless pit of silence yawned between them. Her voice rose. Now sarcasm was barbed with anger. "Rule number three: do not ask questions. The past is taboo and the present confusing, which indicates an uncompromising future." Frustration vibrated through her. "Keep your secrets, Ramsey."

Ramsey gave her a sharp look over his shoulder. Her voice was thin, like a rubber band that had been stretched too far. "It's not a secret," he said soothingly. "Just an old bone I can't stop picking." His shoulders heaved. "Claire was a vibrant, loving person. Our first years were wonderful. When Tess came, I discovered that Claire's love could only focus on one person at a time. Her first thoughts were always for Tess. I got seconds...maybe." He spoke slowly, carefully, as if he were picking his way over pieces of his heart.

"As she was dying, Claire's last words were for Tess. I waited at her bedside for her to turn to me. I tried to tell her...." His voice cracked and broke, emotion running thickly through his words. "Oh, God, there were things I needed to hear her say, but she closed her eyes on me, just as she'd closed her heart years ago. I was a fool evicted from paradise, and I spent fourteen years wondering why and looking for a way back in. I swore I'd never settle for leftovers again."

Sabrina's chest ached at the sound of his misery. To have and trust someone and lose her without knowing why... to examine everything he said and did, looking for faults...how cruel. She stifled her impulse to go to him, hold him, cry with him; if she touched him, she wouldn't be able to let him go. "Do you—?"

Ramsey cleared his throat and turned around. A corner of his mouth slashed upward, deepening the grooves in his cheeks. "Hold it against Tess? For about ten minutes. I felt robbed, cheated of my wife, the future I'd hoped for...my dreams. I was madder than hell and full of self-pity." He sighed heavily. "I love Tess. I couldn't punish her for something that wasn't her fault."

Sabrina plucked at her robe. "Thank you for telling me. I can see why you're suspicious of my motives." She felt weariness as deep as her soul. "It strains my imagination to wonder how long it would take... what it would take for you to believe—"

She moved abruptly. "We're back to blind faith. It seems we both require it, yet find it a difficult thing to give." Walking toward the open door, Sabrina reached for the knob, needing something solid to hold on to. She couldn't take any more. She wanted to burrow under her covers and sleep—forget... just for a little while. "Good night, Ramsey."

Apprehension fizzed up Ramsey's spine. Somehow he knew that if she left him now, their chances would diminish. Hope flared as she paused and turned slightly—and died when she spoke again.

"I don't know whose devils are worse—yours or mine." She shook her head. "It doesn't really matter. Either way, the results are the same." A small sound escaped her as she looked at Ramsey, who was staring out the window into the aspen grove where they'd held each other as if their embrace had to last for all eternity.

Her gaze circled the room, stopping at the bed. She could almost see him there, a book slipping out of his hands as he dozed. If they were on that bed together, he wouldn't be reading, and neither one of them would care about sleep.

Low and husky with regret, his voice reached for her across the chasm. "It does matter. You were right about time running out. What a crime to waste what there is of it for the sake of safety."

His heart felt like a lead weight as he watched her, poised for flight, looking so damn breakable, isolated, her pride and strength corrupted ... by himself and the complications of his life. He'd have to do more than babble philosophy if he wanted her to stay. The thought of having nothing but his imagination to hold in the night—any night, for all the nights to come—stretched before him, endless, frozen and colorless, like a bleak winter sky.

Sabrina's hand tightened on the doorknob. He wasn't going to try to stop her or convince her to stay. They'd both been running for so long that they didn't know how to stop. For a while they had been going in the same direction. Now they were giving up, going away from instead of toward each other, because the course was too long and full of pitfalls. Her thoughts had the flavor of unpalatable truth. Each was losing. By default.

Ramsey felt her withdrawal, and his muscles tensed. He was suddenly ready to rob her of choice, pick her up, toss her onto the bed, become as much a part of her as she was of him. *Good, Jordan,* he thought sardonically. *Why not bean her with a club? Drag her by the hair? Show her who's boss? Play caveman to the hilt.*

Or, a voice whispered slyly, *give her the words. She needs the words. Doesn't everyone? Just engage your brain, open your mouth and string syllables together into a coherent, convincing message.*

He couldn't do it. Sabrina had offered him everything once, but he hadn't been able to trust her. If she offered again, the gift would have to be freely given. It wasn't something he could beg for or borrow or get in response to a bribe, a declaration hastily delivered during a critical moment. Ramsey closed his eyes, waiting for the end of something that had barely begun.

CHAPTER THIRTEEN

SABRINA STOOD on the threshold and stared into the empty hallway. Together. Ramsey had said she was "together" that day at her house—the day they'd discovered something in each other that they'd both needed. But togetherness was the opposite of being alone or apart. She was not together without him.

She remembered the pretty storefront on the Sixteenth Street Mall with its warm wood and mullioned windows. *No fantasies for sale.* Only the reality of cold floors and bare walls. She knew she couldn't stay without a return on her emotional investment. She wanted the unqualified granting of her wishes, absolute fulfillment of her dreams—everything—with a no-risk, heart-refundable guarantee. She wanted perfection, but that was something promised for immortality, not for now.

She closed the door, resting her forehead on the solid wood.

Ramsey stiffened, then sagged as he heard the sound. He'd played his game of pride and lost. He'd been disqualified, because he'd been afraid to commit his emotions.

He turned, intent on going after her and offering all he had to give. Shame lodged in his throat as he saw her standing there. Incredibly, Sabrina had closed them in instead of locking him out.

She was an incredible lady. A special woman. A woman worth loving. Her simple act had given him full title to herself; she'd asked for nothing but the moment in return. His chest tightened with humility, his heart swelled with joy, and the blood boiled in his veins. When had he last felt so much? When had he ever been given so much?

He went to her, stopping her from taking the next step alone. She lifted her arms to his neck as he wrapped his around her waist. Then Sabrina heard her name spoken in the merest wisp of a sound. Looking at him, she saw what words could not express. His brandy eyes glowed richly with a thousand meanings. Was this reality? she wondered. Or her own dreams being reflected back at her?

His lips moved but his voice was quiet, barely disturbing the air. "I love you, Sabrina."

This was reality.

She sighed as she continued to probe his expression, seeing the depth and dimension of his sincerity. Parting her lips to meet his kiss, she moved her hands to his head, and ran her fingers through his hair. Her tongue smoothed the inner textures of his mouth before joining his in a sweet mingling. Trailing down, her hands caressed his shoulders, then parted his shirt to graze the swirling patterns of his chest hair, coarse and soft all at once, making her palms tingle.

Untying the belt of her robe, Ramsey slid his fingers under the straps of her nightgown and slipped both garments off her shoulders. As they floated to the floor, he stepped back, his breath a gasp in the silence. He could look at her forever. . . .

Sabrina allowed him to look, the touch of his gaze as exciting as the feel of his hands. Did he find her pleasing? Closing her eyes, she felt the progress of his exploration—over her breasts, already swollen in anticipation, then to the curve of her waist, her hips burning with inner fire. Her abdomen contracted and quivered as he ran his finger down from her navel to her curly black hair....

A whimper escaped her at his withdrawal. She had forgotten the cesarean scar, a reminder of their conflict forever engraved upon her body. They would not be allowed to forget, even in moments when all existence but their own should fade. With a sigh of regret, Sabrina opened her eyes to face passion recanted, rejection. Instead, she found Ramsey kneeling before her.

Poignant joy rippled over her, overflowing as he enfolded her hips in his arms. Tears flowed down her cheeks and her body trembled in passion. There was comfort in the gentleness of his mouth as he kissed the length of the scar, accepting the role she had played in his life, long before their hearts had become acquainted. And she knew his hunger as his tongue trailed down her stomach, then lowered to taste the heat between her thighs. His hands molded her hips and skimmed her sides to circle her breasts as he rose to taste her mouth.

Love and primitive excitement ran through her veins. His mouth drew on her nipple, sending charges of electricity along her nerves. Encouraging his own hardening response, she rotated her palms over his chest, first lightly, then firmly, then lightly again as she pressed her belly against him, feeling his heat.

Feathering her hands down his torso, Sabrina worked his pajama trousers free and they, too, dropped to the floor. Her fingers savored the firm, hair-roughened flesh of his legs, and she placed small, biting kisses

along his thighs and the hard length of his desire that
was straining for release.

Gasping, Ramsey pulled her up, knowing a pleasure
beyond the physical in the feverish flush on her body,
the burning violet flame in her eyes, the absolute giving quality of her every move. He led her to the bed and
urged her to lie down.

Sabrina resisted, kneeling in the center of the mattress to watch him, painting his portrait in her memory. A smile tugged at her mouth. He was avoiding her
gaze. Self-consciousness stained his cheeks. The unexpected shyness gave her another revelation of the inner
man. She smiled and whispered to him, "You're so
pleasing to the eye and the hand and—"

His eyes met hers, revealing surprise and pleasure. He
hoped he'd never get used to her frankness. She made
him feel as unique as she was. He growled and pressed
her to the covers, kissing her with a depth of feeling he'd
never experienced.

Sabrina absorbed him, felt him with every sense. He
was texture—hair-roughened skin, calloused hands,
hard muscle—and he was color—warm brandy eyes,
rich bronze flesh, luxurious sable hair. He was beautiful in endless variations of light and shadow.

Ramsey's fingers were learning her textures. She was
smooth ivory, ebony silk, puckered rose velvet, moist
satin—hot and throbbing. She was a woman, of the
earth, molding and flowing around him....

"Ramsey..."

Quieting her plea with his mouth, he accepted her
invitation, penetrating her with plunging strokes,
learning her secrets, feeling her tremors, encouraging
them, responding with his own. And Sabrina became
complete, was fulfilled, a woman reborn to fit only him.

Reaching farther and farther to catch her star, her body communicated with his in gentle sighs and fevered moans of pleasure, expressing pure love and a need to give, as well as a desire to take greedily, hungrily.

Ramsey lifted her hips and plunged deep, holding her tightly as he reached the peak with her and they bathed in brilliance together. Then, looking into her eyes, her soul, Ramsey spoke to her without words, in the old way, before words were made. And the blanketing comfort of his body, the reverent touch of his hands conveyed a message older than time. *We are one.*

In those misty, gentle moments after their lovemaking, she could believe in perfection....

Almost.

Floating on clouds of wonder, Sabrina breathed deeply the manly smell of him, listened to the tympanic beat of his heart, savored the memory of his kiss. Her fingertips circled lightly over his chest, filling her senses with him, avoiding any thought at odds with the moment.

Bitter reason—at rest for now—recoiled at her determination, yet remained poised to strike again if aroused by heavy-footed reality. A small sound escaped her.

Alerted by her barely repressed whimper, Ramsey immediately propped himself up on his elbows, hoping her distress was physical. Her breathing was soft and measured, careful, as if she were walking bare-legged among vipers.

"Am I too heavy?" he asked reluctantly, hating the idea of leaving the home her body had made for his, full of acceptance and giving, warmth and excitement. In this single joining he'd learned what belonging meant. He wasn't prepared to go out into the cold again. He knew he never would be.

At his movement, Sabrina tightened around him, holding him with her body, her legs twined with his in a lover's knot of sensual bondage. "No. Stay with me, Ramsey." At his questioning look, she smiled and brushed the hair off his forehead. "It's such a perfect moment," she said simply.

Emotion grew in his throat, tightening his vocal chords. He swallowed convulsively several times as he lowered his head to blink away the haze that was blurring his vision. All he could see was the emotional poverty of the past—and the wealth she gave him, just by being.

Ramsey cleared his throat. "You've taught this fool that paradise is as close as you are, Sabrina. If you don't throw me out, I won't—"

Grasping the back of his head, she urged his mouth to join her own, stopping the promise she was afraid to hear. She would pin her future on it. A sense of loss nudged, taking its place beside the contentment she'd known so briefly. Her emotional independence was gone, drifting aimlessly between Ramsey and the uncontrollable nature of life. How many perfect moments could she gather? Enough to fill her small share of eternity?

The grim truths she'd learned so many years ago crowded into her consciousness. Moments were the merest ripple in time. Perfection was a transient illusion. She could reach out for it, but her hand would touch nothing.

The grandfather clock chimed in the foyer. Sabrina strengthened the kiss, striving for control, desperate to change it from one of gentle communication to an act of mind-blotting passion. Dawn was the true witching hour. Soon the sun would peek over the horizon to violate their sanctuary. Before then, she would explore each moment of the night and claim it as her own.

They hadn't solved anything. Nothing had changed. They'd simply applied a Band-Aid, hoping it would hold until they could find a cure.

Sensing the troubled patterns of her mind, Ramsey drew his mouth from hers to study her expression. The warm, contented mush she'd reduced him to curdled at what he saw. In his male arrogance, he had wanted softness, dreams, loving. He found tension and feverish urgency, as if she were frantic to capture the brass ring, before the post it hung on rotted away. "Dammit, Sabrina, you're doing it again."

"What?" Warily her gaze met his. She shifted slightly, settling him more firmly in the cradle of her hips. "This?" Her hand trailed downward, raking him lightly with her nails, teasing the sensitive skin of his lower abdomen. "Or this?" Her fingers closed around him.

Feeling his body stirring to life again, he caught her wrist and brought up her hand to hold it on the pillow next to her head. "You're thinking again."

"Of course I am. Aren't you?"

"No. I bloody well am not." The quiet timbre of his voice held more force than an enraged bellow. "We've beaten each other with words. You're thinking this thing to death. Has it done any good? Have you found any solutions?"

"No." She sighed.

"More confused than ever?"

"Yes."

"Then cut it out, before you bury us in logic ... please." He punctuated his words with small nibbles on her lips, her ears, down the length of her neck. "Sabrina, give us a chance."

"Ramsey..." Sabrina fumbled for a way to make him understand and yet she knew it was unnecessary. The comforting stroke of his thumbs over the lines of worry between her brows, the empathy clouding his eyes with inner pain, the frustration in the way he held her wrist, all told her he did understand. He just didn't agree.

"Sabrina, love isn't comfortable or reasonable or organized. You can't analyze it, then file it in a Rolodex. You can't aim it at a particular market during a specific season."

"You're right." Smiling, she erased everything from her mind except for the here and now. "I suppose I'll have to become more tolerant of high altitudes. Common sense and practicality are pretty thin up here."

"Up where?" Ramsey asked, distracted as he kissed the tip of her nose, her forehead, her eyelids.

Wistfulness drifted across her face as she pointed upward. "Cloud nine. I've never been this high before."

Ramsey took her mouth quickly, deeply, hotly before grinning down at her. "Well, I've flown past it once or twice, but this is the first time I've ever landed." He eased away from her with a groan and rose from the bed. "Stay put."

Bemused, Sabrina watched him disappear into the hall. Where else would she go? This room had become her world, Ramsey the only other life in it.

He returned with a single spoon, a quarter-full tub of chocolate ice cream held carefully away from his naked flesh, and the anticipation of a little boy gleaming in his eyes. "Wanna share?" Plopping onto the bed, he dug out the first spoonful, magnanimously offering it to her.

Rising on her elbows, Sabrina opened her mouth eagerly, then squinted when the cold stabbed an icy finger into her eye.

They alternated bites until the last spoonful vanished into Ramsey's mouth. He rolled it around, savoring the creamy richness, letting it melt on his tongue, seep into his taste buds and trickle down his throat. He wanted to make it last as long as he could.... Staring at Sabrina as she licked a bit off her lips and peered into the tub, he sighed with regret. "It's the pits," he murmured.

"What?" She leaned over him to set the container on the nightstand, and paused on the way back to kiss the corner of his mouth.

"That we can't live on love and chocolate ice cream."

Sabrina lifted her head as her hands stilled on his chest. "Yes," she agreed, laying her head on his shoulder and holding him tightly. "The pits."

CHAPTER FOURTEEN

"TESS, I DON'T THINK this is a good idea," Jenny Logan whispered. "The last time you took off, your dad had a major cow. What if he finds out?"

"I'm not taking off," Tess retorted, then lowered her voice and looked around the room to make sure the other girls were still asleep. "All I want to do is talk to Seth. I'll be back before everyone wakes up."

"It's awfully early. You'll wake him up."

"No, I won't. He's always the first one at the office, especially since Daddy's been gone on that search party. By the time I get there, Seth will be getting ready for work."

"On a Sunday?" Jenny asked skeptically.

"I told you, Jen. Daddy's been out of town. That means twice the work for Seth."

"Tess, I really think you should wait 'till this afternoon. Go see him at the office."

Tess shook her head. "No! I don't want anyone to know about this. If Daddy found out, he really would have a cow. It would spoil everything." Leaning forward, she squeezed her best friend's hand. "Come on, Jen. Chill out. It'll be okay. I promise."

AT THE FIRST PEAL of his doorbell, Seth rolled out of bed and stepped into the jeans he'd left on the floor. By the second ring, he was stumbling toward the front door as he pulled them up and struggled with the button fly. He jerked open the door then, on recognizing Tess, shut it partway, his left hand still trying to fasten his pants. "Oh, boy," he muttered.

"Hi, Seth. Can I come in?"

Hi, Seth? It was seven in the morning, Tess was underage, here without Ram—his friend and almost-partner—knowing about it, and she says *Hi, Seth?* His first impulse was to pull her into his town house as fast as he could, and check both sides of the street to make sure no one saw her. His second impulse was to shut the door, go back to bed and hope he was having a nightmare.

"Seth, it's cold out here."

He could imagine. Tess looked nice . . . for a Saturday night date. She had on some glittery thing with her jeans that proved beyond a doubt that she was a woman—physically. That look in her eyes was a glaring reminder of just how young and innocent she really was. That look was a clear invitation for trouble. A mature woman would know that, and any mature man with brains would be scared to death by it. He'd just developed a yellow streak down the middle of his back. "Go home, Tess." *Please,* he added silently.

"I have to talk to you. It's important."

"I'm not dressed."

"I've seen you without a shirt, Seth." Before he could say any more, she walked in.

Holding the top of his pants shut with one hand, Seth took a quick glance up and down the street and closed the door. With his back to her, he used both hands to fasten the rest of his buttons. He hadn't felt this awkward since a lady MD had given him his military physical. He walked toward the kitchen. "I need coffee."

"Me, too." She followed him into the kitchen, and made a great show of looking capable as she pushed the button on his already filled coffee maker.

His mouth tightened. "You don't drink coffee, Tess." He opened the dishwasher to find a glass, and realized that he hadn't run it lately. A quick rummage in his cupboards, and he found a highball glass and a beer mug.

"Here." He handed her the glass with his last two ounces of milk in it.

Absently Tess accepted the milk as she stared at the basket full of laundry he hadn't gotten around to folding yet. "Your socks need darning."

"I'll throw them away and buy new ones."

"I'll fold your laundry then."

Uh-oh. His hands shook as he poured his coffee into the beer mug. "Leave it, Tess." He didn't mean to sound so harsh, but it made him nervous when a female—any female—came into his home and started trying to take care of him. His personal space might be a little disorganized, but it was his clutter and his mess, and if he wanted feminine hands putting it right, he'd hire a maid.

Three quick gulps of caffeine made him more alert to his predicament, but did nothing to bolster his courage. He had to do something fast. Tess was filling the dishwasher with soap and turning it on. Next she'd be trying to make his breakfast or—heaven forbid—make his bed. He steered her into the living room. He'd cleaned it yesterday.

Tess plumped cushions and dusted a table with a napkin.

"Cut it out, Tess. This is me, remember? I was there when your dad had to threaten you with bamboo under your fingernails before you'd clean your room." He knew as soon as he closed his mouth that he shouldn't have opened it in the first place.

Stiffening, Tess whirled on him. "Don't talk to me like that, Seth. I'm not a kid."

"Tess..."

She drew back her shoulders, and she put her hands on her jeaned hips. "Look at me. I'm *not* a kid anymore." She spoke quickly, keeping him from saying anything else. "I love you, Seth. I...I thought you had a right to know."

"I don't know what to say to you, Tess," he said honestly, feeling like a rather pathetic excuse for a man. It had been years since he'd been at a loss for words with a woman. But this very young, very sweet, very sincere girl defeated him. He hurt for her. He hurt for himself because deep down inside, he knew that he could easily develop feelings for her that weren't in the least bit filial, platonic or casual...if she were older, and if he were looking to settle down—and a lot of other ifs.

"You can't. Not now. I know that," she said calmly, as if she had it all figured out. "I'm underage. But in two years I'll be legal. Four years after that, maybe three, I'll be out of art school. That's not so long. You said yourself that you don't want to settle down yet."

Was this where he was supposed to be sensitive and gentle? Seth wondered. *How?* He finished his coffee and wanted to pitch the mug across the room. "I don't suppose you'd listen if I told you basic truths about age differences and how people change?"

Tess stared at him, her expression mutinous. "I'm not dumb either, Seth." She clenched her fists. "Why doesn't anybody understand? Sabrina's the only—"

Shaking her head, Tess stopped herself from going on with that particular tack.

"Sabrina—" he grabbed at her name as if it meant salvation in the face of doom "—would understand. Have you talked to her about this?"

"She said it takes time," Tess temporized. "Anyway, this is between you and me."

Seth grimaced, feeling as if he had on a collar that was too tight.

"I was afraid of that." He sighed. "Okay, Tess. Let's get to the bottom line here. I'm a—" he smiled drily "—relatively young man. I'm enjoying the hell out of being a bachelor. You're a young woman who has her eye on a dress for your prom. Were you planning on going alone?"

Tess stared at her feet.

"Right. Most of the world's activities are for mixed doubles. Agreed?"

Tess glanced at him warily.

"There's nothing either one of us can do about our...this...situation for at least two years. Why don't we put this on the back burner 'till then and see what happens?"

He held up his hand, trying to stop the hope he saw in her eyes, trying to do this right and keep them both from being irrevocably injured. *Trying.* "Don't get me wrong, Tess. I don't know what will happen in two or five years. I do know that right now I like my life the way it is. And you have a lot of ambitions for yours. None of that is going to change in the near future. Neither one of us is in a position to make promises."

"But, Seth, I..."

"No promises, Tess. We'll make a pact instead. In five years we'll talk about this again. Not before."

Knowing he was playing dirty, Seth touched her then, a simple touch of his forefinger to her chin, hoping it was enough to keep her from making any more declarations. "As you said, this is just between us."

Tears shone in her eyes as she stepped back. Her voice was defiant. "Don't you dare pat me on the head, Seth. Don't you dare think I'm being silly. I've thought a lot about this. I love you, and it hurts so bad, I want to die sometimes."

Picking up another cushion, she punched it and arranged it on the sofa just so before facing him defiantly. "And don't you dare think I'm too young to know what that means. Daddy fell in love with Mom in high school, and they got married when they were old enough. Sabrina had me when she was sixteen, because she was in love with an older man...." Her voice faded, as if she realized that Sabrina was perhaps not the best example to use.

"I do know what love means," she continued fiercely. "It means hurting every time you touch me because I want more. It means not caring if I go to the prom or not. I want that dress for *you*, Seth. I want you to see me in it and want to touch me. And it means that I'll do anything you want, because I care more about you than anyone else in the world."

Watching her pull a tissue out of her pocket and wipe her nose, Seth swallowed to clear the lump of fear from his throat. If he'd been scared before, he was terrified now. Tess's words sounded better to him than they should. There were too many promises in those words, promises Tess would outgrow. He was realistic enough to know that if he let himself, he'd be dreamer enough to wait around—and hope that she wouldn't. He wasn't blind. Tess herself was a promise of beauty and sweet-

ness and challenge and fire. Someday she would be a
woman to dream about . . . all night long. A woman to
meet every morning with.

But he was almost thirty, and she was not quite seventeen. The numbers were all wrong. He had a bad
feeling that someday he was going to regret that.

Jamming his hands into his pockets to keep them
from wiping away the tears that were running down her
cheeks, Seth paced the width of the room once, then
stopped in front of her, relieved that his voice sounded
steadier than he felt. "I'm not patting you on the head,
Tess. I'm trying to tell you that the timing is bad. I
can't—I won't—let this go any further. It's obvious that
you've given it enough thought to understand the reasons why. We can't change those reasons, Tess. . . ."

The doorbell rang again. Pulling away from her with
a guilty start, Seth groaned. It was barely past eight in
the morning, and he'd be willing to bet the only place
busier than his town house was the city dump on a Saturday afternoon. He peered cautiously out the window
to make sure it wasn't Ramsey, standing there with a
shotgun in his hand.

Seeing the snappy little convertible parked on the
street, he groaned again. Didn't women need their
beauty sleep anymore? His caller spotted him and
waved. Resignedly, he opened the door.

Janet Temple surveyed his rumpled appearance.
"You forgot."

"Oh, hell." He had forgotten. He and Janet had
ended a night of dining and dancing by making a date
for breakfast. "I . . . overslept," he improvised lamely.

"Not to worry," she said brightly. "You don't even
have to dress." She held up a white box tied with string.

Janet's frown alerted him that she had seen Tess. He gave Janet credit for recovering quickly. "Hello, Tess," she said, as if there was nothing unusual about finding a sixteen-year-old girl alone with a half-dressed, sleepy-eyed man.

"Hello, Ms Temple." She gave Tess credit for managing to sound almost polite. The waver in her voice vibrated through him like an earthquake, shaking him, tearing him apart, killing him with the pain he knew she was feeling. He squeezed his eyes shut for a moment, grieving because he knew that a part of her was dying, too.

After a brief, assessing glance at the pair, Janet smiled and glanced at her watch. "Actually, I should have been at my office ten minutes ago." She handed Seth the box. "Sticky buns. Enjoy," she called as she retreated to her car.

Tess hadn't moved. Her back was straight, her head high, but her eyes were stricken. "You like her a lot, don't you?"

Leaving the door ajar, Seth moved back into the room. He tossed the box onto the nearest chair and nodded. "I like her, yes. We have a lot in common."

"Like age?"

"Among other things," he said quietly. He had to get her out of here. His arms ached with wanting to hold Tess, soothe her, tell her everything would be all right. But she wouldn't believe him, and she'd take his action to mean . . . more. "Tess, I can't change the way things are."

She straightened even more, standing tall and proud, her dignity clearly held together by fragile, silken threads. "You don't really want to, Seth. But that's okay. I can handle it." Very carefully she walked out the door, shutting it softly behind herself.

Seth didn't move as he listened to the most complete silence he'd ever heard and wished that she'd thrown a fit—anything—to remind him of how young she really was. Suddenly he needed a reminder....

A car door slammed. Hard. When he heard Tess gun the engine of Jenny's car, he bolted for the door, ready to stop her from taking off like a bat out of hell. He reached the porch just in time to see her fasten her seat belt, carefully look over her shoulder for oncoming traffic and sedately drive away. Shaking his head at the vagaries of the female of the species, he headed for the shower.

There were days when it really didn't pay to get out of bed.

DAYLIGHT FILTERED through Ramsey's eyelids, soaking into his awareness, rolling up the shades of sleep with a snap. His mind hummed with contentment as he felt Sabrina's hand still nestled within his under the pillow. They'd fallen asleep facing each other, their hands clasped between them. Perfect moments, Sabrina had called them. They'd stolen time from a demanding world, had mated their souls just as surely as they had joined their bodies.

He rolled onto his back and made a wild grab for the headboard to keep from falling off the bed. Easing into a more secure position, he gently nudged Sabrina. She was sleeping like a queen, sprawled on her back, arms and legs everywhere, staking claims on everything within reach. She turned and rested her head on his shoulder. Insinuating one leg between his, she rubbed her foot over the length of his calf. Her hair felt like satin against his cheek and her breath puffed on his neck. Her skin was soft and sleep-warm against his own. The scent of woman and the feeling of satisfied passion filled him like an aphrodisiac.

Ruefully he glanced down at the visual display of his anticipation and need rising beneath the sheet. His gaze moved back to Sabrina's peacefully sleeping form. He couldn't. She needed the rest. Gritting his teeth, he set his mind to planning the day's activities for the three of them. Funny how he automatically thought of himself, Tess and Sabrina as a unit....

It was good waking up this way, knowing there was an "us." It was better having to fight for his share of the bed than finding cold, empty places on the sheets every time he moved; better to hear another heart beating in the silence of the night.

Sabrina's hand came up to flick away a strand of hair that was tickling her nose and moved down again, skimming his chest and abdomen, stopping just north of the source of his discomfort. He groaned and shifted. Her hand slid along his hip. His temperature shot up. Breathing through his teeth, he forced himself to lie still. *Easy, Jordan. You're forty years old, for crying out loud, not an adolescent who can't think past his hormones. You can wait until she wakes up. It's just a case of mind over matter.*

Grimacing, Sabrina buried her face into his chest, as if she were trying to burrow more deeply into her dreams and escape the intrusion of a new day. She drew up her knee, pressing lightly against the fullness between his thighs.

There were times when matter definitely overwhelmed the mind.

Seeing Sabrina's lips curve in a smile, feeling her sigh ruffle the hair on his chest, Ramsey called himself an inconsiderate bastard and slid down to nibble and taste his way over her body. He grinned, hearing her second sigh grow into a soft moan of pleasure as he teased her breast. Somehow he didn't think she minded having her rest disturbed.

He raised his head to meet her gaze—misty violet, drowsy, sexy as well. As she moistened her lower lip with her tongue, his desire grew. Her barely whispered words nearly incinerated him.

"More, Ramsey...please." Her hand enclosed his arousal, inciting his body to riot.

Forcing his restraint, he shuddered. "Sabrina, take it easy, sweetheart. It's too soon...too fast."

"No." In one fluid motion, she opened herself to him, her hand bringing him inside her, to know her wanting was as hot and demanding as his. He took her mouth. She took his body. There was no time for protest, no time for gentle love play. There was no time, no world...nothing but themselves, creating one out of two.

Ramsey's sight blurred into a vista of fiery color, flaring, blazing, searing. Sound roared like an inferno in his head. Thought turned to ash, carried away by waves of pure sensation. They moved with a primitive rhythm—wild, feverish, consuming. He reached flash point as she melted around him....

Sabrina's shuddering breath and the tremors in her body told him that she was as unraveled as he was. Rising on his elbows, he framed her face with his hands. Words formed in his mind, looking for a voice to free them. All the reasons why they shouldn't be said clawed and pushed, forming a painful lump in his throat. He wanted to say them, make them a reality, prove to Sabrina that there would be more than frantic leaps from one "now" to the next.

"There has to be more," he said, echoing his restored ideals, believing in them again, vowing to make them so.

"Yes," she answered, unconvinced.

Sometimes I have to leave a dream behind.

Ramsey protested with a shake of his head. Not this time. She'd made it his dream, too. He wouldn't let it go.

The clock radio flooded the room with the mellow baritone of a disc jockey. "For all you lucky people who are waking up to a morning after the night before, here's Frank Ifield with 'I'll Remember You.'"

A mirthless smile touched Sabrina's face. Growling, Ramsey jerked the cord out of the wall socket, then rested his forehead against hers.

"Ramsey, it's time to wake up." Her tone was steady and clear; sorrow hid behind the words.

A high, shrill beep followed, sounding like a wail of protest. Easing away from her, Ramsey silenced the pager. His muscles grew lax in defeat, landing him on his stomach. He turned away from Sabrina and buried his clenched fists under the pillow. He spoke on an expelled breath. "Yeah. Time to wake up."

Damn it, he thought. Seth was supposed to take any calls, handle any problems. Weren't there any normal people in his organization who did mundane things such as eat, sleep, read the Sunday funnies . . . make love?

The bed moved as Sabrina touched his shoulder, then withdrew. With a twist he sat up on the side of the bed and clasped his hands between his outspread knees. "I love you, Sabrina," he said quietly. She was a part of him now, and she'd made him more than he ever thought he could be.

"I know."

Why did she sound so miserable? Dumb question. They were going to have to walk through more than fire to do anything about it. He'd seen Tess's face last week, heard the censure in her voice. And apparently she'd made a couple of comments to Seth, indicating her feelings on the subject. She wanted him and Sabrina to get along so that she could see Sabrina. She did not want him to become seriously involved with any woman to the point of adding another member to their family.

He told himself that Tess was in love. She should understand what it was like. She should, but teenagers, he knew, had a blind spot. They couldn't see—or didn't want to see—that there really was no difference between themselves and adults other than age. Tess had obviously figured out what roles each person in her life should play and when. The only problem was that she hadn't bothered to ask any of the players if they liked her script.

In one way Sabrina was right. They would have to go slowly, ease into things, show Tess that three were better than two and that when she was grown and gone, two would be better than one. At least it would be for him, with Sabrina making up the difference.

Rolling onto his side, he propped up his head with one hand. "Sabrina, Tess will come around. She likes you—"

"You have a phone call to make," Sabrina interrupted, her voice like gold leaf, bright but peeling away.

"Screw the phone call."

She went on as if he hadn't spoken. "I'll bathe and pack while you're at it."

"Dammit, Sabrina, don't treat me as if I were a gigolo you hired for the night." Alarm scraped along his spine and tightened its fingers at the base of his neck as her words caught up with him. "Pack? Why?"

Sitting back on her heels, she gave him a reproachful look, reminding him of life beyond the bedroom door, of others who owned pieces of his heart.

"Never mind. I know why. Naturally, you're right." His finger drew a line from her collarbone to the tip of her breast. "It's just that you belong here... with me. While I was gone, I missed you as if I'd been with you every day of my life, and that was the first time I'd been away from you." His mouth lifted whimsically as he shook his head. "It was the craziest feeling. That's when I decided to quit fighting and explore the possibilities." Somber now, he held her gaze. "I need you, and I think you need me."

Sabrina lowered her head, her hair falling around her face. Could he be right about Tess learning to accept her? The girl's attitude didn't inspire faith. But what did she know about kids?

They're human, she told herself. *They respond to love. And they're territorial, willing to share until told to do so... just like adults.*

She wasn't encouraged. Grasping the sheet, she pulled it over her breasts, suddenly feeling very naked and exposed. "Ramsey, could you risk Tess's well-being to have what you want?"

"No." His answer was unqualified.

"I can't either, for the same reasons." Blinking furiously, Sabrina managed to keep her tears at bay, only to have them flow through her voice. "I tried to forget her for sixteen years. For odd periods of time I thought I'd succeeded. Then it would be her birthday or Christmas or Mother's Day, and I'd have to start all over again.'' Taking a deep breath, Sabrina met his gaze. ''She was a could-have-been and an if-only that hit me especially hard whenever I was vulnerable to loneliness, guilt and wishful thoughts. I know now that I did the right thing in giving her up. The guilt is gone and I don't want it back. I can't live with it. Not anymore.''

Right then, looking at Sabrina was like having a glimpse of a very private room. For the first time she was allowing him to see the guilt and anguished doubts she'd lived with for so long. Some women gave up their babies without a backward glance. Others kept them, but paid a price. He knew one unmarried mother who had three children by three different men. She'd kept them, supported them on welfare and raised them with bitterness and neglect. Why didn't people ever hear of the ones like Sabrina, who paid for their mistakes with subtle and continuous forms of emotional self-torture?

Tess's appearance had been a second chance for Sabrina. He couldn't blame her for being afraid to lose that. Second chances were rare. Third chances were miracles. ''You said once that when you gave up Tess, it was like she had died.''

''Yes. Death without finality. There was no gravestone. There were no memories. Only sixteen years of relentless mourning.''

''Oh, God.'' Ramsey closed his eyes as his open hand pressed gently against the scar on her abdomen. ''This scar goes all the way through you. It will never heal, will it?''

Sabrina didn't answer. He opened his eyes. When she showed surprise at his understanding of her feelings, he felt a kick in his chest. It hurt to know that she hadn't expected him to understand.

"Ramsey..." Her hands covered his on her belly. "It doesn't hurt anymore—not like it did. I lost her childhood, but if I'd kept her, she might not have had one. I've seen it happen—children having to grow up too fast, because their parents are children themselves. I'm so glad she had you . . . and Claire."

Before he could say anything, do anything, the pager wailed again, this time insistently. The night was definitely over. Smiling diabolically, he disabled the instrument and lobbed it into the waste can across the room. Starting today, things were going to change. Tess needed more than a token father. He needed more than a token life.

Both of them needed Sabrina.

Smiling as if to lighten their burden of ponderous thoughts, Sabrina pressed a gentle kiss to his lips and rose from the bed. "I have to hurry if I'm going to get any work done."

Jerking on his pajama bottoms, Ramsey glanced at her over his shoulder. "On Sunday?"

"Mmm." Sabrina drew on her robe. "I have a showing tomorrow night, remember?"

"Does that mean I won't see you until then?"

As she opened the door, her shoulders heaved with a sigh. "Probably. Unless you bring Tess for our final run-through tomorrow afternoon. In that case, I'll treat you to a cup of coffee and a stale doughnut." They were being so casual, as if they woke up together every morning to make love and talk before going to work— as if they'd be coming home to each other at the end of the day...as if life was Ours instead of Mine and Yours.

"Am I invited to your showing?" All of a sudden he felt as if he was talking to her long-distance.

"I put an invitation in with your mail. Black tie, and bring your checkbook." Mischief lighted her eyes as she turned to look at him with an angelic expression.

"Why?" he asked suspiciously. She was spending his money. *Is that,* he wondered, *a good sign?*

"A few original designs will be sold for charity. Tess is madly in love with two of them. I'm giving her one. You can buy her the other one for Christmas." With that, Sabrina left the room, wondering what it would be like for them to choose Christmas presents together.

"Which charity?" Ramsey followed Sabrina into the hall, colliding with her as she stopped. He grasped her arms, turned her to face him and held her there, so close that their toes touched.

"A scholarship fund for unwed mothers." She looked down to see his toes disappear beneath the hem of her robe, and up again to look at his face. Such a little thing to cause excitement, their feet side-by-side...as they'd been last night...in bed.

Ramsey wrapped her in his arms, holding her tightly. "There will be more, Sabrina. Much, much more." His kiss promised as much as his words, then he released her and loped down the hall toward his study.

Sabrina lingered over a hot bath, soaking her tired muscles while forcing her mind to focus on the hundred and one last-minute details for the showing. For that she could be logical, make lists and follow them. For the better part of two days she would—hopefully—be too busy to worry about later. She'd be in control...in between thoughts of Ramsey.

And she'd try very hard to believe that there would be more.

Leaning back her head, she closed her eyes. Memories rushed through her. Had it been only last night?

Clear as it all was, it seemed distant, part of another time, another life, drifting farther out of reach, never to be reclaimed, never to be repeated.

Was that the penalty for stealing a night in paradise?

Angry with herself, she flipped the lever and left the bathtub. *No.* This was one dream she'd not willingly give up, as she had so many others. This one she would fight for until it become a reality.

Or hope died.

Leaving the bathroom, her gaze touched the face that Tess had painted on the mirror. Diluted by the steam, its features ran like tears down the glass, distorted, grieving, a formless mass of garish color.

CHAPTER FIFTEEN

THE LIGHTS in the showroom dimmed. Colorfully illuminated by gelatin-filtered spotlights, the runway stage glowed like the brilliant heart of a black opal. The muted roar of over two hundred voices lowered until there was finally silence.

Sabrina entered from a side door, her gaze immediately drawn to Ramsey in the front row. She had caught glimpses of him from backstage and had admired the fit of his custom-tailored tuxedo. It always took her by surprise to see him with the trappings of a wealthy businessman—the Ferrari, the gray suit, the elegant tux.

As she'd watched, she'd seen that he was acquainted with quite a few of the guests—department store owners, local media personalities and society figures. All these years, they'd moved on the fringes of each other's lives, and very likely had passed within moments of actually meeting.

She smiled as he tugged at his collar and shifted as if his feet hurt. Poor man. He really was more at home in blue denim and Nikes. If only she could reach out, loosen his tie, unfasten the onyx studs on his pleated shirt. She sighed. For the better part of two days, only her memories had felt his touch, only her thoughts had touched him. Thoughts and memories weren't nearly enough.

For the better part of two days she'd wrestled with herself. She could either give in to her fear of being hurt and walk away, or she could stick around and live with that same fear, until it was either proven justified or unfounded.

Losing by default wasn't her style.

Ramsey stared at his hands, as if he were contemplating the secrets of the universe. Actually he was contemplating the complexities of Sabrina: her independence, strength and stubbornness as well as her vulnerability, sensitivity and insecurity. Her strengths and weaknesses balanced each other, interlocked, completed a picture.

The merest rustle of cloth caught his attention like a whispered invitation, and he knew Sabrina had entered the room. His head jerked up, and the sight of her held him transfixed.

Sabrina saw his lips part on an indrawn breath, his eyes widen and spark with deep amber fire as he stared at her. A femme fatale she'd never known existed in her nature surfaced to give him a naughty wink and a slow, wicked smile behind the cover of her notes. It was worth all the hours she'd spent making the gown just to see his admiration.

The red silk—sheer as breath, shimmering like an iridescent flame—had been a nightmare to work with, but when she'd tried on the finished dress, her reaction had been one of admiration for the classic simplicity of her design, the beauty of the fabric, the seductive allure of the whole. *Did I do this?* she'd asked her image in the mirror. *Oh my!* Little had she known then that she would be wearing it for the man she loved beyond description.

Was it a dress or an illusion? Ramsey's mouth snapped shut as he squirmed in his seat. The fabric conformed to her body like a lover's hand—his, two nights ago. He strained to get a closer look at her. The strapless dress covered all the intriguing places he'd caressed and stroked and tasted, without seeming to cover anything at all.

He looked around the room, wondering how many of the men present were trying to see something they shouldn't. He heard appreciative murmurs and applause, saw relaxed postures and professional interest, but no one looked ready to jump her bones. Were they blind? Remembering that this was the fashion crowd, used to seeing gowns like Sabrina's, Ramsey forced himself to relax.

Relax? She was enough to make an eunuch come to attention. Sitting next to him, Seth released an almost silent wolf whistle, earning a narrow-eyed glare from Ramsey. With a knowing smirk, Seth elbowed Ramsey's arm and nodded toward Sabrina. "She's starting." Ramsey turned his head to see her slide on the glasses she wore for close work and step up to the podium. Vowing to concentrate on the show, Ramsey leaned back in his seat.

Except for the five times Tess came onto the stage, he concentrated on Sabrina. She was beautiful... talented ... pure class. His.

Finally the lights came on and applause filled the room. Voices joined in an incomprehensible babble as clients gravitated toward Sabrina and Marty. Waiters appeared from out of nowhere, serving champagne and directing people toward the buffet tables. The models strolled into the room to mingle with the guests and offer a closer look at their garments.

Ramsey's stomach did a slow roll. The tinkle of china, crystal and silver, and the compelling odors of food brought him out of his trance. He'd fantasized his way through the entire presentation and auction. The only thing he remembered was bidding on the gown that Sabrina had told him Tess was "madly in love with." He couldn't remember what he'd paid for it, and didn't think he wanted to. Tess would probably wear it once and then wail that she couldn't wear it again, because all her friends had seen it.

With a bemused look, he followed Tess's progress from one group to another. She was answering questions and accepting compliments with a practiced, sophisticated air. If it weren't for her occasional slips into the language peculiar to teenagers or the excited, slightly awed sparkle in her eyes, she might have fooled even him into believing she was an experienced model. He grimaced and tugged at his collar. It was like seeing a preview of the woman Tess would become: independent, confident and too damn beautiful for a father's peace of mind.

Ramsey's jaw clenched. Twice, a tall, dark, superstud type wearing a waiter's uniform had approached Tess. Dishonorable intentions were written all over him. Both times, Ramsey had been too far from her to do anything about it. Tess had met Superstud's first approach with an appraising once-over, had shot a comparing glance at Seth and excused herself. Undaunted, the jerk had tried again. Whatever Tess said to him had caused a mixture of discreet coughs and amused smiles among the people standing nearby.

In the midst of his ruminations, a tall woman with queenly proportions appeared in front of Ramsey, offering him a glass of punch and a commiserating smile.

He welcomed the drink and the woman with equal relief. He'd liked Marty Jensen immediately. She made
him think of a comfortable pair of leather slippers: soft
and of good quality, with tough, durable soles.

When he'd arrived, she'd introduced herself, ap-
praised him, asked a few pointed questions—which he
should have resented—then had nodded imperiously, as
if she were a monarch giving her approval. "You'll do,"
she'd said. He'd had to bite the inside of his cheek to
keep from laughing. Do for what? he'd wanted to ask,
but she'd already gone.

"I smell a slow burn over here. What is it, Ramsey—
the monkey suit you're wearing—or the ape serving
drinks?"

Casting a malevolent eye in the waiter's direction,
Ramsey noted that he did resemble an ape with his too-
long hair and too-short sleeves. "If that smart-aleck
goes near her again, I'll plant his head in the nearest
wall."

"He'd have to have the hide of an elephant to try
again."

Ramsey's eyes narrowed in suspicion. "What did she
say to him, or am I better off not knowing?"

"She checked him out and told him he had absolutely nothing to offer her."

His mouth twitched in spite of the stern expression he
thought he should have put on. His gaze roamed over
faces and between bodies—he wanted to check on Tess
again—and unerringly homed in on Sabrina.

She looked up, meeting his gaze, and clung to the
sight of him. And she spoke to him with the special te-
lepathy shared by those who love. *I've missed you,* her
look told him.

Ramsey's mouth slanted in a roguish grin as he returned the wink she'd given him earlier.

He saw Tess stiffen as if she'd been slapped. She must have been watching the byplay.

"I hope you're a patient man, Ramsey." Marty's voice held amusement and warning.

"What? Oh...no, I'm not. Why?" Under protest, he dragged his attention away from Sabrina once more.

"First of all, Tess considers you and Sabrina her private properties—like a home and a summer house. One is for living in and one is for playing in. It's going to take a while to convince her you should be connected."

"I know. I heard." He exhaled in a short gust of frustration. "I had a whole list of problems made up, but I didn't think Tess would be one of them." Studying the high gloss on his shoes, he changed the subject. "You said 'first of all.' What's second?"

Marty patted his arm. If he'd been shorter, Ramsey had the feeling that she would have done the same to his head. "Sabrina and Tess aren't going to be free for at least another hour."

Interrupting Ramsey's groan, Seth walked up to them, producing two cigars from his inside pocket. "I guess that means we have time to go outside and smoke these."

Ramsey nodded in relief. "Sounds good. Will you excuse me, Marty?" He'd had enough of wall-to-wall people for a while. It would feel good to loosen his tie and breathe in something besides the mingled scents of every perfume known to man, not to mention aftershave, cologne and hair spray. One lady smelled of mothballs. "Give me a good cigar any day," he said.

Then, he bumped into someone soft and sweet-smelling, the vanilla and spice scent of Shalimar a subtle hint rather than an all-out assault. His senses recognized her before he could focus on the woman he held loosely, keeping her from falling. The body pressed against him was the one he'd known for one night and in the dreams of a lifetime. Sabrina.

Ramsey touched her cheek with his lips in a trailing caress that led to the softness under her ear. "You're beautiful," he whispered.

Every time she thought of him, saw him, desire trickled through her, gathering in the secret places of her body. At his physical touch, the sound of his voice, hit her like a tidal wave. She turned her head just enough to kiss his cheek. To anyone watching it would look like a greeting between friends. In this crowd, people handed out kisses like salesmen handed out business cards.

He gave her a look full of hidden meanings that only she could find. And then he bent over to speak into her ear—it was difficult to hear above the crowd. "Let me take you away from all this . . . to my car, where we can neck in the back seat."

"The Ferrari?" she whispered back, enjoying his outrageousness and the adventure of flirting in the middle of a crowd, with no one the wiser.

"You're right. How about your van?"

The royal blue gown Tess was wearing flashed into view. Sabrina drew away from Ramsey. "Behave yourself, Ramsey," she said lightly, her smile stiff, as if it had been starched to hold its shape.

"Marty said you'll be free in an hour, more or less."

Sabrina checked her watch. It was eleven-thirty. "Less, I hope. Go smoke your cigar, Ramsey and—" her smile returned "—take off your tie. You won't be the only one." She cocked her head to indicate several men who had already made themselves more comfortable.

He followed her suggestion with unconcealed relief. "I'll be back in thirty minutes." A corner of his mouth slanted in another roguish grin. "Maybe less." He glanced around to check on Tess and found her studying the buffet table. The waiter was on the other side of the room. Touching Sabrina's cheek with the back of his fingers, he sent her a silent promise and left the building in long, determined strides.

Seth relaxed for the first time since the show had ended. As soon as Tess had entered the showroom, he'd been acutely aware of the way she'd watched him, the tension and misery in her manner. Once she'd headed toward him, only to stop dead in her tracks as Janet had come up to him, wearing an intimate smile and carrying two glasses of champagne. Tess had looked brittle, ready to shatter as she'd stared down at her gown. He didn't want to be the cause of Tess's hurt. Because of that, he'd been distracted and brusque with Janet. Removing his tie, he stuffed it into his pocket. What a mess.

Ramsey unfastened the top two studs from his shirt and slipped them into his pocket as he and Seth strolled along the green belt that wound through the industrial park. Winter was sneaking up on Denver, and he was glad they'd stopped at the cloakroom for their topcoats. He hadn't buttoned his, though. He needed a cold shower, and the frosty air was the next best thing. He shouldn't have touched Sabrina. It still took him by surprise how much he craved physical contact with her. It was as though he needed to tell her how he felt with his body, because words weren't enough.

He veered in the direction of a park bench, sat down heavily and bit off the end of his cigar. Seth puffed on his as he lit it, then held out a match for Ramsey.

"That's some dress Sabrina seems to be wearing," Seth said casually.

Ramsey's eyes reflected the match's flame as he saw her in his mind, a sorceress veiled in red mist, enchanting, bewitching, all the magic in the world in her eyes. He stretched out his legs, wishing he could take off his shoes. "Mmm."

"Is she worth it, Ram?"

"Who?" Ramsey asked, caught up in thoughts of warm sheets and forget-me-not eyes.

"Sabrina."

Ramsey's face softened. "Yeah. She's worth it." He registered Seth's cautious tone. "Worth what?"

"Uh, Tess saw you and Sabrina in there...and she didn't look too happy with what she saw."

"She saw me run into Sabrina."

"And kiss her. I don't know how anyone in the vicinity could have missed the heat waves rising between you two." Seth rose from the bench and paced in front of Ramsey. "Ram, Sabrina is one hell of a woman. I don't blame you for having the hots for her but—"

"Shut up, Seth. You don't know what you're talking about." Ramsey didn't try to keep his feelings for Sabrina from his expression. Short of slugging his soon-to-be partner to make him drop the subject, it was the best he could do.

After a short moment of penetrating scrutiny, Seth lowered his gaze. "I'm sorry, Ram. I didn't think things had gone that far. I hope it works out for the three of you."

Walking over to a streetlight, Ramsey glanced at his watch. He ground his cigar stub under his heel, then picked it up to toss it into a litter can. "Let's go back in. It's almost midnight."

"Is that when you turn into a frog?"

"I did that in another life, partner. This time I'm going for—" Ramsey stopped abruptly as he heard a squeal of brakes, followed by the crunch of metal. Marty was hurrying toward them with a worried frown on her face.

"Ramsey...out back...Sabrina...trouble."

WATCHING Ramsey and Seth disappear outside, Sabrina had the fanciful notion that the room had dimmed. But she hadn't. She could feel the light inside herself growing brighter with every word and look and touch, until she thought she might glow in the dark.

As she turned back to the showroom, her gaze collided with Tess's. A sound of pain escaped her as she drew in her breath. Betrayal and condemnation hit her like lethal weapons, immobilizing her, killing all sensation but that of Tess's pain, and hurting twice as much because she knew she had inflicted it.

Sabrina shook her head, silently pleading with Tess. It had been such a natural, simple thing to show affection to Ramsey, an instinct older than she was. All her fears were real now.

Now her instinct was telling her that it was all too much for Tess, coming on the heels of other problems and insecurities.

Sabrina saw the tall, dark-eyed waiter approach Tess with his tray of champagne. With a too-bright smile, she accepted a glass as he whispered into her ear. Her gaze, full of antagonism and resentment, was still fixed on Sabrina.

Unease shivered through her. The waiter had something in his eyes now besides an interest in impressing a pretty girl. Marty had told her what Tess had said to him. Twice Tess had struck at his pride, and now he obviously wanted to reassert his masculinity. And he wanted revenge. Though Tess hadn't responded in words, Sabrina had the impression that she had, nevertheless, given him an answer.

Sabrina watched the waiter resume his circuit of the room. A frown shadowed Tess's brow as she stared after him uncertainly, then slipped out the backstage door.

The waiter's gaze followed Tess, his eyes gleaming in satisfaction. With a quick glance at his employer, he set down his tray and headed in the same direction.

Sabrina knew what was happening, what was going to happen as surely as if Tess had given her a signed, notarized document announcing her intention. Urgency prompted her to follow. She'd known others like the waiter. Men with pubescent mentalities, their thoughts seldom rose above their belt buckles, and they assumed that everyone else was just like them.

Ignoring a client who called to her with a compliment, she twisted and turned her way through the crowd, seeing nothing but the door she sought to reach, hearing nothing but the silent pleas that she repeated over and over again. *Tess, don't do this. He's not playing games.* Sabrina's chest constricted at the realization that Tess couldn't hear her, and wouldn't listen if she could.

When she finally reached the door, she slapped it open and lunged across the threshold, her protective instincts blazing. Pausing, she probed the brightly lighted corridor and strained to hear any sound that might lead to Tess.

Sabrina crossed every portal, checked each room, her dread piling up with each failure to locate Tess. Why were her rebellions so extreme? Why did she lose her usual grip on maturity to slip into such thoughtless, reckless action? If only she'd throw temper tantrums, instead of performing defiant acts that had the potential to harm her!

Old enough to know better, and too young to care. Sabrina could almost hear her father saying that, the bitter words reaching across the years, censuring her, following her like a guilty conscience.

The longer Sabrina searched, the louder her instincts screamed. All her senses were stretched as she listened for the rustle of taffeta and kept an eye out for a flash of the gown Tess had loved—until she'd begun to hate the woman who gave it to her.

Finally there was only one door left. Sabrina's skin felt damp and cold, her throat dry. The door led outside, to the rear parking lot . . . to cars.

Cars. If Tess drove away with the waiter, she would be trapped between her own impulsiveness and the waiter's need to prove his manhood. For the sake of spite and anger she would lose what should only be given in love. And more . . . so much more.

How could she stop her?

Sabrina's resolve stiffened and held her courage upright. It didn't matter what she did. If need be, she'd hog-tie Tess and lock her in a maintenance closet.

"Whatever works," Sabrina muttered as she wrapped her fingers around the metal door handle and peered through the small window in the door. They were at the far end of the parking lot, standing beside a car, locked in an embrace. The waiter's hands were all over Tess. And she was squirming in his hold, trying to free herself. He opened the car door and pushed her inside.

Sabrina's mind seemed filled with sand, sifting away all thought as she heard the engine start. They were so far away. She had to stop them, prevent that waiter from harming her child... Ramsey's child.

A cloud of exhaust rose; Sabrina could almost smell the fumes, hear the engine idle as he allowed it to warm up for a scant moment before backing out. Her fingers curled as if they were around the waiter's neck, squeezing. Her nails cut into her palms, and she wished they were clawing his face instead.

Was this a nightmare? Would it go away if she said her prayers and concentrated on pleasant thoughts, leaving only a passing shudder to mark the memory?

The car backed out, maneuvering recklessly between a car on its left and the caterer's truck on its right.

Sabrina ran outside, knowing that if she didn't stop them and Tess was hurt, she would feel it, too—every day for the rest of her life. Tess had changed her mind. She'd been struggling....

He *would* hurt her.

But how could she stop a moving car? She looked around frantically. Superman wasn't bursting onto the scene, ready to save the day, his muscles rippling.

There was only Marty in the doorway, framed by light. "Sabrina? What—?"

"Marty!" Sabrina called over her shoulder as she ran toward the far end of the lot. "Find Ramsey... *now*!"

Marty's face reflected her confusion, but she seemed to grasp the urgency of Sabrina's words, the panic in her voice. Sabrina saw her pivot and hike up her long skirts, running with a speed belying her age and girth.

Gasping sobs tore out of Sabrina as she ran toward the car. She heard the squeal of brakes, the sound of tires skidding on the ice-frosted asphalt. The car was close enough to touch, close enough to give her a glancing blow on the hip, spinning her out of the way as it fishtailed across the lot. Her legs folded under her like cloth.

Light danced crazily over the area as she watched the car jump a speed bump and plow through the temporary fence separating Cachet property from that of a newly constructed building. She heard the crunch of metal, the splintering of glass, a hiss of fluid running out of the radiator. Billows of steam drifted upward as the car landed nose down in a ditch.

The new building, a monolith of stone and glass, filled her vision at a peculiar angle. Fighting a sudden dizziness, she turned her head to meet the grim stare of the cloud-whiskered moon.

Her forehead burned. Her hip throbbed. Her cheek felt sticky and warm. The air bit into her with sharp winter teeth. Something hard and grainy supported her neck. Looking to the side, she saw a dark stain obliterating a name on a parking barrier. It seemed important to focus on the name before it disappeared.

Her name. She sighed at the irony of landing there, of lying in her own parking space. Spurts of brightness exploded behind her eyes. Sabrina frowned in concentration, trying to remember why she was there, how it had happened. Only shadows glided through her mind....

Then came recall with increasing clarity. Tess. Betrayal. Anger. The waiter. Tess. Sixteen years old. Losing part of herself, becoming less than whole. *No!*

Sabrina found a focal point—the car, its rear end protruding from the ditch, its wheels spinning in the air. It was going nowhere. From the near distance she heard an anguished shout and the sound of running feet. Strong, warm hands moved gently over her body. Brandy eyes, dark with pain, spilled moisture onto lean, ashen cheeks.

Ramsey. She had to tell him...he didn't know about Tess. Sabrina shrank away, slapping her hands at those gathered around her. They didn't belong here...not here, but over there...the car. Her mouth opened and words formed. "In the car...Tess...oh God, help Tess." Over and over again, Sabrina screamed, obsessed, possessed by visions of what might be happening.

Something warm was draped over her. It smelled like Ramsey. She fought him when he held her down and tried to pull herself up.

"It's all right, sweetheart. Relax. I promise, it's all right."

"No. Tess. The car."

There were other voices now. She knew them and hated them for being so close to her and so far away from Treasure.

Marty. Marty would surely hear her.

"Marty...please..."

Sabrina heard Seth's voice, and she looked toward him, willing him to listen to her. Before she could appeal to him, she saw Ramsey embracing someone, heard him speak sharply. "For crying out loud, Tess, tell Sabrina you're safe!"

"I'm okay, Sabrina. Please lie still. I'm not hurt."

Discordant bells rang in Sabrina's head. Not bells. Chimes. From the clock tower in the new building. She counted them. Midnight. Nothing was real before the clock struck twelve....

Feeling the warmth of Ramsey's body still clinging to the overcoat that covered her, she listened to Tess's voice. A small smile lifted the corners of her mouth as a dark and silent shadow gathered her into its embrace.

CHAPTER SIXTEEN

SABRINA DRIFTED AIMLESSLY in sleep, soothed by emptiness and silence and lack of involvement with the rest of the world. But awareness found her and would not be denied, as it drew her insistently from the void that separated Then from Now. Reality began to return. Memories intruded upon her peace. Voices penetrated—distinct, yet muffled by distance and walls. She wanted none of it. Especially not the memories...the fear.

There were so many things to be afraid of in life: the bogeyman and things that went bump in the night; lying wide-awake after her mother had said, "Sleep tight and don't let the bedbugs bite," wondering if bedbugs were bigger than she was. She had overcome all that and more, but never until now had she stared at the face of fear and dropped her eyes first.

Tess couldn't have found a better way to punish her if she had conducted market research and planned for a year. Had she known, or had the waiter simply been the immediate means to an end?

He would have hurt Tess. Sabrina had seen it in his eyes. He was too shallow to be aware or interested in how deeply he could hurt others. People like him lived on the surface of life, never knowing anything but their own needs, because they had nothing inside.

Opening her eyes, Sabrina looked at darkness and recognized night. A digital display of numbers glowed in the comforting shadows. 8:07 p.m. Which night? Familiar shapes were arranged around her, exactly as she remembered them: a tall armoire, a quilt rack, two easy chairs grouped by the fireplace at the end of the room. Ramsey's room. She could smell him on the pillow, the sheets, the soft cotton clothing her. And she remembered his body heat beside her, around her, inside....

She felt sharp thrusts of pain and a squeezing pressure in her head and vaguely recalled being periodically awakened. Had she suffered a concussion? Muscle spasms twisted in her hip and thigh. A dull throbbing overlaid her body like another skin.

Sabrina listened to the voices coming from the den—Ramsey's and Seth's and Tess's—in short spurts. Ramsey's voice reached out to her, called to her, drew her. Rising from the bed, she found her mind as wobbly as her limbs. Thoughts darted in and out too quickly for her to grasp. Finding no robe, she shrugged and pulled the top sheet off the bed. Having no toothbrush, she used mouthwash to rinse away the dryness and taste of sleep.

Wrapping the sheet around her shoulders, Sabrina left the bedroom to face whatever came next.

RAMSEY PROWLED HIS DEN like a beast of the wild, confined and maddened by his own helplessness. Each time around, he paused to stare down the hall and listen for the rustle of bedclothes, for Sabrina to call out, for anything to indicate she was finally coming out of it . . . coming back to him.

She'd been sleeping since he'd brought her home
from the hospital emergency room early in the morning...over twelve hours ago. She hadn't even moved in
her sleep, but had stayed in a curled-up-on-her-side position as if she were afraid to move, afraid to wake up.

Minor injuries, the doctor had said. Her forehead
had needed stitching, but there were no fractures. Her
hip, thigh and side were badly bruised—ugly but not
serious; nothing that stitches, ice packs and time
wouldn't heal. Her stockings had suffered more damage than she had. *Thank God.*

And by the grace of God, Tess had escaped with
nothing more than the fright of her life. He'd had three
doctors check both of them before he'd been satisfied.
They had tactlessly suggested that he see the trauma
psychiatrist instead of Tess. With the resiliency of
youth, his daughter was holding up just fine, but it appeared that he wasn't....

The worst had been when Sabrina had come to in the
emergency room, screaming and fighting, hysterical
because she was still living the horror of seeing the car
nose-dive into a ditch not quite twenty-four hours ago.
She'd fought the effects of the injection they'd given her
until she'd seen Tess for herself. The time since had
passed her by unnoticed.

For the sixtieth time in as many minutes, Ramsey
checked his watch. He couldn't stand it; the waiting, the
quiet, the fury and the fear were mangling him. What
if the doctors had missed something? "Damn it," he
said to Seth. "How bloody long does it take to sleep off
one little shot?" He needed to hear Sabrina's voice and
see the light of life burning in her eyes, just as he
constantly needed to watch Tess moving about.

And later, when he had a chance to calm down, he and Tess were going to have a talk about what had happened. Judging from the nervous glances Tess kept throwing at him, he had a feeling he'd have to ground her for a long time. First she'd run away to Jackson; now there was this. She was setting dangerous precedents for future behavior.

"About as long as it takes to sleep off a good drunk," Seth responded as he sat at the bar, staring into his empty mug. "Those little shots can pack quite a wallop if you're not used to them."

"The doctor said it would wear off in a few hours," Ramsey argued stubbornly.

"Take it easy, Ram. The sleep is therapeutic. She'll wake up when she's ready."

Ramsey listened without hearing. Seth was trying to reason with him, but his reasoning processes weren't working worth a damn. He looked at Tess sitting cross-legged on the carpet, a game of solitaire spread out before her. Everything seemed so normal—a quiet evening at home. Normal? The woman who had given birth to Tess was asleep in his bed—this time without him. He loved her against all reason. She had run headlong into a moving car to protect Tess.

Tess had been in the car with that slab of meat disguised as a man. If the waiter hadn't already been unconscious, Ramsey probably would have seen to it by the time the ambulance arrived. He'd still like to have five minutes alone in a dark alley with that son of a bitch. Ramsey looked down the hall again. He didn't have to ask what had happened. Between the snatches of information Marty had given him and Sabrina's hysteria at the hospital, he had a pretty good idea of the whys and wherefores.

Sabrina had been right about Tess's attitude. So had Seth and Marty. He should have listened. And done what? Given up Sabrina? No way. Disregarded Tess's feelings? Equally impossible.

A fist gripped the inside of his chest. He looked up at the ceiling. Perspiration ran from his pores like blood. He couldn't shake the memory of last night: Marty charging through the crowd without ceremony or apology; Sabrina's screams for Tess; his legs turning to lead as he ran toward her . . . too late; Seth pulling Tess from the wreck—and the implications of it all, hitting him like a boulder between the eyes. Tess had clung to Seth and then to him, sobbing, her face appearing almost translucent in the moonlight.

How long would it take him to forget? One lifetime? Two? Never? A voice had whispered "Never" morbidly into his ear when he'd seen Sabrina's blood erasing her name from the parking barrier. He'd been afraid that it was an omen.

Absently Ramsey crouched beside Tess to put a red eight onto a black nine, then flick away a stray curl from her cheek. Tess had calmed down and had refused to leave Sabrina in the hospital. She'd held her hand and reassured her that she was okay. Out of guilt or love? It didn't really matter. Tess cared, even though she wasn't about to admit it right now. She didn't want to care, just as he hadn't wanted to fall in love, but emotions didn't distinguish between wanting and not wanting. They simply were.

Once she had known that Sabrina was all right, Tess's resentment had come back redoubled. Her sullenness had grown in direct proportion to his own concern for Sabrina's prolonged sleep.

His gaze strayed to the hall. Why in unholy hell didn't she wake up?

Tess's voice reached him. "You shouldn't have brought her here, Daddy." She avoided meeting his gaze, as she had all day.

Ramsey crooked a forefinger under her chin, forcing her to look at him. "Where should she be, Tess? A hotel room?"

"Marty is her partner," she mumbled.

"Marty's husband has a nasty case of the flu. Do you want Sabrina to be exposed to that on top of everything else?"

"No." The cards scattered in all directions as she stood up. "I'll go check on her again."

"Tess," Ramsey said quietly as he picked up the cards, carefully stacking them in their box. "It's Sabrina, not *her*. You might remember that, at the same time you remember she saved you from an ugly situation."

Tess stopped midway to the door, her fists clenched at her sides.

Seth sputtered on a mouthful of coffee as he raised his eyes. He wiped his chin and smiled in relief. "Uh... Ram..."

Ramsey glanced over his shoulder, then rose abruptly and stared. After all the hours of waiting, he wasn't quite sure that Sabrina was really awake and standing so close, swaying on her feet, alternately blinking and squinting at him, as if she were trying to focus in the brightness of the room.

Wanting to reassure herself that Tess was really there, really safe, Sabrina reached out her hand to touch her. Tess turned away, going to stand by Ramsey—to pro-

tect him and hold Sabrina off? Sabrina lowered her
arm, feeling unsure . . . lost.

In that static moment, Ramsey forgot the others in
the room, dismissing everything except Sabrina. Her
cheek was scraped raw, a bright, angry red. She sported
a shiner that would do any street kid proud. The bruise
extending to her knee showed through a parting of the
sheet she had wrapped around her like a cloak. Blend-
ing with her pallor, a white bandage covered most of her
forehead to keep her hair from catching on the sutures.
There would be a scar. . . .

She'd never looked more beautiful.

Sabrina remained on the threshold as she watched
Ramsey and Tess. The people who added meaning to
her life stood before her, together, holding each other,
while she stood alone.

That, she admitted to herself, was the root of her
fear. It was a fear of always standing alone, of never
belonging; a fear that she would have to walk away
from them and leave her heart behind.

Afraid she'd disappear if he looked away, Ramsey
clung to her with his gaze. He held out his hand in invitation, and she saw that it was a plea, a need.

Sabrina's heart tripped. Her breath trembled at the
look in his eyes, devouring, absorbing her presence. She
took a step toward him, her entire being craving the
strength and protection of his arms, the support of his
solid chest, the shelter his body offered. His eyes shone
brilliantly, proclaiming his love. Her hand reached for
one of his, so she could touch him all the sooner. Their
fingertips brushed and then his hand enveloped hers.

Winding an arm around her shoulders, Ramsey held
her close. His emotions found release in a bark of
laughter that suspiciously resembled a sob. She moved.

She breathed. He could hear her heartbeat. Or was it his own, reawakening, pounding hard in the aftermath of a nightmare?

Ramsey kissed the pulse that fluttered on her neck and caressed her back, feeling the warmth of her skin through the sheet. Then he traced the gentle ridges of her spine and found the delicate lace at the top of her panties. He remembered undressing her when they'd come home in the morning, how his hands had stilled at the sight of her underwear, a wisp of black silk and lace—barely enough to mention.

He buried his face in her hair and groaned. "You scared me half to death. I thought I'd lost you."

Feeling boneless, formless, Sabrina melted against him. This was why she'd left the bed and followed his voice. This was what she'd needed and wanted: reality to dispel the nightmares.

Stiffening at her father's words, Tess moved closer to him, shifting her weight, coming between them, showing Sabrina that there was no room for her in Ramsey's embrace... in his life.

Easing away from Ramsey, Sabrina went to the bar, curling her fingers over its edge as she stared blindly at the stained glass panel behind it.

Ramsey hated letting Sabrina go, but he'd felt Tess grow stiff and unyielding. He hadn't missed her rejection of Sabrina. *I'm terribly afraid there will never be an Us,* she'd said once. She was still afraid. And with good reason. One third of Us was Tess—angry, threatened and afraid of being left out. Sabrina would tell him they shouldn't have held each other, have given Tess visible proof of the emotion binding them, but he wasn't about to insult Tess's intelligence by trying to hide what she already knew. There wasn't any point.

Sabrina saw movement out of the corner of her eye and felt the weight of an arm across her shoulders. Seth was beside her, raising a mug of coffee to her lips, urging her to drink. Sipping the coffee, she also drank of Seth's compassion, his attention, his support as he guided her to a chair and tucked a crocheted afghan around her legs.

It came from the wrong man. But unless Tess accepted her, Ramsey would be the right man only in her dreams.

Ramsey held Tess at arm's length, frowning at the bitter look she tossed at Sabrina before lowering her head. It was all well and good to know and understand his daughter's feelings, but it did zilch in helping him figure out how to handle them.

He watched Seth taking care of Sabrina, bringing her more coffee, adjusting the afghan more securely around her. He should be doing that, he thought. Not Seth. Not anyone else.

Ramsey's bitterness turned to wry gratitude as Seth led Tess out to the kitchen to make some sandwiches. Tess followed Seth like a faithful puppy. She'd reacted every bit as negatively to Seth's show of tenderness toward Sabrina as she had to his own display of feeling.

Terrific. Tess was feeling threatened on two fronts. That meant double jeopardy for Sabrina and, right now, she didn't look capable of handling even a cup of coffee. Ramsey forgot his restraint and crouched in front of her. Tentatively, carefully, he traced the injuries on her face. "I'm sorry. I wish it had been me. It should have been me."

The liquid in her mug rippled as her hands began to shake uncontrollably. "None of it should have happened." He thought her voice sounded like a sentence written with a pen that was running out of ink. Grimacing with the effort, she clearly tried to find some measure of control and failed. "We knew better. We were crazy to believe we could plunge right in without testing the waters first. We've been reacting instead of thinking. Too much impulse and not enough discretion..."

Ramsey took the mug from her hand and set it on the end table. "You're babbling, Sabrina, and not making sense," he said gently.

"I'm not? But..." Her voice faded and she looked confused, as if she were wondering how that could possibly be. She always made sense—until she'd become someone she didn't know.

Covering her clasped hands with one of his, Ramsey tucked her hair behind her ear. "Regrets, Sabrina?"

At least a thousand. The only regret she didn't have was loving Ramsey. She stared at her hands wrapped in one of his. The only place she felt warm was in his arms....

Tess and Seth came in, carrying a plate of sandwiches, a jar of pickles and a bag of potato chips.

Sighing, Ramsey reached into his shirt pocket for a small brown plastic bottle and shook out a pill. "The doctor wants you to take these for a day or two, so you can rest comfortably."

She gazed blankly at Ramsey, then at the pill, and wondered if easing the physical pain would help anything at all.

"Sabrina, you're fighting a losing battle. I know you hurt. Take this. Please." Relieved that she didn't argue with him, he smiled as she swallowed the pill. "Be sure to eat something. On an empty stomach, these little buggers will hit you like a fifth of Scotch."

Nodding, Sabrina drank the rest of her coffee. Her mind was clearing, registering things. The sudden silence in the room screamed louder than a shout. Tess still refused to look her way. The bottle of pickles gave a short hiss and pop as Seth opened it. Ramsey selected a sandwich and lifted a corner of the bread.

Smiling ruefully, he offered it to her. "PB and J again."

"Daddy, shouldn't you call Marty? You said you would."

"I'll do it," Seth said as he picked up the phone on the bar.

Sabrina ate the sandwich, tasting nothing. "Tess, are you really all right? You weren't hurt?"

"She's fine," Ramsey answered, and frowned at Tess for ignoring Sabrina.

"Ramsey? How long ago was it?" It seemed forever, yet in her mind it was still happening.

Ramsey sighed. Sabrina was coming back to him at last. More importantly, she was coming back to herself. "Last night. You slept the day away." He watched her focus on Tess and tilt her head the way she always did when she was thinking. She straightened in the chair. Her color was returning with every bite she took.

"I'm glad you weren't hurt, Treasure," Sabrina said, then realized how idiotic that sounded. Of course Tess was hurt. She and Ramsey had inflicted the damage.

Tess turned her back on Sabrina. "I told you not to call me that."

Hanging up the phone, Seth found an interesting spot on the ceiling.

"Tess..." Ramsey walked over to his daughter and grasped her arm. "I've had enough of your smart mouth for one day."

"Maybe you've had enough of me. Maybe you'd like to trade me in for *her*."

At a loss as to how to handle Tess, Ramsey convulsed like a dog shaking down his hackles. Now he knew what divided loyalties meant. Tess had just issued what amounted to an ultimatum. She had no right to do that, yet he understood where she was coming from. It was going to take more than a few minutes of heavy-duty communicating to banish her insecurities, and this wasn't the time to start.

Seth coughed and frowned at Ramsey. Ramsey frowned at Tess. Tess glared at the wall. Their expressions reflected various shades of grim.

The afghan slid to the floor in a heap as Sabrina rose from the chair. The room seemed to be at an angle, like a sinking ship. She was going to be the first to desert. The medicine had hit her as Ramsey had predicted it would—like a fifth of Scotch. The combined effect of her weakness and Tess's hostility had looted her of all strength. If she didn't get into a bed soon, she would join the crocheted fabric lying on the floor.

One by one, heads turned in her direction. Holding her palms up, she gave a self-deprecating laugh. "I don't know what to do with myself. I can't think."

Tess checked her instinctive movement toward Sabrina and erased the concern from her face.

Alarmed by Sabrina's admission, Ramsey strode across the room. He reached her side as her eyelids fluttered and she swayed, groping behind herself for the support of the chair. Ramsey grunted with the effort to sweep her into his arms. It wasn't going to work. The best he could do was catch her under the arms. Trim and sexy she might be, but he wasn't Rhett Butler, and she topped Scarlett by several inches. Sighing, he draped her arm over his shoulders and wound his arm around her waist. "Sorry, sweetheart. I'm out of practice. You'll have to walk." Scowling at Seth's amusement, he guided her down the hall to his bedroom.

Tess's gaze followed their progress until they were out of sight. She was worried about Sabrina in spite of the hurt over Ramsey's endearment. Sweetheart. That was what he'd always called *her* . . . and Mom, a long time ago. He had no right to call Sabrina sweetheart. Worse, she shouldn't be caring about Sabrina. Sabrina wasn't her mother. Sabrina wasn't anything.

Her breath shivered in and out like hiccuping sobs after a long bout of crying. Only she wasn't crying. She wanted to, but everything hurt too much. She'd never felt so alone—not even when Mom had died and Daddy hadn't seemed to be there anymore. Everyone had somebody, except her. Daddy was all wrapped up with Sabrina. Tess's mouth tightened. He was all wrapped around her, too. And Seth had Janet. None of them were interested in her—what she did or what she was feeling.

They didn't like the things she'd done, but they didn't seem to care why she'd done them. Last night, she hadn't thought . . . all she'd wanted was to feel that somebody wanted her. It had been important to be wanted, to belong somewhere—even with a stranger. Lately, everybody seemed like strangers to her. Even herself.

Everything had been okay after she'd run away . . . until Sabrina. She didn't even have Seth anymore. He'd always treated her as though she was important, special, as though he understood, like a friend. Now that she was in love with him, they weren't even friends. He wasn't interested in her at all . . . not since Sabrina had introduced him to Janet.

It was as if she'd been shoved into a box, out of the way. Daddy hadn't told her that he loved Sabrina, as if it didn't matter what she thought about it. She could have told him she understood about love. Maybe if he had talked to her about it, she would have been glad. Maybe. She hadn't really had a chance to think about it before finding out. . . .

Why hadn't they told her, instead of going behind her back?

Seth watched Tess as she stood there, looking so . . . displaced. He felt the same way. She hadn't spoken to him since last night—not even in the kitchen when they'd been making sandwiches. He'd suddenly become the invisible man. Tess had always been special to him, since the first time he'd met her. He'd been eighteen and Tess five. She'd been so pretty at five. And so polite. She'd called him ''sir,'' making his chest puff up, his ego expand, his heart warm. Despite the thirteen years between them, they'd always been friends. . . .

Tess blinked and turned around. Her gaze skipped off him as she sat in the chair farthest away from him and stared down at her hands, reminding him of how she used to cover her eyes when she'd done something she shouldn't have, reasoning that if she couldn't see anyone, they couldn't see her, either. He'd always known that she'd been into mischief when she'd done that. And she'd gotten into plenty when she was little. Nothing big or serious, just kid stuff, reminding everyone that she was a kid, even though Claire had expected a lot from her—too much from a child. Tess had tried so hard to please her mother—and when she hadn't, she tried to hide. Like now.

He knew what Tess was thinking, as surely as if balloons of dialogue had been suspended above her head. He knew her so well. And he'd known Claire. That lady had been so good at raising Tess by the book. Only the book hadn't said anything about teaching her child the multiples of love. What was far more tragic, Claire couldn't have taught anyone that particular lesson. She just hadn't been capable of opening her own heart that wide; she had been so jealous of any closeness between father and daughter. Now Tess was lost and confused in the middle of all the surprises life was throwing at her—taking a crash course in coping.

He went to stand in front of her. "Cut it out, Tess."

Automatically her gaze met his, then skittered away again. "I'm not doing anything."

"Yes, you are. You're busy being worried and guilty and humiliated. And you're pretending I don't exist, that you never told me you loved me." He crouched down, meeting her at eye level, making sure she had to look at him. "Last I heard, love meant communicating and trusting."

Swallowing, Tess blinked furiously and tried to look through him. "I changed my mind."

"Good. Then maybe we can get back to what's really important . . . like being friends again." He had her attention now. All he had to do was come up with the right things to say. All of a sudden his mind was blank. "Tess, I could use a little help here." He sighed at her continued silence. She was back to not looking at him. "I guess I really screwed up on Sunday."

"Could we not talk about it . . . please?"

"Not yet, honey. You have to understand first." Lowering himself to the floor, Seth crossed his legs Indian style.

"I understand, Seth. I'm too young," she said, her quivering chin canceling out the bitterness in her voice.

"You're too young," he agreed solemnly. "But that isn't your fault. There's no reason for you to feel humiliated or silly or inadequate. You have everything but age going for you, Tess. I could have told you that the other day, but I didn't want to say all the usual things about how flattered I was or how I'd love you if you were older. I *was* flattered. As for the other... how do I know what I'd do if you were older? Hell, if you were older, *you* might not feel the same way."

Taking her hands into his, he stared up at her, feeling damned inadequate. Nothing he had said or could say was going to make things easier for her. He couldn't protect her, and that was exactly what he needed to do. "Tess, the bottom line is—"

"I heard the bottom line the other day," she pointed out.

His mouth slanted in a lopsided smile. "That was just the subtotal, Tess. The important thing for you to remember and believe is that I haven't rejected you. No one has. You're loved, as my friend and Ram's daughter and Sabrina's—"

"I'm not Sabrina's anything."

"No? Are you absolutely sure?" His eyes narrowed at her closed expression. Closed and locked up tight. "You're not ready to hear this, are you, Tess?" Jerking back as she rose abruptly from her chair, Seth lost his balance and made a three-point landing on his elbows and behind.

"I'm not ready for any of this. I'm so sick of everyone pretending. All my life, Seth, people have pretended. Don't you think I know?" She spoke in a low, controlled voice, like that of someone who had felt too much pain and was using all her strength to fight it. "Isn't anyone real?"

"Who is anyone, Tess?" He scooted back far enough to lever himself off the floor.

"Everyone." She waved her arm in a wide arc. "Sabrina pretends that she cares about me, then she sneaks around with Daddy and pretends that they're just friends, getting along because of me. You pretend that we can be just like we were, but you know we can't. It'll never be the same. I do feel silly, Seth, and you feel sorry for me. Last night at the showing, Janet pretended that nothing had happened and she hadn't seen me at your place."

Seth barely moved and kept his mouth shut, letting her talk, sensing that if she didn't bring it all out into the open now, it would be lost inside her, and she'd never have the courage to face her fears again.

"All of you are being so careful now, pretending that it isn't my fault that Sabrina was hurt. Ever since I can remember—pretending. Mom pretended that she loved Daddy, that everything was perfect. Daddy pretended that he was happy—" Tess clamped her hands over her mouth, one on top of the other. Her eyes were wide, stricken; her head shook back and forth, as if she were denying what she'd always known, yet had tried so hard to ignore.

"Tess . . ." Seth moved to hold her, as he'd done in times past when she'd been hurt or confused or angry.

Vehemently she shook her head one final time, rejecting him and what he offered. She wouldn't be able to stand it if he touched her. And she wouldn't be able to stand it if she broke down in front of him. . . .

"I'm going to bed now," she said in a tiny little voice as she moved around him and walked stiffly to the door.

Wanting to keep her there, Seth let her go, knowing that there was nothing he could do for her. She was so angry—and so right about some things. Too right. She was wrong about Ram and Sabrina, though. And about himself. It was going to be hard to watch her discover that and struggle with pride and independence—and with her need to do the right thing. "Oh, Tess," he whispered, "you're too young to be so old."

CHAPTER SEVENTEEN

STILLNESS. There was nothing—not the rustle of leaves nor the stirring of creatures. Nothing but a silence as deep as eternity. The very air seemed to be sleeping.

In the bottomless hours before dawn, Sabrina discovered that man, or woman, could indeed be an island. Happenings were reincarnated with sharp clarity, and they haunted her in Technicolor nightmares. Recently returned from the numb side of fear, she experienced it all over again, the emotions of a lifetime tearing her to pieces.

When she finally awakened, she sought the familiar shadows of Ramsey's room, and struggled to escape the memories that were plaguing her like phantom pain. Slowly the shadows materialized into discernible substance, giving her better memories to dwell upon. A chair held the irregular shapes of her clothing, a reminder of the moments when Ramsey had brought her here from the hospital—was it only yesterday morning?—and undressed her with such tenderness and love.

His hands had trembled as he'd whispered promises and bits of nonsense. She'd been only half-aware, exhaustion making powder of her strength and medication drugging her muscles. Too groggy to do more than limply obey his commands, she had stored the rest for more lucid moments.

"Bend your head, so I can reach this hook. This dress...like flame ...a few snags...fix it. Make another the color of your eyes for our wedding...forget-me-not eyes." His hands had shaken as he'd folded the gown and caressed the fabric that still held the warmth of her skin. Heat rushed through her as she remembered his caught breath, his eyes glittering when he saw the red lace and satin Merry Widow molding her waist and hips and lifting her breasts into a full, inviting curve.

Ramsey had first cursed as he fumbled to unfasten the many tiny hooks that were concealed down the front, then praised the garment that enhanced rather than merely covered her form. "This is the sexiest thing I've ever seen." His finger had traced the satin garters before he slipped the catches open. "Buy one for every night of the week." Unmindful of their delicacy, he'd slid the silk stockings down her legs. "Stockings ruined...don't need them...skin like hot silk." He'd paused to press tender kisses onto her thigh, her shin. "Bruises...thank God...only bruises."

Sabrina had closed her eyes, feeling loved and cherished and taken care of for the first time in her adult life. At the very center of her being, she throbbed and grew liquid, completely aware of his gaze flowing over her breasts, her waist, and the panties that were as delicate as a wish.

Breathing deeply, she absorbed Ramsey's scent as his pajama top subtly caressed her skin—the same top he'd worn the other night. The golden fabric was a little faded, a little threadbare...like her dreams....

Sabrina fixed her gaze on the ceiling, willing her mind to blankness. Succeeding for a while, her eyes slowly closed in unguarded sleep. Would she always see Tess's unhappiness and a wrecked car in her dreams? Whichever way she faced, she saw choices closing in on her—none of them easy, all of them potentially disastrous.

Ramsey would be shocked to know how many times she'd weighed the possibilities and let the impractical voice of instinct dictate her choice. He didn't know how much a creature of instinct she really was. Somehow, she'd always managed to land on her feet. But this time, she felt like a cat who had used up all her lives but one.

A slight noise alerted her to another presence in the room. She knew it was Ramsey before she opened her eyes. She always knew when he was near. Had he found his own island too solitary to bear and come to share hers?

A dark silhouette backlit by the night-light that was plugged into the wall socket, he stood in front of his dresser, holding a framed picture in his hands. Claire's picture. His gaze never left it, but she sensed that he was really staring into himself, as if he'd discovered something that hadn't been there before. After a time, he bent and placed the photograph in the bottom drawer, his sigh like the final breath of a storm—peaceful, relieved. It was a farewell that had been too long in coming.

Ramsey straightened and turned, as though he'd somehow felt the touch of her thoughts. In his eyes, she saw acceptance of the goodbye spoken by his mind and heart to the face in the picture. Claire would always live in his memory, but her power to hurt him was gone, replaced by the force of Sabrina's love and his own.

"How do you feel?"

Sabrina wanted to tell him not of physical aches and pains, but of the ones of her spirit—more permanent, less tangible. Choking on the tears that had finally come, she turned her face away from him, her plea so softly spoken that she was sure only God could hear her. "Please, I need you to hold me."

Strong arms eased her up and Ramsey hugged her close to his heart. Between sobs, she poured her misery into Ramsey just as Tess had done with her a month ago. "I'm angry. At myself. At you. At the waiter. And Tess. She had no right to do that to herself, or to us. She knew it would hurt us, but she didn't know how much more she would hurt herself. I couldn't let her do it . . . Treasure . . . my child."

Letting her talk and cry, Ramsey rocked her, smoothed her hair from her face, wiped away her tears and felt her anguish soak into him, become a part of him. "I know, sweetheart. I know."

Quieting by degrees she fell asleep again, grateful that he hadn't offered her meaningless platitudes.

MORNING SLICED through the center section of the drawn curtains. Opening her eyes, Sabrina winced at the pain that was stabbing at her face. She moved her head cautiously and tried to stretch the soreness out of her leg and thigh. The smell of fresh coffee made her aware of the dryness of her mouth. Filtering through the distant sounds of early-morning activity, she heard Ramsey's voice, low and even, then Tess's, higher and flat.

Sitting up, Sabrina adjusted the pillow behind her back and stared at the narrow beam of sunshine, content with the peace of the moment. Her mind was clear, her headache nearly gone. But in the bright light of day, she knew, she'd slowly recall past events and they would seem even more significant than they had previously.

Tess walked into the room, bearing coffee, juice and croissants on a tray. Several items of clothing were

draped over her arms. Confrontation was clearly on her
mind. As her daughter stalked across the carpet and set
the tray over her lap, Sabrina wondered if she was going
to go for a calm and rational approach or a down-and-
dirty one.

"Daddy said to bring you this stuff." Tess looked
highly combustible, ready to flare up at the slightest
provocation.

Unsure whether a simple thank-you would be non-
flammable, Sabrina drank her juice rather than take the
risk. She sensed that the clothes that lay folded on the
chair represented provocation for Tess, not to mention
the fact that she, the intruder, was lying smack in the
middle of Ramsey's bed, his pajama top covering her.
She could imagine how...proprietary it looked.

Tess's gaze darted from the Merry Widow to the pajama jacket and back again. Apparently, she was
drawing conclusions as if they were Connect-a-Dots.
"You're making it with Daddy," she stated bluntly.

Down-and-dirty. Not the best way to start the morning. She wouldn't even be able to finish her coffee before giving Tess a piece of her mind. With a last effort
at control, Sabrina wrapped her fingers around the
handle of the carafe and concentrated on getting most
of the coffee into the cup. "Thanks for bringing this in,
Tess."

Her lips thinning, Tess let the jeans and sweater drop
to the floor. "You've taken over everything. Seth and
Daddy fall all over themselves for you and keep talking
about how special and how gutsy you are. It's *disgust-
ing*."

Gutsy? How so? Sabrina wondered. As in courage?
All she wanted to do was run and hide. As in nerve?
She'd had a lot of that, believing for one minute that she

could gorge herself on chocolate ice cream without getting sick.

It was easier to let her thoughts wander than listen to Tess's outburst, but some thoughts lacked the strength to do that. She could still hear every word being spat at her.

"You lied to me. You're just like the others, using me to make points with Daddy." Tess's eyes were flinty gray. "Right now you've got him fooled, but it won't take him long to figure it out...just like he did with the others."

"Right now, Tess, I don't like the way you're acting." Slamming down her cup, Sabrina moved the tray and rose from the bed. Pivoting, she faced Tess who stood in open-mouthed, wide-eyed disbelief. "You're behaving like a self-centered, manipulative little girl doing stupid, destructive things when life doesn't suit you. What you need is a good paddling."

"I don't have to listen—"

"You'll listen if I have to sit on you. God knows, I've listened to you. I listened when you barged into my life needing a shoulder to cry on, a sympathetic ear and a weapon to use against Ramsey. You used *me*, Tess, not the other way around. You didn't give a hoot in Hades for me or my feelings. I was just a surefire way to get your father's attention."

As she always did when she was under stress, Sabrina needed something to do with her hands. The bed cried out to be made. Stomping to the other side, she grabbed the tray and shoved it at Tess, then began yanking the sheets into some kind of order. "I listened when you said you 'really' liked me. Boy, did I listen. In my imagination I'd watched you grow up for sixteen years. Every wish I'd ever made had just come true. I believed in wishes, Tess. I didn't expect them to turn on me.''

Sabrina made trip after trip around the bed, smoothing nonexistent wrinkles, fussing endlessly to have the sheet precisely even on either side. "I listened when you said you wanted Ramsey and me to be friends.''

"I did want you to be friends.''

"Right. Friends, but not too close. Get along, but not too well. We were not supposed to have room in our hearts for anyone but you." Sabrina tucked a pillow under her chin to straighten its case. "We broke all the rules and fell in love. And we do love each other, Tess. You can make us suffer for it and cause us no end of misery, but you can't change the way we feel.''

"Daddy loves Mom. He'll never—''

"He loved her, Tess. But she's dead now." Sabrina said the words gently. "His feeling for her can't grow anymore. Love has to grow or it dies. And if it's healthy, love multiplies when shared. Your father and I have found something very special. You'll be depriving yourself by refusing to be a part of it.''

Tess shook her head. "Why don't you leave? Daddy will forget about you. We don't need you here. I don't ever want to see you again." She was flailing desperately in the midst of conflicting emotions, refusing the aid of Sabrina's truths—truths she knew, yet refused to accept for fear they might be lies. That first day she'd felt so close to Sabrina...closer than she'd ever felt with anyone. Sabrina had told her it was all right to make mistakes, to not be perfect. It was all right to be just . . . Tess.

Now she felt as though she'd been disloyal to Mom. Now she was afraid to believe that Sabrina hadn't been pretending, too. And now she was afraid that Daddy and Sabrina would be so wrapped up in each other that they wouldn't have time for her...that there wouldn't be room in their lives for her. Just like Mom hadn't had room for Daddy. Tess kept her mouth tightly closed, fighting the tears. Somehow she'd always felt as if it was her fault that Mom hadn't cared about Daddy. That was really why she'd run away.

Sabrina slapped the pillows into position and jerked the spread over them. "I see. I'm disposable now that my usefulness is over. You've wiped your feelings all over me, and now I'm just a worn-out doormat. It's time to throw me away. Does that about sum it up?" Straightening, she placed her hands on her hips.

"Yeah. Just like I was disposable. You put me in a plain brown wrapper and threw *me* away."

The verbal blow knocked the breath out of Sabrina. A small whimper escaped her, conveying more pain than she could bear, the sound of dying dreams that never should have been. Swinging around, she blinked away tears that she knew would never stop if she allowed them to fall, and stared at the empty sky outside the window. "I can forgive you a great deal, Tess." Unaware that a single drop of grief was sliding down her cheek, Sabrina turned back to look at Tess. "But to forgive you for being so deliberately cruel...that might take a while."

Tess's gaze fell to her feet, then lifted again. She looked stricken, confused, regretful. "I didn't mean..."

"No more, Tess." Sabrina swallowed the lump in her throat. It settled in her chest, hard and cold and aching, like a piece of stone. "Please. No more." Feeling moisture at the corner of her mouth, she licked the tears away, tasting heartbreak.

Sabrina mechanically walked toward the bathroom. On the threshold, she looked over her shoulder. "Would it have been so bad, Tess, to have one more person loving you?" Closing the door softly, she unbuttoned her top and shed her panties. As she stepped into the shower, she heard Tess leave the bedroom. Then she heard footsteps running down the hall, the slamming of a door—and heartbreaking sobs that echoed in her soul.

She wouldn't forget again that nothing worthwhile came easily. Sometimes it didn't come at all.

Dressing, she focused on decisions unconsciously made, consciously agreed upon. She couldn't allow a single moment to overwhelm her, when there were so many more waiting to be lived. She had to draw a line and keep her toes on it, making no detours into fantasy, no excursions into sensuality. There would be no loitering in the past. She had to learn to live without Ramsey. Without Tess. Without.

How could something so good and right for her be so bad for everyone else?

Ramsey appeared in the bathroom doorway as she was brushing her hair. She stopped him before he could smile, speak or touch her. If he touched her now, she would break. "Ramsey, I'm going home." Her voice was firm, uncompromising.

Ramsey became very still. His smile faded. Just like that, she'd said what he hadn't known how to say. Actually hearing the words was a shock. But he knew Tess needed time. Time to trust her father again, before she could accept his love for someone else. Time to calm down and understand that no one could replace her in his heart. Time to undo the damage that he and Claire had done to her.

Claire, he realized, bore her share of responsibility. Her overindulgence had spoiled Tess, and he had allowed it. His own actions of the last two years had undermined Tess's emotional security. He and Claire had created a monster out of their own selfish needs. The only thing they'd done together in the last sixteen years had hurt the only person they'd both loved ... and Sabrina had been caught in the cross fire.

Ramsey cleared his throat. "The doctor said you should take it easy for a few days ... rest." His voice drained away with his argument. Sabrina was staring at him, her expression blank, as if she were pulling plugs, disconnecting her emotions, leaving him.

"No, Ramsey. Today."

In an abrupt movement, one that was uniquely his whenever too much weighed heavily on his mind, Ramsey bowed his head. Sabrina was right. It was necessary to put a little distance between themselves and the situation. On the other hand, necessity meant zilch to his emotions. He and Tess would have each other, but Sabrina would be alone. "Alone" was a lousy place to be at any time, but when there were problems to be sorted out and pain to be lived with, "alone" was another word for hell.

Lifting one arm, he wrapped his hand around the back of her neck to knead the tightly knotted muscles. "Why the rush?"

Why was he making this so hard for her? he wondered. They weren't talking about forever.... His mouth quirked. *We interrupt this dream to bring you a brief message from real life.* The truth was, he was afraid to let her go, afraid that she would think herself right out of his life permanently, afraid she would convince herself that it was the most practical solution.

Sabrina pressed her hands against his chest, unable to resist his warmth, his strength. "It's been too much of a merry-go-round lately...too wild a ride. I can't hold on anymore."

"You can hold on to me." Still he argued, knowing he was wrong and hating it. Hearing the longing seep through the cracks in his voice, he gathered her close, needing her to depend on him as much as he depended on her. Feeling her hold him so tightly told him more than words. She did need him. Sabrina carried around her control like a security blanket, an extra layer of protection from the unseen hazards that her vulnerability exposed her to. She just hadn't realized it until she'd met him and Tess. It gave him power over her. That kind of power came with built-in responsibilities. Could he fulfill them?

He'd gladly try—for the rest of his life.

"You can hold on to me," he repeated, but felt her shake her head against his chest.

"No. Tess is the one in danger of falling."

To raise and nurture with love, patience and understanding... A phrase written into the adoption agreement. At the time, he'd wondered about a sixteen-year-old girl who would think to insist on it, and then he'd forgotten the words, taking their meaning for granted. *Tess.* His first promise to Sabrina, signed, notarized and duly witnessed before he'd ever known her.

"Tess is trying to work up a good hate for you, Sabrina. I don't think she'll succeed. What you said to her tore her up. If she really didn't care about you, she'd be mad or indifferent instead of hurt."

"I was...not nice to her, Ramsey."

"I heard. She deserved it, Sabrina." He spoke quietly as he stroked her back and rested his chin on the top of her head. "She asked for it. Tess has to learn that making other people suffer for her problems won't solve them or make them go away."

Sabrina released a sigh, ragged from unhappiness and triple-edged pain. Her head throbbed to the ends of her hair. Anguish clawed at her heart, and yearning flowed through her voice. "I love her so much, Ramsey. The adoption papers...I didn't sign away my feelings for her."

Ramsey wanted to wrap himself around her. Gently cupping her chin, he urged her to meet his gaze. "It'll work out, Sabrina. I promise. Will you give me a little time, to heal some old wounds and keep new ones from opening?"

"I'll wait until hope dies, Ramsey. Then I'll go on without you."

Without you. The words closed around his heart like a clenched fist. She didn't believe they had a chance. The only way to convince her was to make it happen. So he'd pick up her fallen dream and keep it alive, until it became their future. "Don't give up on the Jordans, Sabrina." His voice stumbled. "We'll both get our acts together. I—"

Sabrina kissed her fingertips and placed them over his lips. "No promises, Ramsey. I'm such a sucker for promises." She sagged in his arms, tired to the bone. It seemed as if she'd lived a whole lifetime in the last month.

Ramsey led her to the bed and, settling her between the covers, shook out a pill from the bottle the doctor had given him. "Take this and go to sleep, while I make arrangements to get you home." After she swallowed the tablet, he lay down beside her, absorbing every detail of her: the feel of her body, which fitted neatly into the contours of his own; the scent of his soap on her skin, and the taste of her tears on his tongue. As he whispered a lullaby into her ear, her breathing gentled to the slow rhythm of sleep, and her body relaxed.

Long after her eyes had drifted shut, Ramsey stood by the bed, reluctant to leave her, his brooding gaze covering her inch by inch, sculpting a perfect image of her in his memory, telling himself he had to let her go.

For now.

Later, Ramsey drove Sabrina to the airport, where Seth was waiting to fly her home in one of the company's Lear Jets. She might have appreciated the sheer novelty of it under different circumstances, and she might have protested the extravagance, if Ramsey had given her the opportunity. But he'd anticipated her argument, and had become the tough businessman who would not be gainsaid once he made up his mind.

He crouched in front of her and took her hands into his own. "I'll call."

She shook her head, showing him Sabrina, the tough businesswoman who had her own ideas on how things should be done. "No calls, Ramsey. Not unless Tess can accept me as more than a visitor in your lives," she said firmly.

Ramsey stood and looked down at her, wanting nothing more than to hold her and never let her go. "What happened to the woman who approaches life with her eyes and her heart wide open?"

"She's out to lunch," Sabrina answered with a shrug.

Ramsey smiled. "Well then, she'll be back soon."

"You're a hopeless romantic, Ramsey."

"Uh-uh. I'm a hopeful romantic, and it's all your fault."

"I'm sorry," she said seriously.

"I'm not," he shot back, just as seriously. "It feels good to be alive again, Sabrina." Turning abruptly, he walked to the door. "Oh, hell." He paused in the aisle and ran a hand around the back of his neck. "Oh, hell," he muttered again as he reversed his direction.

His parting kiss took Sabrina by surprise. It was harsh and tender, brief and penetrating, a farewell and a vow.

"Soon, Sabrina," he promised thickly and left the plane.

Soon. She was such a sucker for promises.

CHAPTER EIGHTEEN

A GENTLE CANDLE FLAME in the window of the universe, the sun shimmered behind a silver pearl curtain of overcast sky. A faithful beacon, it would soon melt down the slopes of the Tetons to reappear somewhere else, offering hope to another waiting soul. Gravid with moisture, the air was thick enough to quench thirst; the energy of a coming storm gave it an almost palpable flavor.

Sabrina stepped out of her car and walked to her mailbox, gazing at the world around her. Home, pillared by stone mountains and surrounded by a landscape of savage beauty. Home, where friends enveloped her like comforting walls.

Sabrina unlocked the front door and entered her house, searching for familiar things, for reassurance that this was where she belonged...that this *was* home.

Home, where a brown Stetson still hung on a sconce as if it were a natural part of the decor...as if it belonged there...as if Ramsey would magically appear from another part of the house.

Pushing the door shut with her foot, she went directly to her answering machine. Listening to the usual assortment of messages, she leafed through her mail, finding only desolation when the words she needed remained unspoken, unwritten. *The pen is mightier than the sword, but silence is more deadly.* She tried to throw off her grim thoughts as she tossed the mail onto her desk, but this seemed to be a day for introspection and reflection.

"Soon" had never come. Time had marched to the slowest dirge, trailing petals of hope in its wake. Days had become a month, then two, leaving Thanksgiving, Christmas and New Year behind. Sabrina had automatically slipped into her old routines, performing the rituals of her life as if they had never been interrupted by visions of something more.

A practical dreamer, Sabrina had always known that some dreams were hothouse fantasies, cultivated to be used briefly, decoratively, then pressed between the dog-eared pages of memory. Others were firmly rooted in the realm of reality, perennials hardy enough to survive the elements and multiply year after year. Until now, she'd always trusted herself to know the difference.

Sliding her feet into shearling moccasins, Sabrina lighted a fire and sat down in one of the chairs in front of the fireplace. Tracing her forefinger along the random gold nubs in her cranberry wool trousers, she absently rubbed her cheek back and forth over the cashmere of the matching cowl-necked sweater. A pile of gifts covered her desk—lovely, thoughtful gifts she had strained to ooh and ahh over. The birthday luncheon her friends had held for her had been wonderful. She had no right to be in such a deep blue funk.

Except that "soon" had never come.

In the first three weeks after her return, Ramsey had sent her several absolutely ridiculous cards, with silly messages that made no sense, yet had always brought a smile to her lips. Right after Thanksgiving, she'd received a large card with a gaudy profusion of flowers on the front and a sentimental message on the inside. That one had made her laugh until she'd cried...all night. He'd written the word "soon" in front of his name.

She'd heard nothing since.

At least not directly. Indirectly, she heard enough through a peculiar conglomeration of sources to keep the Jordans firmly entrenched in her thoughts. During her weekly telephone conversations with Marty, she learned that Seth was now a full partner in Ramsey's company. And the business section of the newspaper announced that Ram Air Couriers had become part of a nationwide alliance of independent carriers. Soon after that, Seth had been in Jackson on business and had shown up on her doorstep with a large pizza, a bottle of wine and the news that Ramsey had kicked workaholism, and could now only be found at his office five days a week.

No one mentioned Tess.

Sabrina's hope was in dire need of CPR.

In all her thirty-two—no, thirty-three—years, Sabrina hadn't had the time or inclination to play the tragic heroine, languishing with despair and wallowing in self-pity. But she'd recently discovered that experience wasn't required to do some things well. She could languish and wallow with the best of them. All she could think about was the last birthday party she'd been to—Ramsey's—and another she would never celebrate in person—Tess's.

She and Ramsey had shared stolen moments, perfect illusions and a love she believed in. But love and promises weren't enough to live on. She had to get by on memories.

So many memories had been created in such a short time. Even her body remembered sensations experienced, as if they were happening all over again. If she closed her eyes, she could almost believe that pleasure was growing and splintering inside her. And when she least expected it, she would be flung across time and distance to see again the betrayal in Tess's eyes, hear the crunch of metal and the breaking of glass and relive the fear that Tess was crushed and broken.

Tess is trying to work up a good hate...she won't succeed. Sabrina had clung to Ramsey's certainty as she recalled long talks, times of reaching out, Tess's stricken look, her confusion and her attempt to reclaim her ugly words. Could Ramsey be right? Sabrina was afraid to add that wish to her list.

The ringing of the doorbell stunned her with a sudden sense of déjà vu. With a self-mocking twist to her lips, she chastised herself. This had to stop. She couldn't live forever on the razor edge of waiting.

As she answered the door, the congenial smile she'd dredged up from who knew where froze, then melted on her face. Sabrina didn't know what to say and felt a ridiculous urge to cry.

"Hi." Tess looked at her with obvious apprehension. "It's been a while."

Sabrina closed her eyes on the memory of her last words to Tess. "Yes. It has. Too long a while."

Hope made a miraculous recovery.

Relief smoothed the lines of anxiety from Tess's face. "Can I come in?"

Holding the door wide open, Sabrina stepped back in silent invitation. "Would you like some hot chocolate?"

"Yes, please."

"How have you been, Tess?" Dropping marshmallows into mugs, Sabrina poured chocolate from the pan she'd kept warm on the stove.

"Not so hot."

"Oh? Isn't school going well?"

"I haven't been there." At Sabrina's look of alarm, she explained. "It's Christmas break."

"Yes. Of course it is. So, what have you been doing on your vacation?"

Tess sipped from her mug and licked away a marshmallow mustache from her upper lip. "Nothing. I've been grounded for taking off with that creep at the fashion show. Daddy had me working at his office, while his secretary was on maternity leave. He said that since I wanted to run his life for him, I ought to spend more time monitoring his activities."

Nearly choking, Sabrina set down her mug and discreetly cleared her throat. "You wanted to spend more time with him," she pointed out reasonably.

"Not that much time." Tess gave her a level stare. "He heard what I said to you."

"I know."

"Every time I griped about not being able to see my friends, he said if I thought he didn't need anybody but me, then I shouldn't need anyone, either. He said it was only fair."

"He said quite a bit, didn't he?"

"Yeah. He should have been a shrink."

Sabrina sat down across from her. "What do you say?"

A shudder escaped as Tess exhaled and gazed down at her hands. "I was a real bitch. I've never acted like that before. I knew I was wrong, but I couldn't seem to stop."

"You've stored up a lot of anger since your mother died, Tess. It was bound to come out sooner or later." Wondering where all this was leading, Sabrina ran her finger around the rim of her cup.

"Daddy said you understood. He told me how you felt about giving me up...what it was like."

"I'm afraid to ask what else Daddy said," Sabrina commented wryly.

"Enough." Taking a deep breath as if she were preparing to run a gauntlet, Tess reached into her purse and pulled out a stack of envelopes in various sizes and colors. "Daddy put these into his outgoing mail at the office. I took them out," she stated baldly as she pushed them across the table. "And he ordered flowers for you, too. I canceled the order."

Sabrina's heart ached at the measures Tess had taken to keep her out of Ramsey's life. "Tess, do you hate me so much?"

"I wanted to. Instead, I missed you and felt bad about what I did." Tess's eyes had a pleading look. "You have to understand. I knew I was adopted, but Mom...well she wouldn't talk about it. When I asked her, all she'd say was that you didn't exist anymore...that the only mother I had was her. She heard Daddy talking to me about it one time and got really upset."

Tess spoke quickly, her explanation gaining momentum, as if she had to say it all before she changed her mind...as if she weren't really sure whether she was doing the right thing, and she was still caught between divided loyalties. And Sabrina listened, her heart in her mouth; she knew that this might be the most important moment they would ever share.

"I *don't* hate you, Sabrina. It's just that Mom...I felt like I was cheating on her, you know? And Daddy...he and Mom weren't close. She spent all her time on me. I thought that he blamed me, and I was just so mad at everybody. It wasn't my fault, but I felt like it was."

"Do you still feel that way, Tess?"

Tess shook her head. "Not so much. Daddy had a fit when I talked to him about it. He was taking all the blame, and all of a sudden it seemed dumb that we were all going around feeling guilty for things we couldn't do anything about." Tentatively she pushed the stack of letters across the table. "I told Seth about what I did."

"But not Ramsey," Sabrina said, hazarding a guess.

"No. I saw his face every day when he checked the mail. I didn't want him to know I'd—"

"Betrayed him?" Sabrina asked gently.

"Yes."

"I won't tell him, Tess. Maybe someday you'll be able to trust him enough to tell him yourself."

"I trust him."

"Not enough to know he'll forgive you."

"I'm scared, Sabrina. He loves you so much, and I stole his letters to you."

"You're his daughter."

Tess shook her head as tears gathered in her eyes. "No, I'm not. Not really."

Sabrina reached out to lay her hand on Tess's. "Yes, really," she said firmly. "In all the important ways. Do you honestly believe that he would have let me go if he didn't love you?" Squeezing Tess's hand, she continued. "Tess, I would have stayed if he had asked me. He knew that. He didn't ask."

"You wouldn't have stayed. You..." Tess's voice trailed off, as if she'd just realized what she'd said. Both

Sabrina and Ramsey loved her enough to do anything, give up anything, rather than hurt her. She closed her mouth and frowned.

Sabrina smiled inside. Tess believed it, though believing wasn't accepting. That might take a while longer. But she was still young. She had plenty of time.

"Sabrina? Are you going to marry Daddy?" Wariness crept into Tess's question.

"The subject hasn't come up." Except in the depths of night when he'd tucked her into his bed and whispered nonsense about a wedding dress the color of forget-me-nots....

Tess uttered a sound of annoyance. "If it does and if you do, what will that make us? What will happen?"

Sabrina heard more—much more—beneath the surface of Tess's questions, and she recognized the teenager's fear that her world would cave in on her, that she'd be left out, that things would change. Sabrina sat back, analyzing her answer before she voiced it. "If I married Ramsey, it would make you his daughter and me his wife, both of us loved equally in different ways. Neither of us would be deprived of our proper place in his heart, Tess. Ideally, you would realize I'm not trying to take your...mother's place, and you'd give me space of my own in your heart."

Tess bit her lip. "I really do like you, Sabrina, but...it won't be easy."

Sabrina wanted to offer absolutes instead of uncertainties. She could use a few absolutes herself. "No Tess, compromises and adjustments are never easy. We wouldn't automatically be tied up in a happy little family knot."

Clouds of thought crossed Tess's features. "We do have fun together," she stated as if she were making a list of pros and cons. "And you understand about clothes and boys. Daddy gets all wrapped around the axle where boys are concerned."

When no cons were added to the list, Sabrina relaxed, her mind engaging in whimsical doodles of thought. Dormant dreams suddenly sprouted, grew and bloomed—dreams of family and belonging and day-to-day sharing; dreams of birthday parties and finding loose change in the cushions and occasional bursts of temper over little things. Dreams of fighting for the covers and of night-to-night loving.

Sabrina thought of Tess's dreams. "How are your flying lessons coming?" she asked casually.

"Fine," Tess said, rising abruptly and carrying her mug to the sink, giving Sabrina no opening for more probing questions.

Sighing unconsciously, Sabrina frowned as another thought suddenly occurred to her. "Tess, you haven't run away again, have you? I mean...because Ramsey punished you or made you spend your vacation working—?"

"Are you kidding?" Tess squeaked. "I don't want to be grounded for the rest of my life. I have a date for the junior-senior prom in May." She stared at her hands and cleared her throat. "Remember when we talked about Cinderella?"

"Yes," Sabrina whispered, knowing that a confidence was about to be shared and not wanting to disturb the moment.

"Seth is still seeing Ms Temple." Tess looked up, a funny little smile on her face that matched the bleakness in her eyes. "There's nothing I can do about it, so I thought about what you said and decided to go to the ball with someone else."

"The football player with the Texas drawl?"

Tess nodded and excitement crept into her voice. "He's a great dancer and he drives the neatest car. I mean, why should I sit around waiting to try on shoes, while everybody else is out having a good time?"

"No reason that I can see." Smiling at Tess's vehemence, Sabrina relaxed, then narrowed her eyes as she had another thought. "Did Ramsey persuade you to come here?"

"Uh-uh. It was the other way around. I had to talk him into bringing me with him."

Sabrina's heart did gymnastics in her chest. "With him? He's in Jackson? Why?"

"He said he wasn't about to spend his declining years alone, waiting for me to invite him to Sunday dinner. He said that he wanted his cake and chocolate ice cream, too, and if he waited for you and me to give it to him, he'd be too old and feeble to enjoy it." Tess gave Sabrina a you-know-how-men-are look. "I've been trying to figure out if I'm the cake or the ice cream."

Sabrina's mouth twitched at Ramsey's way of handling things. Patience was definitely not one of his virtues. "Does it matter, as long as they go well together?" she asked.

Tess appeared to give the question serious thought. "I guess not. Do you think we will?"

"Go well together? Not all the time, Tess. Marriages—any kind of relationships—aren't made in heaven, but right here on earth. If they were perfect, we'd take each other for granted and have no reason to try and no reason to be thankful when we succeeded."

"That's what Daddy said."

"If Daddy says any more, he'll likely get laryngitis."

"That would be nice," Tess said with a straight face.

Sabrina laughed, delighted with Tess, amused by her observations and just plain happy with the world in general.

"Daddy's out in the car."

In the car. So close. Sabrina's laughter died. A frenzy of sensations rushed her, churning her blood, accelerating her pulse, lobbing her heart right over the sun. Pushing away from the table, she retrieved her boots, which were drying on her glass-enclosed back porch. "There's pop in the fridge, and you know where the television and stereo are. Make yourself at home, Tess." Feeling reckless, she gave Tess a hug and a smacking kiss on the cheek on her way to the front door. "I'm going for a walk."

Sabrina stopped abruptly. As persistent as an unrealized dream, words pounded in her head. She turned to face Tess, giving them freedom. "No matter what, I love you, Tess...always."

"Sabrina, I—" Biting her lip, Tess blinked away fresh tears. "Happy birthday, Sabrina." Her gaze clung to Sabrina, saying more, so much more that she couldn't put into words...yet.

THE SNOW WAS as pristine and uncluttered as a new beginning. A long shadow glided up beside Sabrina's, and she was fascinated by how right they looked together.

Ramsey cleared his throat, calling her back from the magic spell cast by shadows in the snow. "Hi."

"Just passing through, Ramsey?" The short glance she'd meant to spare him grew longer, lingered, savored, devoured. He wore his sheepskin coat over a fisherman knit sweater and his usual Levi's. Except for the large box he carried, he looked the same as he had the first time he'd come here. The only thing missing was—

"Just passing through," he agreed solemnly. "I thought I'd drop by to propose and make sure you hadn't burned my hat."

"No. I plan to use it for target practice . . . spit nails at it."

"You're ticked off." He gave a long-suffering sigh.

"Enough to spit nails," she confirmed. "You should have warned me, Ramsey, given me an idea of what to expect."

Halting, Ramsey grasped her arm and pulled her around to face him. "And give you a chance to think? No way." His eyes narrowed. "Why didn't you answer my letters?"

"I . . ." She stopped herself from telling him she'd received only those few cards and then, nothing. What Tess had done was best revealed by Tess herself. "I was too busy thinking."

"I knew that," Ramsey said, rolling his eyes. His shadow moved with hers, joining it, though their bodies never touched. He looked at her in her hooded fur jacket and knee-length boots. "You look great." His tone held a surprise that was tinged with resentment.

A smile teased the corners of her mouth. "What did you expect—jutting bones and haunted eyes?"

"I lost ten pounds," he announced as if he were showing off an injury.

Not for anything would she tell him she had a tendency to eat when she was unhappy. He didn't need to know she'd gained eight and three-quarter pounds. He'd never let her live it down.

"Sabrina, will you please stop a minute?"

She gazed at him with mild interest after his shout brought her up short.

"This bloody box is awkward. Will you please open it, so I can put it somewhere and hold you instead?"

"What is it?"

"Your birthday present."

"My..." She swallowed a lump of emotion. "I thought you were my present. You and Tess."

Stunned, Ramsey caught his breath, then gave her a smile wide with pleasure at her words, an open smile, full of love. "Open it, Sabrina," he ordered softly.

Lifting the lid while he held the box, she peeked inside, blinked, then stared. A blush crept up her body as she remembered him undressing her. *Sexiest thing I've ever seen... buy one for each night of the week.* In assorted colors—white, pearl gray, indigo, rose, crimson, black and forget-me-not blue—were seven lace and satin Merry Widows, each embroidered with the name of a day of the week. How had he found them? "It must have been something to see—you in a lingerie shop!" she said, chuckling at the image.

Laying the box on a tree stump, Ramsey grinned. He framed her face with his hands and stroked her cheeks with his thumbs. "I promised the owner our patronage for life if she'd have these made up. You'll have to marry me, so I can keep my word."

Her laughter died as suddenly as it had begun. Slipping her arms inside his coat, Sabrina wound them around his waist and under his sweater. She soaked up the warmth of his skin, enjoying the supple muscles of his back and wondering if she'd get enough of him in only one lifetime. Mischief danced in her eyes like fireflies on a warm night. "I can't marry you. You haven't asked."

"Mmm, I haven't? Are you sure?" He nuzzled her neck, breathing deeply as if he would inhale her into his body, imprison her in his senses, make her forever a part of himself.

"Ramsey..." She tilted her upper body away from him. Her voice was breathless when she said, "I'm a great believer in tradition."

"Huh?"

"You know. Passionate declarations made on bended knee, dramatic gestures, soulful looks—that sort of thing."

"What?" He choked in disbelief. "You're out of your mind! There's snow on the ground—cold, wet snow. It's not practical," he added triumphantly, as if he'd said the magic word.

Sabrina sighed. "But it's such a simple thing." She didn't see the calculated gleam in his eyes or the sly curve of his mouth. She was too busy receiving the messages his body was transmitting.

"The only simple thing around here," he grumbled as he gingerly lowered himself to one knee, "is the mind that thought this up." Grabbing one of her hands, he planted a smacking kiss in the vicinity of her wrist.

"You call that a passionate declaration?"

"I call this a dramatic gesture." With a controlled yank, he pulled her off balance so that she landed flat on her back in a snowdrift. Before she could do more than issue a startled squeak, he moved over her, supporting his weight on his elbows and fixing her with a reproachful glare. "Sabrina, you make me crazy." Lowering his head, he nibbled gently at her lips. "And hungry."

Sabrina's protest at his cavalier treatment of her dissolved into a gasp. She nibbled back, and her hands again found the heat of his bare skin under his sweater.

Satisfied that her words—probably a chewing out—
were lost for a second or two, Ramsey whispered to her
between the tiny kisses he strung around her throat like
a necklace. "You hog the bed, you know that? It's
frustrating as hell to have an argument with you...." He
groaned as she moved her hands up to his chest and
teased him with her nails. "You think too much, and
you have a nasty habit of trying to ride on cloud nine,
while dragging one foot on the ground. There are times,
sweetheart, when losing control is absolutely necessary
to enjoy a moment.... Sabrina, move your hand any
lower, and I'll teach you all about losing control."

Her palms skimmed up his sides and over his chest
again, caressing him as she had dreamed of doing for
long, empty days and frigid, lonely nights. "You've already taught me, Ramsey. I haven't been in control
since I met you."

Lowering himself onto her, Ramsey pressed his chest
against her breasts, groaning again as her nipples responded, sending tiny stabs of pleasure through him.
He held her tightly, feeling the rhythm of their hearts
harmonize and beat as one. His voice was a throaty
growl. "In spite of the above-mentioned faults, I love
you."

"I don't have any faults, you wretched man, just ec-
centricities."

"Quiet, woman. I'm trying to bare my soul."

"You're heavy," she complained, moving her leg between his and nudging him suggestively, tormentingly.

"And getting heavier by the minute," he muttered.
"You'll get used to it," he promised. Unable to resist
her exaggerated pout, he bent his head to drink deeply
of her mouth, leaving no crevice untapped by his
tongue.

Sabrina trembled with more sensual energy than an approaching storm. Their breath mingled, turbulent and hot, fogging the air around them. Her hands flexed on his hips, urging him closer until the fierce strength of his arousal strained against her.

Ramsey tore his mouth away from hers, then returned for one more taste. His body shuddered, fighting the pull of gravity as their shared passion drew him higher and higher. Smoothing the hair away from her face, he stared down at her. "I dreamed about us every night and woke up every morning, needing to see the reality." He laughed dispiritedly at the memory of two months, one day and an assorted number of hours without Sabrina to enrich the time. "Reality was cold sheets, a mangled pillow and a big bed, swallowing me up with loneliness and memories."

Listening to the sweet everythings he uttered in a husky whisper, Sabrina's eyes radiated love. She'd been afraid to believe, but the proof was there in the promises and vows that were implicit in his words, the expression on his face. Reality was created from dreams, after all. . . .

"No more stolen moments, Sabrina. We can claim our own. They might be less than perfect, but they'll be ours."

"No more stolen moments, Ramsey," she agreed.

"Will you marry me, Sabrina?" His voice was as intense as a night of passion.

"Yes." Sabrina smiled up at him and shifted her body, seeking a warm spot on the icy bed. "Ramsey?"

"Mmm."

"Tess is almost grown. I realize you might not want to raise another child. . . ."

A corner of his mouth slashed upward in a crooked smile. "I'm forty years old—slightly used, but not used up. I think I still have what it takes." He sobered, answering the question he saw in Sabrina's eyes. "Claire couldn't carry a baby to term. She was pregnant four times before the doctors advised surgery."

Sabrina placed her fingers over his mouth, silencing any further explanation. Four babies lost. How had they stood it? "Ramsey?"

He arched an eyebrow and changed the subject, lightening the moment. "Horses for the kids—yes. Dogs—yes. I draw the line at rodents, reptiles and ant farms. I can change diapers and mix formula—if you want to nurse, I can't help you—and I can keep a rocking chair going. If you cook dinner the night before, I'll serve you breakfast in bed the morning after. I'm hell on wheels with a dust rag. I've done the passionate declarations, gestured dramatically and knelt at your feet. Anything else?"

Sabrina shifted again. "Yes. My back is cold . . . and wet."

Ramsey's shout of laughter seemed to bounce off the air. Snowflakes began a lazy, floating dance around them. "I thought love was supposed to keep you warm."

"My front is warm. The rest of me has turned into a Popsicle."

Dropping a kiss onto the tip of her nose, Ramsey rose and held out his hands to her. "If I can put up with the six inches of bed you leave me, you ought to be able to handle a little discomfort in the name of romance," he stated peevishly as he brushed clumps of snow off her back. "I'm beginning to think you have an attitude problem."

Sabrina's rejoinder faded as she heard a door slam. She glanced at the house. Tess was leaning against the porch rail, her shoulders slumped in dejection. There was a lost, left-out quality in the way her gaze fell to her feet.

Ramsey frowned as he watched his daughter. She didn't understand yet what he'd always sensed. An almost tangible bond existed between Sabrina and herself. Tess had suffered over the rift with Sabrina without realizing why. In time, she'd know it was all right to love more than one mother, just as it was all right for him to love more than one child or take another woman into his life. Thanks to Claire and himself, Tess hadn't learned much about the expanding properties of love or its infinite possibilities, but she was beginning to. Meanwhile, he thought wryly, some days were bound to be a little dicey.

His eyes met Sabrina's. A look linked their thoughts. Smiling along with her, his actions mirrored hers.

One snowball landed with a splat on Tess's foot. Another hit her arm. Startled, she looked from one flattened missile to the other. Raising her head, she stared at Sabrina and Ramsey, seeing their grins wide in invitation to join them. And she did.

Tall evergreens rose from the ground, serene and graceful in their lacy white shawls. Trees bare of leaves swayed to the music of the wind. Enameled with glaciers, jeweled with sapphire and amethyst shadows, the Teton Mountains met the sky in jagged splendor, a barbaric crown atop the earth's head. And in the magic glow of winter twilight, three people played and laughed together, determined to weather whatever storms might gather around them. Nature stood in silent witness as three hearts reached out to one another.

It was a time to be remembered, recreated and treasured . . . forever.

EPILOGUE

IT WAS a special place, fronted by rich wood and mullioned windows. Etched glass and tapestries of silken threads depicting magical figures adorned the walls. Carved antique bureaus and wardrobes took the place of stock drawers and clothing racks, and were filled with everything from lingerie to formal wear in the finest fabrics. Accessories created specifically to complement Sabrina's new line could be found in unexpected places throughout the shop, encouraging clients to browse in every nook.

The entrance had been altered into a large bay window, in which a diamond-paned glass door was centered between four faceted display windows. In the corner of each one, like the signature of an artist, the name of the elegant establishment—Fantasy—was painted in gold.

This time, Sabrina was on the inside looking out.

From the first time she'd seen it, the storefront had captured her imagination; it had been an empty place waiting to be filled. The idea had been Tess's and Ramsey had encouraged it. Marty had reluctantly, skeptically, agreed to making it a part of their company. Marty's skepticism had, in the two years since the shop had opened, turned to amazement. Three more stores were scheduled to open in different cities in the coming year.

Sabrina locked the doors and sighed. Ramsey stood behind her, waiting for her private moment to pass. She smiled up at him, as he put an arm around her shoulders and turned her to face the interior of the shop.

In an alcove hung with silk and furnished with three short divans scattered with jewel-toned pillows, Marty and her husband, Tess, Seth, Lenore and Hap were waiting for the celebration to begin. Fluted crystal champagne glasses—a gift from Seth—sparkled on the table as Marty filled them. The name of the shop was etched on each glass, and stood out against the pale amber liquid inside.

Ramsey lifted his glass to give the first toast. "To three years of paradise," he said, his eyes burning with a fire that never dimmed. "Of course, even in paradise, the roses have thorns reminding us not to take their beauty for granted, reminding us that someone is always there to soothe the hurts and ease the healing."

Barely wetting her lips with the champagne, Sabrina rested her head on Ramsey's chest, hearing his heartbeat and knowing it was hers as well. Making an Us wasn't easy. As soon as one problem was dealt with, another took its place. Yet each solution, compromise or adjustment spun a fragile silken thread to strengthen their three-way bond. Tess might never call her Mother, but attaching labels to their relationship didn't seem important. It was enough that they had one.

"To sentimental men," Marty said, saluting Ramsey. "And successful partnerships . . . and profits. May they be fruitful and multiply."

"Amen." Seth seconded her toast and turned to Tess. "To the next designer in the Jordan family. May you never run out of paper."

Tess flushed with pleasure as her gaze went to the gown displayed in the window. It was her creation, designed and executed in her class at the Art Institute.

"I'd have never guessed this place would make it," Marty's husband said. "But then I didn't think Cachet would, either. I'm proud as hell of both of you." He hugged his wife and embraced Sabrina with his smile. "As a banker, I don't understand how you did it."

"Didn't I tell you?" Sabrina raised her glass to Ramsey. "Ramsey has a fairy godmother on the payroll."

A secret look passed between Tess and Sabrina. "Sabrina, are you going to tell them now?" Tess said. "The only way I'm going to keep this to myself is to leave town."

"Tell us what?" Lenore focused on the contented smile on Sabrina's face, then whispered into Hap's ear.

Always ready to argue, Hap opened his mouth, but said nothing as he watched Sabrina turn to Ramsey and kiss the corner of his mouth. "Yep," he said. "Looks like you might be right this time."

Raising her glass, Sabrina clinked it against Ramsey's as she unconsciously, instinctively pressed her hand on her stomach. "To all the empty places we've filled with life."

Passersby on the Sixteenth Street Mall looked around, startled to hear the sounds of cheering and a loud whoop coming from so elegant a place as Fantasy. Several peeked into a diamond-paned window and saw a tall, handsome man embracing two striking, dark-haired women, a wide grin on his face, his eyes gleaming with moisture.

He looked like a man who held the deed to paradise.

Harlequin Superromance.

COMING NEXT MONTH

#378 THE HONEY TRAP • Pamela Bauer
Veronica Lang was frightened. Her estranged husband
had suddenly defected, and now someone was watching
Ronni and her daughter. Ex-CIA agent Logan McNeil
had offered his protection. But Ronni wondered if he
could be trusted. He was laying some kind of
trap...but for whom?

#379 RAMBLIN' MAN • Barbara Kaye
Cowboy George Whittaker was the sweetest man Laurie
Tyler had ever known, but he was—in the argot of the
country music Laurie loved—a genuine ramblin' man.
She knew she should get out while the getting was
good. She could already hear those hurtin' songs....

#380 WOULDN'T IT BE LOVELY • Eve Gladstone
Reporter Liz Grady would have done anything to make
peace with lawyer Brad Kent, including burying the
story she'd uncovered. But her conscience wouldn't let
her, because beneath the elegant idyllic surface of
Ramsey Falls, something was terribly wrong—wrong
and dangerous....

#381 EMERALD WINDOWS • Tracy Hughes
"You can't go home again" was a truism that stained-
glass artist Brooke Martin had lived with for too many
years. Driven from Hayden, Florida, by the scandal of
her teenage involvement with her art teacher, Nick
Marcello, Brooke had paid in spades for the lies told by
the townsfolk. Now she had a score to settle with the
town...and with Nick

COMING IN OCTOBER

SWEET PROMISE

Erica made two serious mistakes in Mexico. One was taking
Rafael de la Torres for a gigolo, the other was assuming
that the scandal of marrying him would get her father's
attention. Her father wasn't interested, and Erica ran
home to Texas the next day, keeping her marriage a secret.
She knew she'd have to find Rafael someday to get a
divorce, but she didn't expect to run into him at a party—
and she was amazed to discover that her ''gigolo'' was the
head of a powerful family, and deeply in love with her....

Watch for this bestselling Janet Dailey favorite, coming in
October from Harlequin.

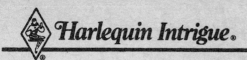

Harlequin Intrigue ®

High adventure and romance— with three sisters on a search . . .

Linsey Deane uses clues left by their father to search the Colorado Rockies for a legendary wagonload of Confederate gold, in #120 *Treasure Hunt* by Leona Karr (August 1989).

Kate Deane picks up the trail in a mad chase to the Deep South and glitzy Las Vegas, with menace and romance at her heels, in #122 *Hide and Seek* by Cassie Miles (September 1989).

Abigail Deane matches wits with a murderer and hunts for the people behind the threat to the Deane family fortune, in #124 *Charades* by Jasmine Crasswell (October 1989).

Don't miss Harlequin Intrigue's three-book series The Deane Trilogy. Available where Harlequin books are sold.

DEA-G

Indulge a Little
Give a Lot

An irresistible opportunity to pamper yourself with free gifts (plus proofs-of-purchase and postage and handling) and help raise up to $100,000.00 for **Big Brothers/Big Sisters Programs and Services** in Canada and the United States.

Each specially marked "Indulge A Little" Harlequin or Silhouette book purchased during October, November and December contains a proof-of-purchase that will enable you to qualify for luxurious gifts. And, for every specially marked book purchased during this limited time, Harlequin/Silhouette will donate 5¢ toward **Big Brothers/Big Sisters Programs and Services**, for a maximum contribution of $100,000.00.

For details on how you can indulge yourself, look for information at your favorite retail store or send a self-addressed stamped envelope to:

INDULGE A LITTLE
P.O. Box 618
Fort Erie, Ontario
L2A 5I3